"I NEVER PUT MUCH STORE IN WOMEN BEING WITCHES," LONGARM SAID ...

"So you still got to prove you're one."

"I promise I weel do thees for you," Clarita replied. She came to the easy chair and stood facing Longarm. ... "So we go to bed, no? Ees best place for show you."

"You sure all you want to show me is that you're a witch?" Longarm asked.

"No," Clarita smiled. "Ees not all . . ."

Also in the **LONGARM** series
from Jove

Chapter 1

"Well, I see you made it to work all right this morning," Longarm told the pink-cheeked young clerk who sat behind the desk in the outer room of the U.S. Marshal's Office.

"Why, of course I did, Mr. Long," the youth replied, looking up wide-eyed from the newfangled typewriting machine he'd been struggling with. "Why shouldn't I?"

"Because I got the idea on the way here that about half the people in this damn town decided they'd rather spend the day in bed," Longarm snapped.

"Is something wrong, Mr. Long?" the young man asked, rubbing his freshly shaven chin as he looked with almost open disapproval at the stubble that darkened Longarm's jaws.

"Nothing more'n usual, I guess." Longarm jerked his head in the direction of the door that bore on its upper panel the inscription UNITED STATES MARSHAL, FIRST DISTRICT COURT OF COLORADO. "Billy Vail get here, too?"

"Certainly," the young man answered primly. "There are very few days when Marshal Vail isn't the first one to arrive."

"Good." Longarm started for the door. "I'll just go have a quick word with him."

Nimbly, the young man popped out of his chair and almost succeeded in getting between Longarm and the door, saying, "I don't think Marshal Vail should be disturbed right now. He's going over the morning mail."

Longarm gently moved the youth aside with a big, calloused hand, and was reaching for the doorknob when the door opened and Vail appeared. His hands were loaded with papers. When he saw Longarm's face, he passed the papers on to the clerk and said, "Go on in, Long. I don't need but one guess to figure out what's on your mind." To the clerk, he added, "We'll go

1

over these later. There's nothing that has to be taken care of in a hurry."

By the time Vail got behind his desk, Longarm had hooked his boot toe around the leg of the red morocco-upholstered chair that stood along the wall, and dragged it up to the desk. He settled into the chair, watching Vail. The chief marshal was rearranging the heaps of papers that covered the desktop, shuffling them around and sorting them into stacks.

Longarm pulled a cheroot out of his pocket and lighted it while he waited for Vail's attention. He stared out the window at the buildings of downtown Denver, their roofs piled high with drifted snow. Sight of the snowdrifts reminded him of his walk to the Federal Building and set him puffing furiously on the long, thin cigar.

Denver's first real storm of the year had swooped across the peaks of the Rockies overnight and left the Mile-High City under a knee-deep snow blanket before moving on to the eastern plains of Colorado.

Longarm had snapped awake when the rising sun's rays, reflected from the sparkling surface of the ground, had brightened the windows of his bedroom in the roominghouse on the wrong side of Cherry Creek. He'd taken one glance at the high, narrow windows and burrowed deeper into the blankets. He wasn't surprised when he saw the brilliantly reflected light that spelled a snowfall. Last night as he stepped out of the Windsor House, where he'd been managing to stay even in a poker game, he'd been sure he smelled a storm blowing in.

Looking across the room, Longarm saw Thomas Moore's portrait staring at him from the label of the bottle of Maryland rye that stood on the dresser, and wished he could reach it without having to get out of bed. Deciding to cut his losses, he tossed the covers off and got to the dresser in one long stride. The thin carpet prickled like ice under his bare feet, and a layer of cold air hovering over the floor nipped his ankles.

Longarm took a healthy swallow from the bottle and deferred the other half of his eye-opener until he'd pulled on his balbriggans. The coarse weave of the underwear rasped against the goosebumps that even a few moments in the chilly air had brought popping out of his skin. He pulled on his britches and wool socks and stomped into his stovepipe cavalry boots before

2

tilting up the bottle for the other half of his morning libation.

Whoever it was that said a man can't walk worth two hoots in hell on one leg sure knew what he was talking about, he told himself silently as the smooth, aged liquor trickled down his throat. It's always that second one that finishes off the job.

Picking up a cheroot from the top of the dresser, Longarm flicked a match into flame across his thumbnail and puffed appreciatively as the flavor of the cigar smoke caressed the afterbite of the rye. Tucking in the tails of his gray flannel shirt, he knotted the string tie that federal regulations now forced him to wear while he was in the city, and rubbed his fingers over his chin. While he brushed his sweeping longhorn-style mustache into shape with a fingertip, his gunmetal-blue eyes studied his image in the tarnished mirror. A shave, he decided, would have to wait until later.

This ain't a day to save a dime by scraping them whiskers off in ice water, he silently told his mirrored image. George'll have a kettle of water hot by the time I get some grub under my belt and get to his shop. And maybe by then I won't feel so all-fired frazzled.

Lifting his gunbelt off the head of the bed, where it had hung through the night as always, within easy reach of his hand, he cinched the belt around his lean hips and slid his .44-caliber Colt Model T out of its open-toed holster.

Pulling the hammer back to the first notch, he spun the cylinder. Its soft, almost silent clicking told his practiced ear that the weapon needed no oiling. He revolved the cylinder more slowly, looking in through the open latch while he inspected the ends of the shells to be sure none of them bore a telltale trace of oil that could seep in around the caps and cause a misfire.

Satisfied, he reholstered the Colt and pushed his hands through the armholes of his vest before picking up the stubby little derringer that lay on the chair seat under the vest. A shackle fixed to the derringer's butt was attached to the chain that held his Ingersoll watch on the other end. He broke the derringer and flicked his eyes over its loads, closed the action, and dropped the gun in his right-hand vest pocket, the watch in the left, letting the chain drape across his vest front.

Shrugging into his full-skirted black frock coat, Longarm

3

set his Stetson on his crisp brown hair at its usual jaunty angle and treated himself to a bonus from the bottle of rye before leaving. Locking the door of his room, he started down the creaking stairway, his bootheels clumping on the steps.

As usual, Longarm was the first of the roomers to be stirring. The front door swung inward, and when he pulled it open, a few blobs of the snow that last night's howling wind had piled against it fell onto the hall carpet-runner.

Let's face it, old son, he thought as he looked across the narrow porch at the unbroken surface of the knee-deep snow that sloped down the steps to the sidewalk and stretched on across the street. You and snow just wasn't ever made to get along on good terms, and that's the size of it.

Longarm was ready to repeat that observation, doubled in spades, by the time he'd pushed his way laboriously as far as the Colfax Avenue bridge. His feet were already getting numb, and his breath, puffing out as vapor, had started to form ice in his sweeping mustache. He moved more carefully across the bridge, for the freezing mist rising from Cherry Creek had covered its surface with a solid sheet of ice before the snow came to cover it. His stomach had been reminding him it was empty ever since he'd stepped out into the cold air so he pushed on.

Quong Choy's restaurant was closed; there was not even a light glowing in Quong's living quarters behind the cafe. George Masters' barbershop was closed too, when Longarm reached it, his stomach feeling heavy with the cold food he'd been forced to settle for—hardboiled eggs and bologna sausage off the free-lunch counter at the Black Cat Saloon. He'd climbed the snow-slick steps of the Federal Building with a feeling that if anything was going to go wrong, this was the day to look for it to happen.

Billy Vail finally got his papers in order and looked across his desk at Longarm. "You're swelled up like a pizened pup," Vail observed. "Did you lose your spare shirt in that poker game you sat in last night, or is your pet corn aching because it's so cold?"

"Damn it, Billy don't go making jokes. You know I don't like snow any better'n a cowhand likes a sheepherder."

"Oh, I knew right away what was biting you," Vail replied.

4

"Even if I'd spent the night shut up in this office and hadn't looked outside, I'd have known it snowed the minute I saw you."

"Now what in hell do you mean by that, Billy?"

Vail glanced with a smile at the Regulator banjo clock that ticked away on his office wall. "Because a snowstorm's about the only thing that'll get you to the office on time, and you're nearly a half-hour early today."

"Quit rubbing it in, Billy," Longarm protested.

Vail reached across his desk and picked up a sheet of telegraph flimsies that he'd put on top of one of the stacks of paperwork. He said, "Maybe this will make you feel better."

"A new case?"

"One that's got your name on it, too. I'd have picked you for it even if you hadn't been the only deputy I've got free right now. And it's in a nice warm part of the country."

"Well, come on out with it, damn it! Whereabouts?"

"Down in Arizona Territory. I'd guess you must have heard about the Gadsden Purchase. Or, maybe you haven't. That was a while ago, back in fifty-three."

"Hell, I was just a skinny kid down in West-by-God-Virginia then, Billy. Big enough to go to the war in '63, though. But if I recall what little I learned in school, that Gadsden thing was when we bought a little slice of land from Mexico."

"Everything south of the Gila River to the thirty-first parallel," Vail affirmed. "That slice of land got twisted out of shape a little bit by the time the dickering was finished, but that's where you're heading for."

"I know about where you mean, Billy. Go ahead. What's going on way down there?"

Vail glanced at the top flimsy. "They've got trouble in a little town just north of the Mexican border. Place called Mina Cobre. I looked on the map, but the only town I could spot in the general area is named Quijotoa."

"I never heard of either one. I been to Tucson, and up in the Four Corners, if that helps any."

"Going by the map, Quijotoa's a good hundred miles or so west of Tucson, and since Mina Cobre's not on my map, I guess it's going to be up to you to find it."

"I tell you the God's truth, Billy, I don't much care where

5

the place is, long as it ain't snowing there."

"Not much chance. That's desert country, as I recall, hot even in the dead of winter."

"Fine. When do I start?"

"Don't get so previous. You don't even know what the case is about yet."

"I'm just waiting for you to tell me." Longarm leaned back, stretching his legs out.

"It's not exactly new." Vail flipped over the top flimsy and looked at the next one. "There's a new cooper mine in Mina Cobre. The outfit that owns it must swing more weight in Washington than in Arizona, or we never would've been called in."

"Which ain't strange, considering the shape the country's in today," Longarm observed. He could feel his feet getting warm.

"As close as I can tell from this message from the Attorney General's office, there's about six sides to everything down there," Vail said.

"There generally is six sides to the cases we get sent on by the Attorney General's paper-pushers," Longarm commented.

The top of Vail's pink, bald head was tipped toward Longarm as he reread the flimsies. "This one's about the same. The way I read things, the mining company must control the county, and I guess they've got a line into the governor's office too, because he's tried to send a squad of militia to Mina Cobre to keep order."

"What do you mean, tried? Don't the governor have charge of the militia in Arizona, same as everyplace else?"

"Seems the territorial legislature's got some say about what the governor can do. Anyhow, they voted against him calling out the militia, even if there has been enough trouble to call for it. There was a state investigator killed not too long ago, and there's been some other shootings."

"Sounds to me like it's Arizona's fuss, not ours," Longarm frowned as Vail paused to read more.

"It's ours now," Vail told him. "There's an election coming along, and Washington wants it to be fair and peaceful."

Longarm exhaled a puff of cigar smoke and a half-sigh at the same time. "Not that I'm complaining, Billy, but this job

6

sure would be easier if all we had to do was run down robbers and outlaws. It's when decent folks get all riled up that a case gets tough to handle."

Vail glanced at the Regulator clock again. "You've got plenty of time to get the express south. The way you've been acting, I expect you'll want to get the first train you can take out of here."

"You just bet I will! But don't you think I better find out where in hell I'm going, Billy? I'd feel like a damn fool if I lit out of here like a spooked jackrabbit and headed in the wrong direction."

Vail stood up and walked over to the map that covered most of one wall of his office. Longarm followed him, and they studied the map together for a moment. The chief marshal put a pudgy fingertip on a spot about halfway between Texas and California, on the Arizona-Mexico border.

"You'll be going somewhere in this general area," he told Longarm. He looked at the map again. "I guess Tucson's about the best place you can head for."

Longarm was examining the area surrounding Vail's finger. He said with a frown, "Hell's bells, Billy, that sure ain't such a much of a piece of country down there. Not a single railroad's got across Arizona Territory yet."

"Well, the cavalry's got plenty of horses at Fort Lowell, and the Engineer Corps office there ought to have a newer map."

"Looks like I'm going to have to go clear around hell's half-acre to get to Tucson," Longarm said. "South from here to San Antonio, and then to El Paso. It'll be a long ride."

"But you won't be riding through snow," Vail reminded him. "I'll have the clerk write up your vouchers and papers. You can stop by and pick them up when you've packed. And do me a favor, Longarm. Try to stay out of trouble, this trip."

Longarm turned his back to the windows of the smoking car until the southbound Fort Worth & Denver City express had gotten out of the snow zone south of Castle Rock. Even then, he glanced outside only occasionally while the train rocked on through the rolling eastern foothills; it was country he'd crossed and recrossed too many times for it to have any novelty.

7

When darkness came as the express gained speed on the level roadbed that ran ruler-straight across the Texas Panhandle to Fort Worth, he dozed. In Fort Worth he had a late supper in the depot's restaurant while he waited for the MK&T local that took him to the junction with the I&GN at Taylor, and at daybreak he woke to look out across the flat farmland of central Texas as the train steamed through the morning hours and pulled into San Antonio shortly after noon.

A quick look at the restaurant in a corner of the elongated mustard-and-mud-brown depot convinced Logarm that he'd be better off finding another place to eat. A film of coal dust covered the stools and counter, and there were no lids on any of the pots that stood on the greasy range behind it. He had three hours to get to the Texas & Pacific station, so he reclaimed his saddle and gear from the baggage room and looked for a hack.

"Where's there a good place to eat between here and the Texas & Pacific depot?" Longarm asked the hackman as he heaved his saddle up into the seat beside the hackie and put his saddlebags and Winchester inside the cab.

"Depends, I guess. Menger Hotel's got a dining room that's pretty good, but it's expensive. Meals run as much as six bits or a dollar there. You can stop at the market plaza and eat at one of the chili stands, if you like Mexican truck. I tell you, though, mister, was I hungry, I'd go to the White Front Saloon. They got better vittles on their free lunch than you'll find at most cafes, and all for the price of a nickel beer or two."

"Well, you know this town better'n I do. We'll stop at the saloon, then."

A cold beer with his lunch—two kinds of hot sausage, accompanied by mustard-smeared bread and pickles—followed by a healthy tot of Maryland rye for dessert, put Longarm into condition to face another jolting train ride. At the T&P depot, he passed his travel voucher through the wicket. The ticket clerk looked up with a frown.

"This voucher covers transportation to Tucson, mister," the man said. "Except we got no rail that far yet. You'll have to take the Southern Overland Stage past railhead."

"If that's what I've got to do, it looks like I'll have to settle for it, then. Just take what part of that voucher I won't get to use for the train, and put it on a stagecoach ticket."

"Well, now, I can't rightly do that."

"You're bound to have tickets, seeing as the stagecoach has got to meet your trains," Longarm pointed out.

"Oh, I got the tickets, but I can't sell 'em except for cash."

"You go find your boss, then," Longarm said quietly. "Tell him that travel voucher covers transportation on official U.S. Government business. I imagine he'll figure out some way to accommodate me."

Two hours later, Longarm was leaning back on the plush cushions of a day coach, the smell of disturbed coal dust in his nostrils, motes of the same dust dancing in the rays of the westward slanting sun as the T&P train chugged toward El Paso and the railhead beyond it. In the pocket of his vest was a ticket for a seat on the Southern Overland Stage from the T&P railhead to Tucson.

Chapter 2

Riding this damn railroad from San Antonio to El Paso wasn't all that bad, Longarm told himself. But this ain't a railroad track anymore. Feels like riding a log down a flume.

At El Paso, he'd changed trains, getting on what the T&P baggagemaster had referred to as the "railhead special." It proved to be a supply train with one passenger coach tacked on at the rear instead of a caboose. A caboose, Longarm thought, would have been more comfortable than the ancient day coach; it had wooden seats without padding or upholstery, and one flat wheel that crashed against the rails with monotonous regularity.

As long as the train was moving across the rolling, dunelike desert country of southern New Mexico Territory, Longarm hadn't paid too much attention to its minor discomforts. Then it reached what he took to be the last-laid section of new track, and for the past half-hour it had gotten progressively worse.

A squealing of twisted couplings reached Longarm's ears in time to warn him, and he clung to the armrest of his seat to keep from sliding into the side of the coach as the special hit another dip in the track and the battered day coach tilted precariously to one side.

With a screeching of wheel flanges against rails that rested on half-tamped ballast and hadn't yet been worn smooth, the coach slowly returned to an upright position. Ahead, the puffing of the engine slowed and the train's forward movement became a crawl as the track grew even rougher. Straightening his Stetson, which had been pushed askew when its brim touched the window at the low spot of the coach's leaning, Longarm looked at his fellow passengers straightening up in their seats again.

11

He'd already counted; besides himself, there were fifteen people scattered around the coach. There were two middle-aged couples whom he tagged as being small-town merchants and their wives. A woman dressed in black widow's weeds occupied a seat by herself; from the momentary glimpse of her face that Longarm had gotten through her veil, she was fairly young. Seated as far from the other passengers as he could get was an Indian wearing buckskin pants and a light cotton jacket; his coarse, shoulder-length black hair was held by a woven headband.

Judging by their looks and clothing, all but one of the others were either ranchers or working cowhands. They were uniformly dressed in duck trousers, faded shirts with neckerchiefs knotted around their collars, boots, and wide-brimmed hats. The exception was a lean, pale-faced man wearing a black-and-white-checked vest and a fawn-colored suit. The big diamond stickpin in his puffy cravat was obviously glass, and from the looks of his pale slim hands, he'd never done a day's hard work with them.

In a day coach built to accommodate sixty, the sixteen passengers had by choice created their own private spaces. The two couples sat together, but the woman in mourning had settled into a seat at the front of the car, the Indian had seated himself at the bulkhead in the rear, and Longarm had dropped into a seat about a third of the way up the aisle. Only the ranch hands showed any community of interest. They'd preempted the center seats and had a low-stakes poker game going even before the railhead special pulled out of the depot. Their laughter and joking comments dominated the car.

When they'd started their game, the thin man in the fawn suit had invited himself to sit in. One of the older ranch hands had looked him up and down, not bothering to hide his contempt. "We don't want you, tinhorn," he'd said quietly. "This is a friendly game, and from the way you look, it wouldn't stay that way very long if you took a hand in it." For a moment the two men had locked eyes, then the tinhorn had shrugged and taken a seat near the front of the coach.

Ahead, the train's whistle tooted sharply, two quick blasts. One of the men in the poker game glanced out the window in the gathering dusk and stood up. Longarm looked out; a cowhand mounted on a pinto, holding the reins of a saddled gray, was waiting a little distance from the broken earth of the right-of-way. The man who'd stood up was making his way to the front of the coach. The train kept slowing. The departing passenger disappeared into the vestibule, and through the window a moment later, Longarm saw him walking toward the waiting rider. The engine puffed faster and the train began to regain the speed it had lost.

A few miles farther on, three more of the passengers alighted. This time the train made a full stop while one of the couples and another cowhand got off. The couple went to a buggy that stood near the tracks; a boy was standing at the head of the horse. The cowhand started walking. As the train began moving, Longarm could see the lights of a small town gleaming a half-mile or so from the tracks.

Hell, this ain't a train, he grumbled to himself, this is a damn streetcar, letting folks off and on like there was street-corners out here. But I guess it makes sense. Don't cost the T&P anything, and they're going to want to do business with these folks, if they ever finish laying their tracks and get real trains running on 'em.

An hour or so and a score of grinding miles later, the train came to its final stop, on the last line of several sidings that branched off the main line. Flatcars and gondolas stood on the nearest of the sidings; beyond them, lights glowed in the converted boxcars that housed the tracklaying crews. Unlaid rails and stacks of ties were scattered beside the tracks. A few dark figures moved around the crew accommodations.

"Stage passengers over here!" a trainman called, waving a lantern in the blackness that the rear signal lights of the day coach barely pierced.

Saddlebags over his shoulder, saddle and bedroll in one hand and rifle in the other, Longarm fell in at the rear of the straggling group of passengers who were following the man with the lantern. Looking at their silhouetted backs, he saw that all but he and two others were ranch hands. The other two were the woman and the tinhorn. Longarm tried to count the cowhands, but they kept changing places. The trainman led them to within a few yards of the stage and stopped while the group moved on ahead.

"All right, friends, now let's step lively!" the shadowy figure standing beside the stagecoach called. There was a ring of authority in his voice, from which Longarm guessed he was the driver.

As they drew closer, Longarm saw that he was a thick-bodied man, full-bearded, with an unkempt, windblown stand of whiskers streaked with gray. His face was shaded by his hat. Like the ranch hands, he wore the duck jeans that Longarm took to be the area's usual garb, and a black vest. A big, old-style Colt Dragoon dangled in a flap-holster at his hip. The trainman turned back when the passengers were within a few yards of the stage, leaving the glow of light from the engine's headlight the only illumination around the coach.

"All right, friends!" the driver called. "We're ready to roll, but any of you needs to look for a bush, you better do it now, because it's eighteen miles to the first stage station, and I ain't aimin' to pull up and wait while you go." He saw the woman in widow's weeds and added in a tone of apology, "Women-folks excepted, a'course."

"Ain't there a place where a man can buy some grub?" one of the cowhands asked. "I been going since noon, and my gut's sure lettin' me know it's empty."

"There'll be hot biscuits and sweetening and fresh coffee at the first station," the driver replied. "And you'll have plenty of time to eat. Better eat hearty, too. We won't get fed again till two stations later, and that'll be a while after sunup."

"My goodness!" the woman exclaimed. "The ticket agent in El Paso told me we'd only have a short stagecoach ride to Tucson from where the train stopped. When will we get there?"

"Well, barring bad luck, we oughta pull in about noon, the day after tomorrow," the driver answered matter-of-factly.

"But how far are we from Tucson?" she asked.

"Right at two hundred miles, lady. And we ain't gettin' no closer as long as we stand here jawing. Now, let's all you folks git aboard so's we can pull out. Lady, you git in first and set in that middle seat facing the team. It's a mite smoother ridin' on that seat than the others."

After the woman had gotten aboard, the other passengers began piling into the elongated coach. Longarm's eyes were adjusted to the darkness now, and he could see that the stage was not the curved-bellied semi-closed Concords used farther north. It was a boxy wagon with a wide center door. Its sides rose just above the backs of its three benchlike seats; canvas flaps that could be lowered to cover the glassless space above the sides were strapped in tight rolls at the roofline.

The seats were arranged so that riders in the front seat faced the back of the coach; the middle seat was a double one with a backrest along its center, and the passengers on it sat back to back. Those sitting on the rear half of the center seat faced the occupants of the back seat.

"Three in a row!" the driver said. "There's room under the seats for your carpetbags and valises. If your legs is too long, sorta lock your knees together."

As the passengers crowded up to get on the stage, the driver began counting, his bushy beard crinkling as he made his tally. Three or four had already boarded before he stepped between those remaining and the wagon and spread his arms to stop them. ·

"Now, dagnabbit, we got too many to ride inside!" he said. "Wagon holds nine, we got eleven! Two of you men is goin' to have to ride on top with me. We ain't carrying no money chest and there ain't no Injun hostiles in these parts no more, so we won't have nobody ridin' shotgun. Two men'll fit in the top seat with me just fine."

Longarm decided at once that with his long legs and wide shoulders, he'd be cramped if he rode inside the packed coach. He said quickly, "Count me for one up in the driver's seat."

Almost at the same time, the cowhand who stood beside him volunteered, "You know I ain't going far, Patches. I'd as lief ride outside as in."

Peering through the gloom, the driver said, "Oh, that's you, is it, Billy? Well, fine. You and the other fellow draws the top, then." He looked at Longarm's gear and added, "You see to your own saddle, friend. Stagecoach company ain't responsible for lost stuff."

Spreading his feet, Longarm heaved his saddle on top of the coach and climbed up to tie a pair of saddle strings to the rail that ran around the top. He laid his bulging saddlebags on top of his Winchester and used another set of the strings to tie both to the saddle. Finished, he dropped back to the ground.

15

He told the cowhand who was waiting, "You can ride in the middle or on the outside, it's all the same to me."

"Might as well set on the outside, then. Like I said, I ain't got far to go." The youth named Billy hoisted himself nimbly up into the seat.

Longarm followed and settled into place just as the driver clambered in from the other side. "You men set?" he asked.

"Set as we'll ever be, Patches," Billy answered for both himself and Longarm.

With a ringing "yay-hoo" that rivaled the war-whoop of any Indian Longarm had ever heard, Patches slapped the reins sharply on the necks of the four-horse team, and the stagecoach lurched forward. A sudden glare set Longarm's eyes to blinking as the stage rolled slowly into the cone of light from the locomotive's headlight. The glare grew dimmer as the horses settled into their harness and the stage moved faster. The headlight became a yellow disc that disappeared as they mounted a rolling rise and dropped behind it. Then the light was completely gone and the night closed around them.

Temporarily blinded by the headlight's glare, Longarm could see very little except the white, blurred faces of his companions on the seat and the rumps of the horses ahead. Gradually his night vision returned and he could see Patches' rough-cut features and Billy's youthful face, and when he looked over the bobbing ears of the lead horses, he could also see the ruts that marked the road to Tucson. He hadn't needed to see the road to know it was mostly ruts; the lurching of the stagecoach had already told him that was the case. He turned to Patches.

"Ever hear of a place west of Tucson, a little town called Mina Cobre?" he asked the driver.

Patches shot a stream of tobacco juice off to the side of the rattling stagecoach before shaking his head. "Nope. Not much wonder if I ain't, though. There's new places popping up in the territory every day."

"It's just beyond a town called Quijotoa, down close to the border with Mexico," Longarm persisted.

"Never heard of Qui-whatever-it-is, neither. Sounds like a Papago town to me. Or maybe Mex, left over from when that part of the territory belonged to Mexico."

16

"Don't this stageline go on west from Tucson?"

"Sure. Clear on out to San Diego, in Californy. But the road follows what there is of the Gila River going on west. I'd guess this Mina Cobre place is a good piece south of the Gila."

"I never heard of it neither, mister," Billy volunteered. "But I ain't been in the territory very long. Never even been to Tucson, come right down to it. Keep telling myself I oughta see what it's like there, instead of going back to El Paso for a spree when I get some time off, but Texas is more home to me than Tucson'd be."

Just then the ruts got deeper and rougher as they crossed an alkali flat, and Patches gave his full attention to the straining team. After they'd rolled on a mile or so past the rough stretch, Billy's eyelids began to droop. His head sagged forward and he began to snore gently, swaying in the seat.

After a short while, the young hand's snores and the swaying of the stage began to make Longarm sleepy. He let himself slip into a light doze that lasted until he felt the driver's elbow nudging him in the ribs. His eyes snapped open and he looked around. The moon had come up, showing a starkly bare landscape, its baked soil cut by the ruts of the road, with here and there a towering saguaro cactus or a rock outcrop. Patches started sawing on the reins. Longarm hadn't seen any kind of landmark, and saw none when the team came to a halt.

Patches said, "Poke the youngster awake, will you, friend? This is where he wants to git off."

Longarm nudged Billy with his elbow. The young cowhand opened his eyes, yawning. He asked, "We there already?"

"Yep," the driver replied. "You say hello to Tom and his missus when you git to the ranch. Tell 'em I'll be looking for 'em to flag me down, next time they head for the bright lights."

"Sure will."

Billy dropped off the seat. Patches geed up the team. The young cowhand waved, and started walking at right angles to the road. Longarm's professional curiosity made him glance back now and then. The desert moonlight was new to him and he kept testing its quality against a time when his life might depend on gauging the range of a rifle shot in the night. He watched Billy until the youth was lost to sight in the darkness, then took out a cheroot and lighted it. He was conscious of the

17

stage driver's curious gaze flicking over him now and again, but did not show that he noticed the scrutiny.

Finally, Patches could hold back his curiosity no longer. "You mind me askin' what your line of work is, friend?"

"Not a bit. Ask away," Longarm replied.

"Dagnabbit, I *am* askin'!" The driver paused long enough to send a squirt of tobacco juice over his shoulder before adding, "You got the look of a lawman or a bounty hunter, but I'm damned if I can tell which one."

Longarm saw no reason for an evasive reply. "Deputy U.S. marshal. Out of the Denver office."

"You're a hell of a long way from home, ain't you?"

"A piece."

"I guess you got a name," Patches suggested. "You know what mine is, from Billy."

"Long," Longarm replied.

"Wait a minute! You ain't the one they call Longarm, by any stretch of the imagination, are you?"

"My friends call me that. Other folks too, I guess."

"I heard about you from Cy Ewing! Me and him was hacking down in Galveston when you busted up Kester's gang! Cy drove you around town there, one night."

"That was a while back," Longarm said. "I guess I disremember your friend."

"Well, Cy never claimed he knowed you, but he sure did know he'd drove you that night." Patches shook his head. "Well, it's a little bitty world, I guess. I'm real proud to have you on my stage, Longarm."

"Thanks. But I'd appreciate it if you'd just sort of keep quiet about me being a marshal. For now, at least."

"Why, sure." Patches was silent for a moment, then he asked, "Headin' for this place you was askin' me about, Mina Cobre?" When Longarm nodded, the driver said, "Guess I give you a right short answer before. Tell you what, you ask the men in the stage station when we git to Tucson. Likely they can tell you how to git there."

"Thanks. I'll remember to ask." Longarm tossed the butt of the cheroot away, and it landed in a tiny flare of sparks on the hard soil. He asked, "How much further before we stop?

I could do with a bite of grub and some hot coffee."

"Just a little ways up ahead now. You can see the station when we top the next rise."

As they reached the crest of the rise, Patches began yelling "yay-hoo" even before Longarm saw lights ahead. His wild calls brought results quickly; lights showed ahead, and as the stage careened down the slope and drew closer to the station, the black, shadowy figures of men showed against the glowing lanterns. They were soon close enough for Longarm to see the stage station, a raw wood shanty that stood beside a pole corral in which several horses were standing. Patches hauled back on the reins. The stage slowed to a halt and he set the brake and swung to the ground. Longarm dropped from the seat on his side of the stage.

"You folks can git coffee and hot biscuits inside," Patches announced. "Conveniences behind the station. The lady goes first, you men can wait. We won't be pulling out for ten or fifteen minutes, so there ain't no hurry."

Two men were leading a fresh team from the corral to replace the horses that had drawn the stage from the railhead. Longarm watched them for a moment, then walked leisurely to the station. Inside the low-ceilinged shanty, the air was hot and laden with the odors of stale bacon grease, sweat, and horse manure. A hollow-faced woman with graying, straggly hair, and dressed in a wrinkled, shapeless wrapper, was handing out cups of coffee and molasses-smeared biscuits from a rickety, unpainted table at the back of the room.

Longarm took his place in line and waited his turn to be served, paid the dime the woman requested for his coffee and biscuit, and went back outside where he could breathe more freely. The fresh team had already been hitched up, but he saw Patches busy doing something to the stage and walked over to look. The driver was removing the back of the middle seat and fitting the two pieces to span the gap between the front and the rear seats. He looked up and saw Longarm.

"Give ever'body but you and me a chance to stretch out and grab a little shut-eye," he explained. "These Celerity Wagons don't quite come up to a feather bed, but a fellow can doze where the road ain't too damn rough."

"I guess it's better'n sitting up," Longarm said, eyeing the bare, uneven boards dubiously. "But I'll keep on riding up by you, if it's all the same."

"If you change your mind, you can git down and nap after we leave the Tombstone Junction stop. There'll be a lot of 'em get off there to wait for the local stage south."

Longarm nodded. "Sure. We'll see how I feel then."

"Excuse me," a woman's voice said. Both Longarm and Patches turned around. The woman in widow's weeds had come up behind them. They could not see her face through the dark veil that shrouded it, but her voice sounded troubled. She said, "Can I talk with you a minute, driver?"

"Name's Patches, ma'am. Talk away."

She looked at Longarm and said, "I mean, in private."

"He's a law officer, ma'am," Patches explained. "I don't guess it'd hurt for him to stay, if you don't mind. If you got some kind of trouble, maybe he can even help you."

"Well..." She hesitated for a moment, then blurted, "It's that man sitting by me, Mr. Patches! He keeps... well, it's awfully dark in there, and he keeps trying to get his hand up under my dress. And he says things, ugly things, whispers to me so soft the others can't hear him. I thought if you talked to him, or maybe changed my seat or something..."

"Just a minute, ma'am," Longarm said. "First off, you mind telling me your name?"

"Moore. Sarah Moore."

"My name's Long, Mrs. Moore. Now, excuse me if I ask you this, but you didn't lead this fellow on any, did you?"

"I most certainly did not!" she snapped. "I kept pushing him away. I... I didn't want to stir up trouble in the coach."

"It'd only have been trouble for him, most likely," Longarm told her. "But I can see it would've put you in a sort of embarrassing position." He thought for a moment, then said, "I'll tell you what. Let's you and me walk back to the station and stand outside the door till he comes out. I'll have a talk with him, and I don't imagine he'll bother you the rest of the trip when I get through with him."

"You want me to call the passengers out about the time you get to the door?" Patches asked. "Maybe you can nab him easier if ever'body comes through the door in a hurry."

"Good idea," Longarm said. He took the woman's arm. "You just come along now, and let's see what happens."

Two or three of the passengers had already come out of the station by the time Longarm escorted the woman back to the door. Patches waited until they stopped, then yelled, "Board up now! We'll pull out soon as ever'body's in the coach!"

Standing in front of his companion so that she would not be seen at once by those coming through the door, Longarm waited for the tinhorn to appear. He grabbed the man by the collar as he passed and swung him around. The fellow's pale face was twisted angrily when he saw the woman standing behind Longarm. He said, "Whatever this woman's told you about me is a lie!"

"How'd you know she told me anything about you?" Longarm asked him. "Seems to me you just convicted yourself of what she's accusing you of doing."

"She invited me to feel her!"

"I did not!" she snapped. "I kept trying to push you away!"

"She's lying!" the tinhorn insisted.

"Shut up!" Longarm commanded. "Now, just so you won't think I'm just butting in, I'm a deputy U.S. marshal, and I'm—"

Before Longarm could finish, the man twisted around, and his sudden move took Longarm by surprise. He'd had only a loose grip on the tinhorn's collar, and he felt the cloth sliding through his fingers before he could tighten them.

Just in time, Longarm saw the man stretching his left hand across his body, reaching for his right forearm as he completed his turn. With a quick, sharp kick, Longarm booted the tinhorn's right arm upward. There was a flat-sounding explosion, and the slug from the tinhorn's sleeve gun cut the air above Longarm's head and thudded harmlessly into the wall of the stage station. Behind him, Longarm heard the woman's belated scream, as he immobilized the man by twisting an arm behind his back.

"It's all right now" he told her. "That trick gun he's got hid up his sleeve only holds one shell."

"But he might've killed you!"

"Only he didn't." Longarm looked around. The ranch hands were rushing toward the station from the coach. Those who

21

wore guns had them in their hands. He called, "It's all right, men!" Go on back to the coach! I'm a peace officer, and I got everything under control. We'll be moving out in just a minute!"

"You sure?" one of them called.

"I'm sure. Go on back now. We'll be right along." Turning his attention back to the tinhorn, he asked, "What's your name? And I mean your real one!"

"Fortner. What . . . what're you going to do with me?"

"Well, if you hadn't been so quick on the trigger, I'd've shook you up a little bit and let you off. But if you're all that ready to shoot a U.S. marshal, I got a hunch you're wanted pretty bad someplace. I'll take you on into Tucson and hand you over to the sheriff there. He can find out pretty fast."

"Honest, now, Marshal, I'm not wanted anywhere! I just got excited when you grabbed me. Thought you were trying to rob me."

"That sounds good, but I don't rightly believe it." He turned to Sarah Moore and said, "Now, you just go ahead and get in the stage. I'll bring this fellow along."

"You're not going to let him ride in the coach next to me again, are you?" she asked.

"I'd be afraid to, Mrs. Moore. If them fellows found out what he's been up to with you, they'd save me the trouble of taking him in. He'd never get to the next station alive."

"I hadn't thought about that."

"You go on now," Longarm repeated. "Patches has fixed the seats so you can sleep while we're traveling. I'll take care of whatever's necessary."

Longarm let the woman get halfway to the stage before he led Fortner after her. Patches still stood beside the Celerity Wagon, waiting for them. The passengers were peering out curiously.

Longarm told them, "Just hang on a minute, men. We'll move out as soon as I take care of this prisoner."

"Take your time, Marshal," One of them answered. "We spotted him for some kind of crook back there on the train, but there wasn't much we could do about it."

Patches asked, "What the hell happened down there? That wasn't you shooting, was it?"

"No. It was this critter," Longarm told him. "Which reminds me, I better take that sleeve gun off of him." None too gently, he pulled Fortner's coat sleeve up and unstrapped the long, tubular weapon from his forearm. Dropping it on the ground, he planted one foot on it and bent the barrel into a sharp angle, then tossed the now-useless gun off into the darkness.

"Won't you need that for evidence, if you're taking him in?" Patches asked.

"Not hardly. Far as I know, it ain't against the law to tote any kind of gun in Arizona Territory. Anyhow, I ain't made up my mind whether I want to take this trash in or not. He might get himself shot trying to get away between here and Tucson."

"Now, wait a minute!" Fortner protested.

"Shut your mouth!" Longarm snapped. He asked Patches, "Them nags broke to riding?"

"Not likely. Most of the stock we get's barely broke at all. Half of 'em, it's a fight just to hitch 'em."

"This is as good a time as any to find out how well-broke they are," Longarm said to the driver. "Maybe you'll give me a hand getting this fellow on one of 'em."

"Whatever you say, Longarm."

Between them, Longarm and Patches managed to get Fortner mounted on the second horse they tried. Longarm took his handcuffs from his coat pocket and snapped the shackles on Fortner's wrists, securing his arms behind his back.

"How do you expect me to stay on this damn horse if I can't use my hands?" Fortner asked.

"I reckon you'll manage," Longarm replied coldly. He turned to Patches and said, "Whenever you're ready. I just didn't want that skunk in the seat with us the rest of the way. His stink would have us puking before we'd gone half a mile."

He joined Patches in climbing to the driver's seat, and the stagecoach pulled out onto the rutted road again.

Chapter 3

Relieved of the need to be constantly alert, watching his prisoner, Longarm dozed much of the time during what remained of the night. He wasn't the only sleeper; several times he woke to find Patches asleep, swaying in the seat beside him. The first two or three times this happened, Longarm worried, but he saw that the team seemed to know the rutted road as well as the driver did, so he stopped letting the idea of a sleeping Patches bother him.

At the next two station stops, while the passengers stayed on the stage, sleeping more soundly with the vehicle motionless, he stretched his own legs and allowed Fortner to walk and relieve himself while the horses were being changed. Both stops were short, lasting only long enough for the tired team to be removed and a fresh one hitched up.

At the last station before the Tombstone crossing, he asked Patches, "Don't you get no relief at all during this haul? Seems to me it's asking a whole lot of a driver to keep going without no rest for two whole nights and the better part of two days."

With a sheepish grin, the driver said, "I was supposed to turn the rig over to my relief at the last station, but I told him to pick up on the next stage that comes through. Why, shit, Longarm, I wouldn't miss seeing how this is going to come out for anything you could give me."

"I can tell you right now how it's coming out," Longarm told him. "We're going to pull into Tucson, and I'm going to hand that fellow over to the sheriff, and that'll be the end of it."

"We're a long ways outa Tucson yet," Patches reminded him. "For all you know, that tinhorn might try to pull some kind of trick on you yet."

25

"If he does, I guess I can handle it."

"That's what I know," Patches chuckled. "That's what I wanta see!"

Longarm had discovered that by bending down over the side of the stage, he could look down into the interior, and several times during the hours of darkness he'd checked on the sardine-packed passengers. When dawn broke, he bent over to look again. Two or three of the ranch hands had dropped off during the night, at station stops or spots where their trail home joined the stagecoach route, so there were now only five men and Sarah Moore stretched out across the improvised sleeping arrangement.

They were still sleeping, the men head-to-foot in a crowded line across the forward section of the wagon, the woman stretched out the width of the rear seat. Longarm grinned when he saw that the men had left the widest possible amount of space between themselves and the sleeping woman.

Sunrise caught them rolling along at the stage's steady pace of about six miles an hour. By Longarm's reckoning, they were roughly halfway between the third station stop and the junction where the local Tombstone stage met the Overland route when the sun came up red and hot. It grew steadily hotter as the Celerity Wagon jolted across the barren land hour after slow hour.

By day, the desert looked even more desolate than it had in the moonlight. Under the cloudless morning sky, the dun-colored earth reflected the sun's hot glare, and anyone in the open found himself being baked from below as well as from overhead. The landscape was still featureless; rolling terrain, broken only by a few red rock outcrops and an occasional towering saguaro cactus or a clump of thorny, low-growing ocotillo bushes.

At the San Pedro River, waterless at this time of year—a shallow gully in a stretch of loose, treacherous sand—Patches wheeled the team across the riverbed and turned the horses' heads toward the low humps that marked the pass through the Whetstones.

Beyond the riverbed, the land began to rise. The heat grew less intense, though only a hardened desert rat would have called the air cool. The stage topped the crest of the rise and

26

the Tombstone Junction station popped into view. There was more to it than there'd been to the night stops; two other buildings flanked the shanty and the pole corral of the station itself.

"That place just past the station's where you and me is going to be, soon as I turn this rig over to the hitch-up team," Patches told Longarm, pointing to a false-front building. "If you feel like an eye-opener, that is."

"A swallow of Maryland rye'd go down real good right now," Longarm agreed. "And I hope that station dishes up real grub for breakfast. My belly's yelling for a big piece of steak and some fried spuds."

"You won't get nothing like that at the station," Patches said. "But that place between the station and the saloon's a cafe. They'll set out just about anything you crave." He jerked his head at Fortner, who was almost lying prone on the broad back of the horse after his uncomfortable night. "What'll you do with him while we're eatin'?"

"Cuff him to one of the stagecoach wheels," Longarm replied promptly. "He ain't likely to go much of anyplace if he's got to drag the wagon with him."

After Patches had set the brake on the coach and the passengers had started walking, bleary-eyed and with unsteady feet, the fifty yards or so from the coach to the station, Longarm got Fortner off the horse and snapped one bracelet of the handcuffs around a wheel spoke.

"How about my breakfast?" the tinhorn whined. "It's bad enough to have to bounce around on that damned horse all night. You don't need to starve me to boot."

"I'll be back in plenty of time for you to get some grub," Longarm told Fortner. Over his shoulder, as he turned to join Patches, who'd already set a beeline for the saloon, he added, "And don't start trying to blame anybody but yourself for the fix you're in."

Young as the morning was, a sizable lineup had gathered at the bar in the saloon. Longarm and Patches found places at the end, and Longarm lighted a cheroot while waiting for their drinks. He ran his eyes idly along the faces of the drinkers, but saw no familiar ones. Most of them had the look of miners or prospectors, though there was a small sprinkling of clean-shaven, neckerchief-wearing ranch hands among them.

Finishing their drinks, the two headed for the restaurant next to the saloon. It was less crowded; only two men sat at the long counter, and one of the three tables was occupied by Sarah Moore. She'd pulled her veil up over her hat while eating, and for the first time Longarm got a good look at her face.

It was a much younger face than he'd expected it to be. Although she was a bit pale, her face was unlined; she had high cheekbones, dark thick brows over large brown eyes, a nose that was a trifle too prominent, full pouting lips, and a firm chin. She nodded smilingly at the two men, and continued eating.

"I got to keep my eye on the coach," Patches told Longarm as he led the way to a table by the cafe's only window. "Passengers is going to be wantin' to go pretty soon, and the bosses get riled if we don't push right along. A'course, we stay here longer'n we do at most stations, it being a breakfast stop. But we can't lollygag if I'm going to pull into Tucson on time."

Longarm glanced out the window. The horse-handlers had taken the tired team to the corral, but hadn't yet brought out the fresh one.

"Looks like we got plenty of time," he said.

He was about to look away from the window when he saw a man walking toward the coach. Longarm frowned. He seemed to recall the man from somewhere, but couldn't remember any passengers getting on at the railhead who'd worn a dusty black suit or who walked with that peculiar, hesitating gait, a hesitation that stopped just short of being a limp.

He asked Patches, "You taking on any new riders here, heading into Tucson?"

"Not as I know of, but I'll lose some. Pullin' out, there'll only be the widow and one cowboy, and he'll drop off up the line a ways. A'course, there'll be you and the tinhorn."

Longarm hadn't taken his eyes away from the window. The man was almost to the stagecoach now. He turned to look over his shoulder and Longarm got a glimpse of a bearded face and a broken nose in the few seconds while the man's face was turned toward the cafe. The beard was strange, but Longarm recognized the twisted nose, and now he recalled why the

28

hesitating gait had seemed so familiar. He's seen it last in a courtroom in Wyoming Territory, where he'd been testifying at a trial.

"Spade Blasdell!" he exclaimed. "He must've busted out and I didn't hear about it!"

"What're you—" Patches began.

Longarm was already in motion. He kicked his chair away as he leaped up and headed for the door, drawing as he ran. He heard but didn't heed Patches' surprised shout.

Fortner was facing the restaurant. He saw Longarm burst out of the door with his Colt in his hand. Longarm could see the tinhorn's lips moving, warning the man approaching him.

Blasdell drew, but instead of firing, he passed the pistol to Fortner, then produced a second gun from beneath his coat. He hit the ground and rolled for the scanty cover of the stagecoach wheels as Fortner fired. His hurried aim was bad. The bullet missed Longarm by a dozen feet and tore splinters from the wooden front of the cafe.

Instinct born of countless gunfights told Longarm to pick Fortner as his first target. His shot rang out and the tinhorn's second shot echoed it.

Longarm's trigger finger had moved a fraction of a second faster. Fortner's body jerked as the heavy slug from the .44 struck him. His gunhand was already drooping when he triggered his weapon, and the lead kicked up dust a yard in front of Longarm's boots.

Blasdell had sheltered behind the wheel to which Fortner was handcuffed, and the tinhorn's sagging body spoiled his aim when he let off his first shot at Longarm. Longarm felt the rush of air as the bullet whizzed past his cheek. He dropped to the ground, looking for cover, but there was none.

Patches was out of the cafe by now, brandishing his big Colt Dragoon. He could see Fortner's body hanging from the wheel by its handcuffed wrist, but did not spot Blasdell under the stage. He stood in the door, swiveling his head in search of the hidden gunman.

Longarm let off a safety shot at Blasdell, more to keep him pinned down than with any hope of scoring a hit. Then he saw Blasdell's arm snake out past Fortner's form, reaching for the pistol that lay at the tinhorn's side.

When he saw Blasdell's move, Longarm snap-shot at the outstretched hand, but the target was too small and the range too great. The slug rang off the wheel's iron tire, and Blasdell got the pistol before Longarm could fire again.

Longarm's shot pinpointed Blasdell's location for Patches. The stage driver began circling away from the restaurant, to get the gunman under the wagon in a crossfire.

Blasdell saw Patches moving and knew that his string was running out. He leaped from his cover with a pistol in each hand, firing wildly, one gun aimed in Longarm's general direction, the other toward the crouched, running driver.

Longarm dropped Blasdell with his next shot. The bullet caught the gunman full in the chest and he toppled over backward as though he'd been poleaxed. Patches' first and only shot cut through the air above Blasdell's prone body.

Keeping his eyes fixed on Blasdell and moving warily, his Colt ready, Longarm stood up and walked to where Blasdell lay. He nudged both pistols out of the gunman's reach before looking down to make absolutely sure of the man's identity. This close, no mistake was possible.

Blasdell's eyelids quivered and his eyes opened. He said in a weak but still angry voice, "Damn you, Long! I wanted you! It was your bullet that give me this game leg when you took me in for that bank job up in Wyoming!"

Patches came hurrying up before Longarm could reply. Longarm motioned the driver to keep quiet. He asked Blasdell, "When'd you bust out of the pen?"

"Two—weeks—ago," the gunman gasped. Longarm could see that his strength was going fast. "Had it all— fixed with Fortner—to meet here and—take as many mine payrolls as we could—till things got—too hot. . . ."

"They got too hot too fast, I'd say," Longarm observed, holstering his Colt.

"Seems like," Blasdell gasped. "If I'd been—two minutes faster—getting that gun to Fortner—you'd be laying here—instead of me. . . ."

Much more quietly than he'd burst upon the scene, Blasdell died. Patches slowly put his Dragoon back into its holster.

"Sorry I didn't make it in time to give you a hand, Longarm," he said.

"You helped enough just by pulling Blasdell's attention off me long enough for me to get him."

With the gunfire obviously over, men were running toward the stagecoach from the saloon and station. Longarm took out his badge and held it up for them to look at. Raising his voice, he said, "It's all over now. There's not anything more going to happen. Just a couple of badmen that didn't make it."

Questions popped from the throng, but Longarm ignored them. He took Patches by the arm and drew him to one side. "Reckon you can get whoever's in charge of the station here to get them two buried? Be a waste of time hauling 'em to Tucson."

"Sure. He's goin' to want me to get moving right fast, and that'll save us hanging around." Patches indicated the curious onlookers. "There's enough miners in this bunch that digging graves for 'em won't be no big job. But you better come along with me while I talk to him. You got the badge."

Arrangements for burying Blasdell and Fortner were completed in less time than Longarm had anticipated. Within a quarter-hour after the last shot had shattered the air of the station, the stage was on its way again. There were only two passengers left now—the rancher who would get off at the trail to his home, and Sarah Moore.

Longarm still rode with Patches; he had no wish to discuss the shooting incident with anyone. He stayed silent in response to the driver's efforts to start a conversation as the Celerity Wagon bounced over the bumps of the Whetstone Pass, and pulled up to let the rancher alight. Before Patches could gee up the team again, Sarah Moore stuck her head out of the stage and looked up at Longarm.

"Marshal Long?"

"Is there something wrong, Mrs. Moore?"

"It's not exactly that there's anything wrong, but I feel so terribly alone in this big stagecoach all by myself. Would you mind riding down here with me for a while?"

"Go on," Patches whispered. "I bet the pore lady's still got the shivers from seeing all that shooting back at the station."

"Well..."

"Git down there now!" Patches urged. "Hell, that lady might git a fit of nerves if she's got to stay by herself!"

31

Longarm swung down from the seat and got into the stage. He hardly had time to close the door before Patches slapped the reins and started the team moving.

"I guess seeing all that shooting and those two outlaws getting killed made you sorta nervous," Longarm suggested as he settled down on the seat beside her.

"Well, it's not exactly what I'm used to. Maybe I shouldn't admit this, but I thought it was kind of exciting. Things like that don't happen very often in Charleston."

Longarm's interest perked up. "Would that be the one in South Carolina, or Tennessee, or West Virginia?"

"West Virginia. Why?"

"Because I growed up in West Virginia."

"You're joshing me, Marshal Long!"

"Honest Injun."

"Isn't that a strange coincidence! For us to meet out here in the desert, in Arizona Territory!"

"It don't happen very often," he agreed. "That's pretty small country, back there. But I been gone from it such a long time, I don't reckon I got any family or friends left there."

"I can't really believe it yet, Marshal Long!"

"If you don't mind, I got a sort of nickname my friends call me by. I answer to it a lot better'n I do to my born name. Why don't you just call me Longarm, Mrs. Moore?"

"Why, of course." She hesitated for a moment, then lifted the veil away from her face and looked up at him. "I . . . well, I suppose you'd say I've got a confession to make."

She paused again and Longarm suggested, "Seems to me I remember something about confessing being good for a body."

"I don't think it's really all that bad." She smiled. But I think you're the kind of man who'd understand. And after all, we're both from West Virginia."

"So we are."

"Yes. Well . . . it's not *Mrs.* Moore. And if I'm going to call you Longarm, will you please just call me Sarah? You see, I'm not a widow at all. I just decided to wear these weeds and veil to keep men from bothering me, traveling alone the way I am. You know, like that one tried to do last night."

Longarm nodded. "Can't say as I blame you. A pretty young

girl like you must get a lot of men running after her."

"I don't think any girl minds having men run after her. Most of us feel flattered, even if we're not supposed to show it. But how flattered we are depends on the kind of man doing the running, as far as I'm concerned."

"I'd say that's a pretty downright way of putting it."

"Well, it's true," Sarah said defiantly. "Any woman who denies it is a hypocrite, and I don't have much use for her." She looked up again at Longarm. "Now, had it been you, instead of that terrible pale thin man last night, I might not have asked you and the driver to stop him."

Longarm managed to whistle around his smile. "You really do put it plain and blunt. I guess I better say thank you. What you just said seems to me like it calls for one."

Sarah caught Longarm's gunmetal-blue eyes with her large dark ones and held his gaze on her face. She said, "I'm not very old, Longarm, but I'm not a skinny little girl in pigtails any longer, either."

"Oh, I can see that real plain," Longarm assured her, his eyes taking in the swell of her breasts that the severely cut, black bombazine dress she wore hid at a glance but emphasized on close inspection.

"You haven't asked me yet, but I suppose you will sooner or later, why I came out here to Arizona Territory."

"I wasn't asking. Or even wondering," he told her.

"You might as well know now that I was sent out here to stay with my aunt and uncle in Tucson to keep my family from being disgraced." She was looking at Longarm with a questioning stare, half defiant, half fearful of the reaction she'd see in his face. When he said nothing and his expression did not change, Sarah added, "You understand, don't you? I'm going to have a baby."

"Now, that's a perfectly natural thing, Sarah. Women have babies all the time, even if they ain't married, which I guess is what you're trying to say."

"Yes. I've been trying to say it to somebody ever since I knew. Oh, my family, of course, I had to tell them, but they try not to talk about it. And I'm sure I'm not the first one who's listened to a man she thinks she's going to marry, and gets ahead of the wedding ceremony."

33

"And won't be the last one, either," Longarm assured her.

She smiled. "It wasn't my first time, with Tommie. Even if he was the first real grown-up man. I was really a skinny little girl with pigtails when I let my curiosity get the better of me. I guess I didn't have any excuse the next time, and then when Tommie realized he wasn't the first..."

"He up and moved on," Longarm finished for her. "It happens that way a lot, Sarah. There's not any need for you to feel so bad about it."

"Oh, you don't know how much better you've made me feel, Longarm, just listening and understanding when I talk about it! Because there hasn't been anybody who'd listen, until now!" She blinked away the moisture that had welled up in her eyes and added, "I could just hug and kiss you for being so nice! And I guess I will!"

Sarah pulled Longarm down to her and found his lips with hers. Longarm hadn't expected the kiss, and when it took place, he didn't expect it to turn into the kiss that it grew to be. Sarah's tongue sought his, and Longarm matched its questing movements. His hand found her breast, soft and full under the stiff, crinkly fabric of her dress. They clung together on the hard, jouncing seat while the stagecoach rattled along in the bright noon sun.

Sarah broke away, panting, her lips parted and her eyes open wide. "Goodness, Longarm! Tommie never kissed me like that. I don't guess anybody else ever did, either. But you've been with a lot of women, I suppose."

"If I have or if I haven't, it ain't something I'd want to talk about," he told her.

"Oh, I wouldn't be jealous. I'm just curious. You see, I don't know all that much about men. *Real* men, I mean. I know I said Tommie was a man, but he was just like a little boy in a lot of ways. He wanted to... well, he wanted me, but he acted like he was afraid of me too. And maybe he was. Maybe he was afraid that what did happen might happen."

"And you weren't?" Longarm asked, gazing at the strange girl-woman Sarah was revealing herself to be.

"Afraid? No. Not a bit. Maybe I didn't have sense enough to be. All I could think of was how I felt, when we'd ride out of town in the buggy and hug and kiss awhile."

Longarm found no reassuring answer to that. When he

34

stayed silent, Sarah put her hand on his knee. He looked down into her upturned face. Her parted lips glistened, and her eyes held a question. Longarm was sure he knew what it was, but he made no effort to answer.

"Longarm..." she said, and stopped short.

"Go on, Sarah. You been bottling too many things up inside you, I'd say. Come on out with whatever you were going to ask."

"Will you kiss me again? I mean, will you kiss me, this time? Before, I kissed you."

Longarm found her lips. They moved vibrantly under his, and again her tongue darted out. He felt the hand on his knee slide up his thigh to his crotch. He was far from being erect, but the kisses had roused him from total flaccidity. Sarah's fingers stroked him, and he felt himself swelling. She felt it too, and sighed in her throat. Longarm returned his hand to her breast, and Sarah twisted her body to give his fingers more freedom to caress her. They broke the long kiss, both of them gasping.

"Can we?" she whispered. "Right here and now?" She indicated the baked desert landscape. "There's nobody to see what we'd be doing."

"Except Patches."

"He's outside. Anyhow, he wouldn't have any reason to peek down and look at us. Even if he did, do you think he'd stop the stage and make us get off?"

"No. Except him looking might embarrass you." Even as he objected, Longarm knew Sarah was in no mood by now to listen. He realized there was little danger of Patches looking into the coach, but he made a final try. He said, "Tonight, after it gets good and dark..."

"No, Longarm! Now!"

Her hands had not left his crotch. She'd kept squeezing and rubbing him while they talked, and Longarm was by now fully erect. Her fingers began working at the buttons of his fly, and he wondered if she'd been as urgent and eager with the boy she called Tommie. She finally loosed the last button and freed him.

"Oh, God!" she gasped. "Is that what a real grown-up man looks like?"

Sarah's hot hands caressing his throbbing erection brought

35

Longarm to a quick decision. He lifted her skirt and petticoat and found the buttons in the waistband of her knee-length knickers. She raised herself from the seat to let him slip the ruffled underthings down and off. He could see drops of her juices glistening in her dark pubic brush.

Longarm clasped his hands around her waist to lift her above him, but Sarah anticipated him. She rolled over and straddled him. She was still holding him and now she released one hand and guided him into her with the other. Then, with a sobbing sigh rising from her throat, she impaled herself on Longarm's upstanding shaft.

He tried to help Sarah ease her body down as he went into her, but she twisted away from his supporting hands. She let herself down slowly, cautiously, then he saw an expression of fear or doubt flicker across her face and she tried to lift herself away from him. He put his hands on her hips and stopped her from rising. Sarah shook her head. She was biting down on her lower lip, her white teeth gleaming. The eagerness she'd shown a moment earlier had drained away.

Longarm held her firmly, feeling her muscles tightening under his hands. For a moment they stayed motionless, then Sarah moved her hips tentatively, gently, as though she were testing the sensation of Longarm's shallow penetration. Her hips began to move a bit faster, and the expression on her face changed from doubt to pleasure as a ripple of quick, gasping sobs escaped from her throat.

Her body shook in Longarm's hands, twisting in a convulsive storm that ended as suddenly as it had begun. He felt her taut muscles relax and her sobs ended in a long, gentle sigh. Longarm supported her limp body while she calmed and the lines that had formed so suddenly on her face vanished. She opened her eyes and looked at him, shaking her head.

In a low voice, she said, "I'm sorry I couldn't take you any deeper, Longarm, but I'd never felt myself filling up like that before, and I was afraid it'd hurt. Does that mean there's something wrong with me?"

"Not a bit. It might just mean you ain't been with a man for quite a while."

"Almost four months. But I'm not scared anymore." She slid her hand between them and Longarm felt her fingers exploring his groin. She went on, "I can take you all the way now. I *want* to take you all the way!"

Longarm raised his hips and slid forward on the seat. Sarah brought up her legs and knelt, straddling him. Then, her eyes closed again, she lowered herself until her spread buttocks were resting on his outstretched thighs.

Sarah was silent for such a long time that Longarm began to feel alarmed. He asked, "Are you sure you're all right?"

Her eyes popped open and she smiled happily. "All right? I've never felt so damned good in all my life!"

She threw her arms around him and locked her lips to his in a hard, grinding kiss. Longarm braced his feet and thrust upward. Sarah quivered and her arms tightened around his neck. He thrust again, and her trembling increased. He clasped her soft buttocks in his hands and lifted her, then pulled her down to meet his next upward lunge.

Sarah's body stiffened and she began shaking spasmodically. Longarm thrust up at an increasing tempo, until she threw her head back, her mouth opening as she gasped for breath while her body convulsed in orgasm. He did not stop, but kept up the quick tempo of his stroking. Almost before Sarah had recovered from one orgasm, she was writhing ecstatically in another.

Longarm held her pulled tightly down to his hips until her spasms ended and she fell forward limply on his chest. Releasing her hips, Longarm put his arms around her and held her close. They stayed that way for several minutes, their only movement the slight lifting of their bodies from the seat as the stage bounced over the rutted road.

Finally, Sarah stirred as though she wanted to pull away. Longarm dropped his arms and she leaned back and looked at him, her face worried. "I ruined it for you, didn't I? I couldn't wait long enough. I'm sorry, Longarm."

"Don't be. I sure ain't."

"But I can still feel you, all big and hard. You didn't—"

"Don't worry about that," he said. "It just takes me a little while longer than it does you. Rest a minute, and we'll start fresh."

"You really mean that?"

"Why, sure I do. You'll enjoy it more, too."

37

Sarah leaned forward and kissed him. She held the kiss, and what had begun as a kiss of gratitude became one of passion. As he caressed her breasts, the stiff fabric of her bodice keeping his fingers from her flesh, Longarm found himself wishing for the darkness, when there'd be nothing between them. He moved and she took it for an invitation. Still holding him in the kiss, she began to twist her hips, pushing down as hard as she could.

Longarm brought his own hips up. His hands closed again on Sarah's warm buttocks and he lifted her bodily, pushing upward with quick, short strokes while he held her suspended above him. He forced himself to hurry, but could not reach his peak before she exploded again in an orgasm lasting even longer than those that had shaken her before.

Sarah broke their kiss and gasped, "Don't stop just because I was too quick again! Keep going, Longarm! I love the way you fill me up so much that I can't think about anything but you going in and out! Keep on, Longarm! Please keep on!"

Longarm was building to his own orgasm now. He stroked faster, his groin wet with Sarah's flowing juices, until, just as he felt her beginning to shake again, he came and kept coming while he stroked harder than before, bringing Sarah to still another wrenching climax before he stopped and relaxed and held her to him while her trembling, sobbing gasps subsided and at last ended completely.

After what seemed a long time, Sarah stirred and asked him drowsily, "Did I wait long enough this time?"

"Plenty long. But don't you think we better get our clothes fixed up back the way they oughta be now? I lost track of how far we come, but there's bound to be a station up ahead, and maybe not too far from here."

"I don't want to move. You still feel so wonderful inside me, you know. But I guess we'd better."

After they'd rearranged their clothing, Sarah snuggled up to Longarm on the seat. "You're such a strange man," she said. "I never have met anybody like you before. You didn't make a move to touch me before I—well, I just threw myself at you like a shameless hussy. Which is what I am, I guess."

"Every woman I ever knew has got a little hussy in her,

and if she don't let it come out now and again, she'll dry up like a prune," Longarm told her.

"You've known a lot of women, haven't you, Longarm?" Sarah no sooner finished asking the question than she shook her head. "No. I don't have any right to ask you something like that."

"But you did. And I'll give you an answer. I don't know as you could say it was a lot, but some. Including a few I'd just as soon not ever have met."

With a wisdom he'd not credited her having, Sarah said quickly, "Oh, I'm not about to ask you a whole string of questions. I know I don't like people poking questions at me."

"You don't seem to mind—" Longarm stopped short, realizing that he was getting into dangerous territory.

Sarah finished for him. "Talking about myself?" She shook her head. "I don't, with most people, but you've got a funny way of letting somebody know you'll understand what they're trying to say, even when they don't come right out and say it."

"Maybe that's because my business is trying to figure people out. Crooked people, mostly, but they're not too different from the rest of us, except for being crooked."

"You certainly understood what I was trying to tell you about Tommie. And the other two boys before him."

"I've known such things to happen before," he told her reassuringly.

Sarah yawned and stretched her legs out in front of her. She said, "You know, all of a sudden I'm getting sleepy."

"Nap awhile, then. Lay your head on my shoulder, if you feel like it, and go to sleep."

"I think I will, Longarm." She smiled. "Because I don't want to waste any time sleeping tonight."

Chapter 4

Longarm lighted a cheroot and studied Sarah's sleeping face after she'd fallen asleep. Old son, he told himself, you got to go real easy with a girl like this one. She's got an awful lot of growing up to do. For all that she's a woman, she still ain't much but a little girl trying to get used to how the world is. She don't understand yet that all she wants is to get that itch between her legs eased. Well, you keep on easing it for her till the trip's over, then bow out fast. Because if you ain't careful, you could could bite off a lot more'n you can swallow.

Sarah slept soundly as the stagecoach rattled on to the next station. She woke when the motion of the Celerity Wagon stopped, and was sitting up, stretching and blinking, when Patches swung off the driver's seat and opened the door.

"I see you two's all right," he said. "You better stretch your legs fast, 'cause this'll be a quick stop. I'm running a little bit behind on account of that ruckus back at the junction, and I got to make my time up."

"I missed breakfast there too," Longarm reminded him. "But I'll get some jerky out of my saddlebag to tide me over."

Although Sarah tried, she didn't quite manage to hide her impatience as she munched on the hard jerky with Longarm. The stage jounced on to the next station, where within a few minutes the teams were changed and they were moving again. Slowly the sun dropped down the sky, its final rays slanting into the stage itself. Just after sunset they reached the next stop, where they ate cold bacon and biscuits and drank strong hot coffee.

Patches came into the station to eat his supper while the horses were being changed. While he was munching on biscuits and bacon, Sarah asked him guilelessly, "Do you mind putting

41

the seats down before we leave, Mr. Patches? I'm so tired of sitting up, I think I'd like to stretch out for a change."

"Why, sure. Glad to oblige you." Patches cocked his head at Longarm. "You aiming to ride inside or up with me?"

Before Longarm could reply, Sarah said quickly, "Don't leave me by myself in the dark, Longarm. I'll feel better if you stay inside."

"You heard the lady," Longarm told Patches. "But those seats ain't going to get any softer when they're laid flat. I'll get my bedroll off the top and spread it out for padding."

Almost before the stage was out of sight of the station, Sarah propped herself on an elbow and leaned over Longarm, who was lying stretched out on his back on the rough surface of the blanket from his bedroll. He'd folded his coat for a pillow, and his holstered Colt lay beside the coat, on his vest.

"I'm glad you didn't change your mind," she said. "I won't be such a baby tonight."

"You weren't a baby before. Pretty much a woman, I'd say."

"It's not too early for us to start, is it?" Sarah whispered urgently. "Even if it's not quite dark yet?"

"It never is too early to start," Longarm smiled. "And I'd like to see how pretty you are before the light's gone."

Lowering herself above him, she offered Longarm her lips. He kissed her, and once more felt the tip of her tongue slipping into his mouth. Longarm stroked her breasts, gently at first, then, as he found too many layers of fabric between his fingers and the swelling globes he was caressing, he started unbuttoning the long line of buttons that ran down her back.

"Are you going to take all my clothes off this time, Longarm?" Sarah asked.

"I was figuring to. Unless it'll make you feel—"

"I want you to!" Sarah interrupted. "I've never been naked with a man before, you know. Just... well, on a buggy seat, like we were a while ago, or standing up in a stall in the barn, hurrying and watching to see that nobody caught us. I told you I was a baby, now maybe you'll believe me."

Longarm pulled the dress away and rubbed his cheek over the soft skin of Sarah's white shoulders. She sat up and helped him to slide away the straps of her camisole and to undo the snaps of the stiff corselet that girded her breasts like a plate

42

of metal armor. When she shrugged out of the straps and tossed the corselet aside, Longarm lowered his head and began to kiss the dark rosettes of her nipples. He felt them bud and roughen and stiffen as his tongue explored them.

As he began working her dress over her hips, Sarah sat up to help him. Her fingers flickered as she unbuttoned and pushed cloth from skin, until she lay naked beside him on the rough surface of the blanket. Supine, her breasts still rose firmly round, their dark tips not yet pebbled. Her skin was a glowing pink in the sunset's afterlight. Her body was lushly fleshed, and as yet she showed no signs of the child she carried. Between her swelling thighs, her pubic hair formed a vee of reddish brown.

Leaning over her, Longarm began to caress her with his tongue, between her breasts and across her flat stomach. Sarah fumbled his belt buckle loose and started to pull at his trousers. Longarm interrupted his caresses. He sat up and took off his shirt, unbuttoned his balbriggans, and knelt on the flat surface of the folded seats, crouching under the low top of the stage. He glanced at Sarah, and found her eyes fixed on him.

"I better not take off my boots," he told her, pushing down his underwear and balbriggans. She leaned forward to help and their hands joined in pushing the underwear down his hips. "If something was to happen and I'd need to get outside in a hurry—"

"Nothing's happened to the stage so far, but I feel like a lot has happened to me. And hasn't stopped happening yet. But I understand about your boots and pants."

Leaning back, Sarah looked at him, straining to see through the fast-fading light. Longarm was only partly erect. She wrapped her hand around him and stroked slowly back and forth. "Do grown men enjoy this too?"

"For a while. To get 'em ready for something better."

Longarm's erection was forming now. Sarah kept up her gentle motion, stopping now and then to squeeze the cylinder of flesh she was fondling. After a few moments she asked, "Are you ready now? I think I like to feel you in me better than I like just holding you, even if it is exciting to watch you swell up. But I'm beginning to ache, I want you in me so much."

Longarm replied by bending to kiss Sarah and, while their

lips clung, let his weight slowly settle on her, pressing her down to the blanket. He held her below him for a moment, his erection trapped between their bodies, with Sarah's hand still clutching him. He raised his hips to free her thighs and she brought them up around his waist, then slid the tip of the warm, pulsing cylinder she'd been fondling into her moist, waiting warmth. Longarm went into her all the way, as she'd wanted him to, with a single, slow, deliberate lunge.

For a full minute he held himself in place before he drew back. Sarah raised her hips to follow his, as though she were afraid he would leave her. Then Longarm drove down hard and suddenly once more. Without waiting this time, he began to stroke quickly, bringing a gasp from Sarah's full lips each time he plunged.

Soon she began to follow the timing of his lunges. She opened her thighs when he started his downward thrusts, then, when he was buried deepest, locked her legs around his back to ride up with the lifting of his hips. When Longarm felt her body start to tremble, he stopped thrusting and held himself in her at full length while, beneath him, her hips twisted and strained as she tried to push him up, to get him to start lunging again.

"Don't stop, Longarm!" she begged. "Not now!"

Longarm shook his head. "Wait awhile, Sarah. Hold on as long as you can."

"No! I can't wait! Don't do this to me! Can't you see I'm about to burst?"

Longarm did not reply. He waited until Sarah lay quiet, and then resumed thrusting, but in a slow, deliberate tempo. In a few moments she began to quiver again, and again Longarm stopped and ignored her efforts to move, holding her pinned firmly to the blanket. Once again he brought her almost to her climax and held himself deeply in her while she urged him to go on, and ignored her urging until she'd grown calm.

Then, when he resumed his slow, deep stroking and felt her body responding, he did not stop, but sped up and plunged into her again and again in an unceasing drive until inarticulate, gasping cries were torn from Sarah's throat. She quivered into her spasm, and then at once began a second shaking orgasm and, when Longarm kept thrusting, went into still a third that

44

kept her shaking and moaning with cries of painful delight until Longarm's own climax came and he lay on Sarah's soft, trembling body, his muscles jerking into relaxation as he drained away.

Longarm did not know how much time slipped away before he became aware again of the jolting of the stagecoach and the thudding of the team's hooves on the baked desert soil. He knew he'd slept, because darkness was full, but had no way of knowing how long he'd been sleeping, whether briefly or long. Sarah was asleep too, her face a dim white oval against the frame of her dark hair and the even darker hue of the blanket.

Longarm stirred and started to raise himself up. His movement woke Sarah, and instinctively she tightened her legs around his hips.

"Don't move yet," she whispered. "Stay where you are, please, Longarm."

"We'd best get into our clothes again," he told her. "We've both been asleep, and for all I know we might be getting close to the next stage station."

"But I don't want to dress! I just want to stay where we are!" she exclaimed. "We'd only have on our clothes a little while, anyhow, until we got past the next station. At least I hope we would."

"We'll undress again, all right," Longarm promised. 'But for right now, we better do as I say."

Sarah sighed, but relaxed her legs and let Longarm withdraw. He adjusted his clothing quickly while she picked up her pantalets, camisole, and corselet and, after looking at them for a moment, tucked them under a corner of the blanket. Then she slid the wrinkled black dress over her head and sat down with her legs folded, Indian-fashion. Longarm had stretched out on the blanket and lit a cheroot.

"I feel so naked," she chuckled, bending to stroke his cheek and run her fingers through his crisp hair. "And absolutely free, and a little bit sinful. Longarm, am I a fallen woman, like my mother said I am?"

"Not no ways at all! You just got feelings and you do what they tell you to when you get 'em. Which is a lot better'n trying to fight what's right and natural."

45

"I've never had anything so wonderful happen to me before!" Sarah said happily. "I hated you every time you stopped, but then, when it kept getting better and better every time you started . . . well, I was still a little girl until tonight, Longarm. Now you've made me a woman."

"You been a woman a long time, only you didn't know it, Sarah. And a real fine one, too."

"You say that like you really mean it."

"I do mean it. I—" Longarm stopped as, from the driver's seat above them, Patches' loud "yay-hoo" sounded to announce their approach to the station. "Looks like we put our clothes on just in time."

"We won't be here long, will we? Because just thinking about what you said a minute ago was right and natural is getting me all excited again."

"Just long enough to change the horses, Patches told me. And we'd better make the most of what time we got after we leave here, because the next station after this one is Tucson."

Both Longarm and Sarah got out while the horses were being changed. When Sarah excused herself and walked down to the shanty that housed the station, Longarm and Patches stepped behind the coach to relieve themselves.

"You and the widow woman comfortable?" Patches asked, his voice carefully casual.

"About as comfortable as anybody can be, when their liver's getting shook out of 'em," Longarm replied. Then he added quickly, "But the bouncing didn't stop either one of us from sleeping."

"I reckon you'll want to go back to sleep till daylight?" Patches' question was in the same casually innocent tone that had been in his voice before.

"I imagine. Why?"

"Well, seeing as this is the last stop before we pull into Tucson, I figured I'd stop around daybreak and put the seats back up, so's you'll ride into town setting up." Then, winking, he added, "Just thought I'd mention it, Longarm."

"Thanks. We'll be expecting you to stop, then."

As soon as the Celerity Wagon topped the first rise beyond the station, Sarah began unbuttoning her dress. She knelt to whip

46

it off over her head, and pushed the stiff garment out of the way, against the stagecoach wall. Longarm had his shirt off and was unbuckling his belt. Sarah moved closer to help him. As they worked his pants and balbriggans down to his thighs, she looked at him, the first time she'd seen him completely flaccid.

"That's how men are most of the time, aren't they?" she asked, weighing him in her palm.

"Unless there's a pretty woman around, feeling of 'em."

Sarah cradled his beginning erection in her hands. "That's what I thought, because otherwise they'd be sticking up so you could see their pants sticking out." A note of puzzlement crept into her voice as she asked, "But why didn't Tommie and the others keep standing up a long time, the way you do?"

"I can't answer that, Sarah. I guess all men ain't alike, that's about all I can tell you."

"Longarm, do you feel as good as I do when you're inside me?" she asked, rubbing her fingers along his increasing length.

"Why, sure."

"Even if you were to be in me a long time? The rest of the night, maybe?"

"I'd like it just the same as you do."

"Will you stay in me the rest of the night, then, Longarm?"

"I can't think of a thing I'd like to do any better. But if that's what you want, we better lay down a little different, because you'll get squashed if I lay on top of you all night."

"How? I mean, how will we lay down?"

"Like this."

Longarm pulled Sarah to him, turning her back to him as he brought her body closer. He cupped her breasts in his hands and guided her to lie on her side, her back snuggling to his chest.

Sarah grasped the idea at once. She raised her leg and snaked her hand between her thighs to slip his almost full erection inside her. Longarm pushed his hips against her buttocks to make his penetration complete.

"You don't feel like you did before," she told him over her shoulder. "It's different. Bigger, somehow. But I like it this way too."

Longarm had begun to kiss Sarah's neck and shoulders

while he kneaded her breasts with his hands. He felt their tips spring erect, and began stroking slowly. Sarah sighed and arched her back to push her buttocks against him more firmly. He thrust a bit harder and in a few moments she was trembling and almost ready to go into her final spasm.

Longarm stopped, and this time Sarah did not object. She did not protest when he stopped a second time and then a third, and then, at last, even though he was far from his own peak, he carried her on past the brink and into an orgasm that rippled through her body and left her lying limp and gasping in his arms.

"Oh, that was the best yet!" Sarah sighed between deep, gusting inhalations. "Even better than before! And I'm ready to start again whenever you are. Don't make me wait too long, please, Longarm. Because I want to remember this as the best and most exciting night of my whole life!"

Chapter 5

Longarm did not linger in Tucson. He left as soon as his business was finished, even though it was late enough in the day for the sun to be in his eyes as he rode west. He'd found nothing to hold him in the old pueblo and former territorial capital after bidding Sarah Moore goodbye.

Sarah's aunt and uncle had been waiting for her at the stage station, and hadn't bothered to conceal their complete lack of enthusiasm for both their niece and her traveling companion. Sarah had retreated into a shell at the sight of her relatives, and her final farewell had been a cool handshake. Longarm smiled as he contrasted the almost imperceptible pressure of her hand with her earlier tearful, clinging goodbyes that had lasted from her first sight of the town's sun-baked adobe houses until the stage was in the city itself.

She'll grow out of being fearful of her kinfolks soon as she understands a little bit more about the way the world is, he told himself as he fished a cheroot out of his pocket and flicked his thumbnail across a matchhead. All she needs is a little more time to think, and figure out that older folks ain't always right.

Patches had proved more of a problem than Sarah. He'd buttonholed Longarm just as he was going out of the station, and kept him standing for a half-hour as Longarm tried to explain why he couldn't stay over for a day or two. When he'd finally been convinced, the driver had insisted on carrying Longarm's saddle out to the spot where the hackney cabs waited and, once there, had spent another half-hour warning Longarm to be careful of the fierce Apaches and Yaquis who still ran wild and warlike on the Mexican border. Only firmness had stopped Patches from getting into the cab and riding with him to Fort Lowell.

49

At the fort, Longarm's federal credentials had gotten him not only a handsome, deep-chested Morgan from the remount depot, but an oversized artillery canteen, two fresh round loaves of garrison bread, and the shank of a smoked ham. The last place he visited at Fort Lowell was the office of the Engineer Corps, where he requisitioned a large-scale map of the huge triangular chunk of desert that lay west of Tucson and south of the Gila.

Mina Cobre wasn't on the map, but it did pinpoint Quijotoa for him; more importantly, it showed the trails and waterholes west of Tucson. After a quick inspection of the map, Longarm estimated that he still had a hundred miles of travel ahead, and decided instantly to reduce that distance by the twenty or thirty miles he could cover during the remaining daylight. With forty-eight jouncing hours of stagecoach travel behind him, the idea of a quiet ride on a horse that couldn't make conversation seemed an appealing prospect.

Longarm didn't hurry as he rode into the declining sun. By taking a sizable bite off the distance he still had to cover, he would be able to reach his destination before dark of the next day, without pushing the Morgan. He stayed in the saddle until the last moments of the long desert twilight were almost gone, and made a dark camp in a dry wash. After his exertions of the previous night, he needed no lullabies. Two minutes after crawling between his blankets, he was asleep.

There was still more than an hour of daylight left the next afternoon, when Longarm reached Mina Cobre. The air hung still and breathlessly hot when he reined in for a preliminary look at the town. For the last half-hour of his sweaty, sweltering trip, he'd followed the bed of a tiny trickling stream that meandered aimlessly across the flat, sunbaked desert. The little watercourse was marked on his map as Sonoita Draw, and the grizzled prospector he'd talked to at Quijotoa had assured him that by following the draw south he'd wind up at Mina Cobre.

Almost directly below him, along the eastern edge of the draw, was a cluster of crude, low-roofed huts made of river reeds plastered with mud. Between the huts and the tiny trickle of tan water, there were cultivated plots to which a few women were carrying *ollas* from the stream and pouring water from

50

the clay pots on the dusty green bushes that grew in the miniature fields.

Papagos, Longarm thought, or maybe Pimas or one of the other river tribes; he knew the names of most of the tribes, but did not yet know how to identify their people at a glance.

A narrow brush-and-pole corral had been erected between the Papago village and the town; it held a horse or two, a number of goats, and a few sheep. The town was a glare of light yellow buildings framed of raw, fresh boards. With the sun in his face, Longarm couldn't tell much about Mina Cobre, which appeared to his squinting eyes as a confusing set of blocks against the bright sky.

Pulling down his hatbrim to shade his eyes, he saw there was more town than he'd realized, for past the newer buildings there was a straggle of adobe structures that looked much older than the frame houses close to him. Mina Cobre was, he supposed as he toed the horse into motion again, like so many places where the adobe towns of the original Hispanic settlers were being replaced by the neat frame buildings of new arrivals from the East.

As the road reached the town it curved, and distantly Longarm saw on a ridge well beyond both the frame and the adobe houses a group of buildings that were much more recognizable, the dull metal walls and low shed roofs of the copper mine that gave the town its name. In Montana and Idaho, Longarm had seen so many similar pit mines that he could tell one the instant he saw the glinting surfaces of the leaching ponds that surrounded the sheet-iron structures.

Well, old son, he told himself, puffing the cheroot he'd lighted when he first reined in, looks like you've got to the place you been looking for. Now if you can just settle up all the trouble they're supposed to be having as easy as you found the town, maybe this case won't be as bad as the last one you had where the folks were fighting it out to see which bunch of 'em was going to wind up bossing the place.

Longarm toed the Morgan ahead and let the horse set its own pace at a slow walk. He wanted plenty of time to look around and try to judge what kind of town Mina Cobre was going to be before he looked for a place to stay.

At first glance, the town had the freshly scrubbed appearance of any new settlement; the buildings looked better than the few people on the street. These were a varied lot: a housewife or two with parcels under their arms, hurrying home to prepare supper; a few loungers in shady spots created by the declining sun; an occasional Mexican wearing the huaraches and light cotton suiting of that section of the border; a Papago, distinguishable from the Mexicans at first glance only because he wore a headband instead of a woven straw sombrero.

Most of the town's fresh look came from the new lumber of the stores and houses. Paint was apparently unknown; the only paint Longarm saw as he rode slowly down the slightly crooked main and only street was on the signs that identified the buildings. All the signs were predictable: cafe, dry goods emporium with a doctor's office above it, hardware, barbershop with its striped pole and the legend "BATHS" over its door. There was a large and sprawling general store in the center of the town, a big saloon across the street from it, and a small saloon at the far edge of town, with a livery stable beyond it.

Aside from the wide main street, there were no others, just a random sprawl of houses higgledy-piggledy, placed wherever their builders fancied. Longarm saw nothing that looked big enough to be a boardinghouse or rooming house, and wondered what the men employed at the mines did for a place to stay. He turned the horse back up the street, dismounted in front of the big saloon, and pushed through the batwings.

A high ceiling and windowless walls gave the interior a feeling of coolness. Longarm ran his eyes along the bar; there were eight or ten men lined up. He noticed that there were no Mexicans among them. The bar was unpainted pine like the walls; there was no ornate mirrored backbar. Shelves behind the bar held a good variety of liquor, though, and among such south-of-the-border names as Orendian and Jose Cuervo, Longarm spotted the friendly face of Tom Moore on a bottle label before he was halfway across the saloon floor.

"Just set that bottle of Maryland rye in front of me, and I won't bother you for a while," Longarm said, pointing to Tom Moore's picture, when the barkeep broke off his conversation with a trio of overall-clad miners to come and take his order.

"Rye whiskey?" the barkeep asked incredulously, his eyes following Longarm's finger.

"Not just rye whiskey," Longarm corrected him. "Maryland rye."

Shaking his head, the barkeep reached the bottle down and put it in front of Longarm, then said, "I guess I'll have to get a corkscrew. Two years that bottle's been setting up there, from the day this place opened up, and you're the first customer that's asked for rye."

"Don't bother about a corkscrew," Longarm told him. He flicked the blue-green revenue stamp off the neck with a horny thumbnail, hit the bottom of the bottle sharply with the heel of his palm, and the cork popped out far enough for him to pull it the rest of the way with his strong yellowed teeth.

"Guess I better give you a glass, though." The barkeep put a glass beside the bottle and looked with unconcealed curiosity at Longarm as he poured. "Come in to work for the mine?"

"Nope. Come in to look around." Longarm drained the glass and refilled it. He tapped the bottle with his forefinger. "Pour one for yourself."

"Well, thanks, but if it's all the same to you, I'll take a cigar instead."

"Suit yourself." Longarm knew that the cigar the barkeep chose from a box under the liquor shelves would be returned as soon as he'd left, and its price put in the barkeep's pocket.

Turning back to Longarm, the barkeep held up the cigar and put it in his shirt pocket. "Just finished one. I'll smoke it later, thanks. My name's Corky, by the way." He looked curiously at Longarm, and when his lead wasn't picked up, he went on, "You say you're just looking around. Business or pleasure?"

"That depends on how good the business turns out."

"Well, now, I wasn't setting out to pry," the barkeep said hastily. "No offense, I hope?"

"No offense," Longarm replied. "A man that don't ask questions don't learn much. Now, if I was to want to stay around here awhile, where'd I look for a room?"

"I tell you, that's a hard one to answer," Corky replied, shaking his head. "There's not a spare room in town that ain't

53

rented out in day and night shifts. The Copper Queen's just getting into real production, see, and men keep coming faster than the carpenters can put up houses." Then, in afterthought, he added, "You might get a shakedown in one of them adobes the Mexicans live in, but I wouldn't advise you to."

"Looks like I'll just have to spread my bedroll down along the creek, then."

"Maybe you won't, at that." The barkeep scratched his chin. "You got any business with the Copper Queen?"

"I might have. It'll depend."

"You go out to the mine, then. Tell Grady—he's the superintendent—what your business is. The Copper Queen's got a little accommodation house out there that the big bosses use when they've got to come here. If there's a spare room in it, maybe Grady'll let you have it. And it'd be a sight better'n anything you'll find here in town, if he does."

Longarm tossed a cartwheel on the bar. "I'm obliged."

"Hope you'll be a steady customer while you're here, Mr. . . ." Corky paused expectantly.

Longarm filled the gap the man had left open. "Long. From Denver."

"Glad to meet you, Long." Corky opened the cash drawer and made change. "Sure hope you make connections all right with Grady."

Longarm retraced his path through town and rode past the adobe houses toward the mine. He guessed the distance as about three miles, but added a half-mile when he came to a long curve the road made to avoid a sizable lake. Closer to the town than it was to the mine, the little stream that flowed through Sonoita Draw had been dammed, a low earth-fill dam that impounded a surprisingly large lake, for desert country. He skirted the lake, following the well-beaten trail that ran along its bank.

As he drew closer to the huddle of buildings, he saw that the mine operation was bigger than it had looked from town. The sheet-iron structures, like the wooden buildings in Mina Cobre, were shiny new, so new that the acid-laden fumes rising from the ore-leaching ponds had not yet begun to corrode the metal. Rising over the buildings on its tall, stiltlike tower was a huge Eclipse railroad windmill. A wooden-stave cistern filled the central area of the windmill tower.

Men, most of them Mexicans, were walking around wherever he looked. Some of them carried loads of one sort or another—buckets or lengths of wood or metal—some pushed wheelbarrows. A surprisingly large number of the men he saw, though, were doing nothing except pacing the outer limits of the mine area. These carried rifles and most of them wore pistols as well. Longarm had no doubt they were guards, and looked for the nearest of them to challenge him as he rode into the area. The rifle-carrying man merely looked at him without interest and continued his patrolling when Longarm rode past.

Now Longarm was in the working area of the mine. He rode by the green-surfaced leaching ponds, their edges froth-foamed. Past the ponds, a small hillock of leached tailings rose from the flat desert soil. Between the leaching ponds and the yawning mine pit there were a half-dozen large buildings and several smaller ones, as well as a sizable corral holding a few horses and a number of mules. Around the corral, deep-bodied ore wagons and Fresno scrapers were scattered.

Longarm had seen enough copper mines in Montana and Utah to have a general understanding of what he saw. The copper ore, mixed with dirt and stones, was taken from the pit with the scrapers, and dumped in the leaching ponds where a mixture of acids separated the lighter ore from the dirt. When the ponds were drained, the ore formed a layer on top of the soil from which it had been leached by the acids. The ore was scraped off to be sent to a smelter, the leached dirt removed and dumped on the tailings pile, and the ponds refilled so the process could be repeated.

All the buildings Longarm had seen so far bore numbers. He guided the Morgan at random around the buildings until he found one that bore the sign "OFFICE" instead of a number. He tossed the horse's reins over the hitch rail and went in. The office was a single room, holding a number of desks and tables, most of them piled high with maps and papers, and one clear desk at its back, where a man sat studying a chart.

"You'd be Grady, I reckon?" Longarm asked.

"That's right." He did not look up from the chart he was examining.

Grady was black Irish, and there'd been an "O" in front of

his family name not too many years ago, Longarm guessed when the mine superintendent looked up a moment later and he saw his face clearly for the first time. He had midnight-blue hair, a set of thick, dark eyebrows, china-blue eyes, and a heavy shadow of beard on a long face with a jutting jaw. Longarm put his age in the middle thirties.

"Well?" Grady asked.

"My name's Long, Grady. Deputy U.S. marshal, out of Denver."

Grady did not stand up or offer Longarm a chair. He asked, "Are you looking for somebody who works for the Copper Queen? If you are, you'd better catch the paymaster tomorrow; he's already gone for the day. He'd be more likely than I would to know the name of whoever it is you're after."

"You're the one I come out here to see."

"About what?"

"My job's to keep the lid on this county until after the election's over. Word's got back to Washington that there's already been some killings."

"There have been," Grady interrupted. He'd been giving his full attention to Longarm since hearing the word *Washington*. "Two men dead, and I'm afraid there might be more. And the whole county's stirred up over it."

"Now, the killings ain't rightly my business," Longarm went on. "But seeing the election's run honest is. That's what I aim to do, far as one man can."

"Well," Grady said, satisfaction in his tone. "I'm glad to know that somebody back East is listening to our complaints."

"Before you go any further, Grady, I ain't on nobody's side in the election. I got to stand right in the middle and see that everybody gets a fair shake."

Grady nodded. "Oh, I understand that. That's all we're interested in, seeing that the majority rules. But we've got—" He broke off and glanced out the window at the sky. "Look here, Long, this isn't the best place for us to talk, and it's time for me to knock off. Are you staying in town?"

"Fact is, I ain't staying anyplace yet. Barkeep in town told me there wasn't any rooms to rent, and said you've got some kind of shakedown out here."

"We have. A company house that our executives use when

they come here on an inspection tour or something of that kind. It's empty now, but the housekeeper and cook are still there, cleaning the place up. They stay in the cottage when the guest house is occupied, but both of them live in town. I'll just have them stay on, and you're welcome to use the place if you want to."

"I'd be right obliged if I could rent a room in it."

"Certainly not! There won't be any charge. The house is just standing there idle. You might as well be using it."

"If that's the way you want it, Grady. But I better tell you, if I do, I won't feel beholden to you for the favor."

"Nobody'd expect you to." Grady stood up. "You rode out, I suppose?"

"Horse is hitched to your rail outside."

"I've still got a few things to do before I can leave, so I'll have to ask you to wait for me to finish up. I've got the guards to inspect, for one thing, make sure they're all there."

"I noticed you had a bunch of sentries out. You looking for trouble from the folks in town, or something?"

"Oh, no. Not that kind of trouble. But you know we're very close to the Mexican border here, Long. They're still bands of wild Apaches and a few bunches of Yaquis that raid across the line whenever they take a notion to."

"So I've heard. Can't say I blame you for standing ready. From the stories I've listened to, the Apaches are as tough as the Comanches, and the Yaquis are worse'n the Apaches."

"That's about right. We've been lucky, there haven't been any raids for quite a while, but that doesn't mean I intend to let our guard down."

"So I seen. You do whatever you need to, Grady. Waiting a few minutes won't put me out a bit."

"I'll go over to the corral and get the hostler to hitch up my buggy. Then you can follow me to the guest house. We'll sit down and have a drink and a private talk there."

Longarm rode behind Grady's buggy to a frame cottage that had been built in a wide wash on the shore of the impounded lake. It was close enough to the mine to be convenient, and far enough away to be private; actually, the cottage stood about midway between the mine and Mina Cobre. A small corral with an open-fronted shed was behind the house, a pony and a burro were in the enclosure. Grady dropped the buggy's ground anchor in front of the cottage and gestured to Longarm to ride back to the corral. The mine superintendent followed on foot.

"I'm afraid you'll have to look after your own horse," he told Longarm. "Whenever there's somebody from the head office here, I let them use my buggy."

"I ain't used to having a horse valet around. I'll look after the nag. It's part of my job," Longarm said, following Grady around the cottage and into the front door.

"Luz!" Grady called. "You've got a guest!"

From somewhere in the back of the house, a woman's light voice replied, "I'll be right there, Mr. Grady."

Longarm looked around. The cottage was furnished comfortably but impersonally; it might have been a hotel room except that no bed was in it. Upholstered lounge chairs, a divan, and a long library table were placed around the square room in no apparent pattern. There were curtains on the windows, and an Aubusson rug on the floor.

He'd barely finished giving the room a quick look when Luz came in. She was more Spanish than Mexican, Longarm saw, small, almost tiny, but in spite of her diminutive size, he saw immediately that she was a woman and not a girl. Her breasts puffed out the peasant blouse she wore, and the fullness of her long gathered skirt emphasized the flaring of her hips. Her features were the classic Spanish-Mexican aquiline nose, dark lustrous eyes, pouting full lips, in a long oval face. Her skin was a creamy tan, and she wore her hair in a coronet of double braids over the crown of her head.

"Mr. Long's going to stay here for awhile," Grady said. Luz nodded. Grady went on, "He's not with the company. He's a federal marshal from Denver."

"Mr. Long," Luz acknowledged. "I'll do my best to make you comfortable while you're here."

"I'll try not to be too much trouble," Longarm said. "Most of the time, I expect I'll be out."

"Suppose you ask Clarita to make coffee for us, Luz," Grady suggested. Then he turned to Longarm. "Unless you'd rather have a drink?" Longarm shook his head and Grady told Luz, "Coffee, then. And Mr. Long will be wanting supper,

I'm sure. I won't stay, though." He motioned Longarm to a chair. "Now, then. I expect you'd like for me to give you a little bit of information on the problem we've run into here, Long."

"Whatever you feel like telling me."

"Very quickly, the situation is that the Copper Queen isn't too popular in Mina Cobre. You might've gotten an idea to that effect when you stopped in town."

"No." Longarm shook his head. "I didn't talk to anybody except that barkeep, Corky he said his name is."

"Well, it's a fact," Grady went on. "A lot of the people who live there were brought in while we were building, and I suppose they looked for their jobs to last forever. Of course, we'd always planned to hire Mexican labor after we started operating. It's a damned shame, but with all this miner's union agitation, the only protection we've got is to hire men the agitators can't talk to."

"I guess the ones you hire live on this side of the border?" Longarm interjected.

"As far as we know, they do. They've got their own place— the town doesn't welcome them. I don't suppose you saw the place we built for them. It's just behind a bluff where the concentrate ponds are located. Now, our Mexicans vote the way we tell them to. I'm sure you understand that's a necessary evil, these days. So we have effective control of the county, and the Anglos have the town."

Longarm nodded. "It ain't a new situation. I've run into it before." He thought of the three-way situation in which he'd gotten involved in Kansas. He'd been caught there in a battle between the Bratiya—"the Brethren"—a Russian religious sect whose members had emigrated to settle on railroad land as farmers, the townspeople of the closest community to the homesteads of the Brethren, and the cattlemen who'd been lords of the range before the Brethren had arrived.

"What's happening," Grady was saying, "is that the people in Mina Cobre are trying to take over the county offices that the Mexicans have always held. And it's turning into a bitter fight. Feelings have been running too high for comfort. In fact, that's one of the reasons I'm glad to see you here. I've got an uneasy feeling that things are close to the breaking point."

"You'd know more about that than I would," Longarm said. "I ain't sniffed around in town yet."

"When you do, I think you'll agree. I'm afraid things are likely to explode any day now, and if they do, Long, you're going to have your hands full!"

Chapter 6

Longarm was still absorbing Grady's words when Luz came in, carrying a tray on which there were two cups of steaming coffee, a sugarbowl, and a cream pitcher. She offered the tray first to Longarm, then to Grady. After they'd been served, she left as silently as she'd come in.

After she'd gone, Longarm asked Grady, "Has something new happened since those shootings? Because they were quite a ways back, the way I heard it."

"There hasn't been any more gunfighting," Grady said. "But the feeling left by those two killings has been getting stronger every day. I feel like I'm sitting on a time bomb."

"Who's to blame for the shootings?"

"Nobody knows. Or if they know, they're not talking."

"Well, now, you wouldn't look for 'em to talk, would you?"

"Of course not. But these weren't like a saloon gunfight, Long. In a showdown of that kind, everybody knows who pulled a trigger. These were backshootings, from ambush, and everybody's under suspicion."

"You're sure those killings were tied to this election that's coming up, I guess?" Longarm asked.

"Dammit, man! It's past any kind of coincidence that both of the dead men were running for office. One was a candidate for sheriff, the other for constable."

Longarm drained his coffee cup and set it down without any comment on Grady's statement. He said quietly, "Looks like I got some digging to do. Can't tell who's on which side till I nosey around some, and that might take a little time."

"Well, you know where my people stand," Grady said. "And the company too, of course."

Longarm decided it was time to turn a few cards faceup.

"I ain't so sure I do, Grady. You don't want the folks from Mina Cobre to get control of the county, I understand that. But I'd sure like to know what your people are doing to take over Mina Cobre and run it."

"Not one damned thing!" Grady said quickly. "I imagine we'd support a candidate for town selectman or constable, if we were pretty sure they'd see things our way. We'd be fools not to. But that's as far as we'd go." He stood up. "Well, Long, I'm sure Luz will make you comfortable. Let me know if I can do anything else. Always glad to help."

"Sure I will. And I'm obliged for the use of this place, even if it won't make me feel like I got to look the other way if your outfit tries to pull anything."

"We've already agreed on that. Good evening, Long."

For a moment after Grady left, Longarm sat puffing on his long slim cigar, then he went back to the kitchen. Luz and another woman were in the midst of a discussion in rapidfire Spanish, too fast for him to follow with his sketchy knowledge of the language. They stopped talking when he came in, and Luz looked at him questioningly.

"You wish something, Mr. Long?"

"No, thanks. What I come back here for is to tell you not to go to any trouble fixing supper for me. I'll be riding into town, and I'll get a bite at the restaurant."

"But Mr. Grady said—"

"I know. But let's just say I changed my mind, if you ain't started cooking anything yet."

"No. But it will be no trouble—"

"It'll be a lot less trouble not to fix anything at all, now won't it? Thanks just the same. Oh, yes. I like steak and potatoes for breakfast. And lots of coffee. I'll see you ladies in the morning."

With a half-bow, Longarm went out the back door and mounted the Morgan, which was still standing saddled outside the corral. He turned the horse's head toward Mina Cobre.

That Grady, he's a real slick article, old son, Longarm mused as the horse moved around the bank of the little lake and started on the trail to town. Wonder how much of what he fed me was true, and how much he made up? And how much he didn't tell me? He sure as hell ducked out fast when

62

I commenced asking about his outfit trying to take over the town. Looks to me like the best thing I can do is set around in the cafe and the saloon for a while and just keep my ears flapping. There's always more'n one side to everything, and so far the only side I've heard is Grady's.

Mina Cobre wasn't much of a town after dark, Longarm decided as he sat in the restaurant drinking a second cup of coffee while he puffed an after-supper cheroot. There'd been only two customers in the cafe when he came in, and they'd finished eating and gone. Now he had the small place to himself, except for the cook, who did double duty as a waiter.

Mina Cobre was also an expensive town to eat in, he discovered as he paid forty cents for a meal that almost anywhere else would have cost only twenty-five. He walked out to the street and looked along its deserted length. Although the evening was still early, the only lights came from the saloon and restaurant, and before he stepped across the street to the saloon, the restaurant's lights went out.

There was a slightly larger crowd in the saloon than there'd been in the cafe. Two men stood at the bar, and at a table in one corner, three others sat at a table. Corky was behind the bar and he came up to greet Longarm.

"Hope you got Grady to fix you up," the barkeep said.

"I did. You was sure right when you told me the place out at the mine's better'n any room I'd've got in town. They hire a woman to keep it cleaned up and another one to cook."

"Oh, they know how to spend money, that bunch does. Where it'll do 'em some good." Corky jerked his head at the shelves behind the bar. "You drinking the same whiskey you had before?"

"Just as long as that bottle holds out," Longarm smiled.

Corky reached the bottle from the shelf and set it in front of Longarm. He said, "You don't need to worry about that. If I remember, there's another five bottles of it in the storeroom."

"I'll buy one of 'em off you, if you'll sell it," Longarm offered. "I like an eye-opener in the mornings, and it ain't going to be so convenient for me to ride in from the mine before breakfast to get one."

"Be glad to accommodate you, Long." Corky watched Longarm as he poured and tossed back half of the glass of rye. Making no effort to hide his curiosity, he said, "I guess you found out you'll be doing business with Grady, since you're staying out at the mine. You figure to be around town awhile, then?" .

Longarm nodded. Riding into town, he'd made up his mind that there was no point in concealing his identity, nor was there any need to do so. In fact, the more visible he became, the easier his job might be. Visibility, he'd discovered, had a way of bringing informants calling.

"I'll be here awhile. Till after the election, anyhow. But I'm not what you'd say doing business with Grady. I'm not in the mining business, Corky. I'm a deputy U.S. marshal, and what I'm here for is to sort of keep the town quieted down so nobody else gets shot before the voting."

Corky's eyes had started bulging when Longarm mentioned his title. He said, "But you told me you're from Denver, not Washington. How come the federals are busting into our business way down here in Arizona?"

"I ain't from Washington. Denver's where I headquarter. Now, Corky, you ought to know there's federal marshals in all the states and territories," Longarm said. "You got one in Arizona, up in the capitol at Prescott."

"Hell, Long, it's damn near as hard to get to Prescott from here as it is to get to Washington."

"Well, maybe that's why they sent me from Denver instead of having the marshal in Prescott come down." Longarm didn't think it would be wise to mention that when a case involved politics, Washington had learned to send a marshal from another state or territory, one who'd have no local ties to affect his decisions.

"If you're a lawman, Long, you'll want to get acquainted with our constable. That's him, Barney Trent, sitting at the table back there. Come on, I'll introduce you to him. Might as well bring your bottle along. I imagine you and Barney'll want to chin for a while."

Picking up the bottle of rye in one hand and his glass in the other, Longarm followed Corky over to the table where the three men he'd noticed on entering the saloon were seated.

They were an oddly assorted trio. One was grossly fat; his chins overflowed the collar of his white shirt, and his twill pants would have served a small man for a tent. Another of the men was stringbean-thin; he wore a frock coat similar in cut to Longarm's Prince Albert, though it was fawn-colored instead of black. The third was bull-necked, with a massive chest and shoulders. He had on a pair of rancher's duck pants and a checkered shirt over which he wore a vest. He was the only one of the three who was wearing a gunbelt.

Corky said to the bull-necked man, "Barney, this man's in your line of work, you being constable and all. I sorta figured you and him better get acquainted. His name's Long, and he's a U.S. marshal. From Denver."

"Deputy marshal," Longarm said quickly.

"Well," the constable said. His voice was flat and without expression. "Quite a ways from your regular territory, ain't you, Long? You chase somebody down here to the border?"

"You'd know how it is," Longarm said, keeping his voice as toneless as the constable's. "You go where your job takes you."

"Damned if you federals ain't the closest-mouthed bunch I ever run into!" Barney looked at his companions. "If it's because these men are listening, you don't have to worry about them. This one here" —he indicated the fat man—"he's Ed Naylor, and he's one of our town selectmen. This other one's Jim Cross, and he's more apt than not to be sheriff, after the votes gets counted in the election coming up."

Longarm nodded at the others. None of them had offered to shake hands, but he put that down to the fact that they could see his hands were both full.

"Well, sit down, Long," Trent invited. "Long as Corky's brought you over, we might as well jaw a little bit."

Longarm put the bottle of rye on the table, set his glass beside it, and sat down in the empty chair that stood between Naylor and Cross. Corky had been looking on with a puzzled frown, but now he shrugged and went back to the bar.

"You still ain't mentioned why you're down this way, Long," the constable said. "Might be something I could help you with."

"It might be, at that," Longarm replied. "Fact is, somebody

back in Washington heard about those shootings you had here. Got 'em all confused. Figured they had some connection with that election you mentioned a minute ago."

"How'd they ever get that idea?" Naylor asked.

"Maybe because both of the men that were killed were going to run in the election," Longarm told him. "That's all the connection I can see, anyway."

"What business is it of Washington's how we run our affairs down here?" Cross demanded. "It's a local election. That's not any skin off anybody's ass back East."

"Now, I wouldn't exactly say the election's all local," Longarm said. "You'll be voting on the President. And there'll be somebody running for the territorial legislature, and they're going to pick out a U.S. senator."

"Oh, who the hell in Mina Cobre pays any attention to them other jobs?" Naylor asked. "All we're interested in is our own."

"Well, it ain't my place to argue with what my chief tells me to do," Longarm said. "You know how that is."

"What're you going to do, Long?" Cross asked. "Start poking into everybody's business, trying to find something that's not there?"

"Maybe if you ask me that after a few days, I might be able to tell you," Longarm answered. "I just blew into town a few hours ago, I need to get my feet on the ground."

"You found a place to stay yet?" Trent asked.

"Thanks to your friend Corky over there, I got lucky. The superintendent out at the mine, Grady, I guess you all know him, he invited me to use that house they got out by the lake."

A dead silence settled over the table following Longarm's words. He took out a cheroot and touched a match to it to fill the gap in the conversation, and was reaching for the bottle to refill his glass when Naylor finally spoke.

"I guess that shows everybody where you stand," the fat storekeeper said.

"You mind explaining what you mean?" Longarm asked.

"What I mean is what I'm damned sure you already know. We don't have much use for the Copper Queen or anything connected with it here in Mina Cobre," Naylor replied.

"Maybe you'd like to tell me why," Longarm suggested.

Before the merchant could reply, the batwings flapped and

all four men at the table looked up to see who'd come in. The newcomer was a Mexican, wearing the straw sombrero, huaraches, and baggy cotton trousers and jacket that Longarm had seen on the workers at the mine. He stopped just inside the swinging doors and looked around; then, with a shrug, he headed for the bar.

"You going to let him drink in here, Barney?" Naylor asked in a low voice.

"Keep your prick in your pants, Ed," Trent replied in the same half-whisper. "He might've just been sent in here looking for somebody. Wait'll we see if he tries to buy a drink."

If the Mexican was aware that the men at the table were watching him, he did not show it. He walked up to the bar. Corky acted as though the man were invisible. The Mexican waited for a moment; then, when he saw that the barkeep was purposely ignoring him, he tapped with his knuckles on the bar's pine top. Corky paid no attention to the tapping. Neither did the four customers.

"*Señor!*" the Mexican called, "*Por favor, quiero bebida.*"

Corky saw that he could no longer ignore the man. He looked around and asked, "You talking to me?"

"*Sí. Una bebida.* Dreenk. *Tequila.*"

Corky shook his head. "We ain't got none."

"*Mira, hombre!*" the man exclaimed, pointing at the bottles of tequila on the shelves behind the bar, "*Hay dos o tres botellas ahí!*"

Again Corky shook his head, this time saying, "*No sabe.*"

"'*Pues, no pense que paga?*" the man demanded. He took a coin from his pocket and threw it on the bar. "*Mira! Tengo dinero!*"

"Well, Barney," Naylor demanded. "you going to do your duty, or ain't you?"

Since the fat storekeeper had begun prodding him about the Mexican's presence in the saloon, Trent had been covertly watching Longarm. Longarm had sat impassively, showing no expression of any kind on his face. Trent stood up and walked slowly to the bar. He tapped the Mexican on the shoulder. The man turned around. Trent jerked a thumb at the swinging doors.

"Vamoose, hombre!" he snapped.

"*Por qué?*" the man asked. "*No hace—*"

"Because I'm telling you to!" the constable said. He flipped his vest open to show his badge. "I'm the law here, and I tell you to git out! Vamoose!"

"Pero, señor—"

Trent cut the man's words off by grabbing his shoulder and whirling him around. With one hand on the Mexican's collar and the other grabbing the slack of his pants, the constable frog-marched him to the batwings and sent him through them with a shove and a kick added for emphasis. He waited for a moment, until he was sure the Mexican was not going to return, then came back to the table. Corky and the drinkers at the bar had paid no attention to the constable's ejection of the Mexican.

"Glad to see you did the right thing, Barney," Naylor said, "even if it did take you long enough."

"Dammit, Ed, I had to wait'll he asked," Trent told the storekeeper. "There wasn't no reason for me to move till he did."

Longarm asked quietly, "You got a law against Mexicans drinking in town?"

"Well, not exactly a law," Trent replied. "We just don't let 'em drink anyplace but that saloon down by the livery. That's theirs to do what they want to in. Cut each other up, for all I give a damn."

"Or kill each other?" Longarm asked.

"Don't go putting words in my mouth, Long!" Trent snapped angrily. "If they break the law, they go to jail like anybody else does! I just don't waste time in little shit when there's a bunch of Mexicans to blame!"

"I see," Longarm nodded.

"You know how Mexicans are, Marshal," Cross put in. "You don't keep 'em in their place, they get uppity."

"There's so damn many of 'em out at the Copper Queen, we can't afford to let 'em get out of hand," Naylor said.

"Them that work at the mine, Naylor, you let 'em buy their groceries and stuff in your store?" Longarm asked.

"Why, of course," the merchant answered, then added quickly, "as long as they stay in their place, don't push in ahead of my regular customers, they can buy whatever they've got the money to pay for."

68

"I don't guess you let 'em live in town here, though?" Longarm asked.

"Hell, they've got their own place out at the Copper Queen!" Cross said. "They don't want to live in Mina Cobre!"

"I imagine it's the same with them Papagos that got their shanties on the edge of town?"

"They'd sooner be with their own kind too," Trent said.

Longarm made no reply. Regardless of his own feelings or opinions, he knew he had no grounds to interfere in a local matter such as this, whether the incident was based on law or custom. Deciding he'd had enough for one evening, he drained his glass and was reaching for the bottle of rye when the batwings flapped open and another Mexican burst in.

Seeing the new arrival, Naylor said in a low voice, "Look out, Barney! Here comes our friend the sheriff, and from the way he looks, he's hot under the collar!"

"Let me handle him, Ed," Trent replied. "Don't you get mixed up in a fuss with Carvajal. Remember, you're running against him."

Longarm didn't need the exchange between Naylor and Trent to identify the man who'd just crashed through the batwings. It was obvious at a glance that he was no mine worker, even without the silver star pinned on his shirt pocket.

Carvajal's attire was spectacular. He wore a cerise silk shirt, and twill britches of a light creamy hue. The legs of the britches were tucked into ornately silver-stitched boots. His California-creased Stetson was also white, and its black leather band was studded with silver bosses. Silver bosses also adorned his polished black gunbelt and the twin holsters from which protruded the butts of silver-chased Colts.

Though the sheriff was of normal build, neither slim nor fat, short nor tall, his face was exceptionally long and thin, and the expression on it was very angry. He covered the distance from the door to the table in two huge strides and stood with a hand on each gun butt, staring at the constable.

"Trent!" he exclaimed. "You have an explanation to make to me! Why have you mistreated one of my people who broke no laws of your town?"

Without shifting position in the chair where he lounged,

69

Trent said, "If you mean that *pelado* I just got rid of, you know damn well why I kicked him outa here, Carvajal."

"I know of no law that allows you to handle an innocent man so crudely! You exceed your authority, Trent! For this I will see that you pay!"

"Well, now, if you feel like we got something to settle, I'll be right glad to settle up with you, Carvajal," the constable said. "Right now, if you've a mind to."

"I will not dirty my hands with a *villano* of your class! You will make your payment when the election votes have been counted, and you no longer have the power!"

"Hell, I don't need no power to handle a blow-off like you!" Trent stood up. He was much shorter than Carvajal, but half again as wide across the shoulders. "Come on. Let's have it out right here and now. Fists or guns, take your choice!"

Longarm felt that he could not sit by and let the argument reach the stage of blows or bullets. He said sharply. "All right, now! That's enough outa both of you roosters! This damn foolishness is stopping, right this minute!"

"Stay outa this, Long!" Trent warned. "It don't surprise me none you're on his side. Hell, the copper company owns him, and it's turning out to look like they got you in their pocket too!"

"I don't belong to nobody, Trent. I'm just doing my job the way I see it's got to be done."

"This ain't no part of your job, Long! You're outa your jurisdiction when you step in between me and the sheriff while we're settling a private fuss!"

"Like hell I am!" Longarm retorted. "Anytime I see two men that's supposed to enforce the law getting worked up to break it, I'll step in between 'em, jurisdiction or not!"

Carvajal transferred his attention to Longarm. "And who are you, *señor*? I see no badge that gives you authority here."

"I don't need to wear a badge on my coat," Longarm told the sheriff. "I'll show it to you if you want to see it, though." He took out his well-worn black wallet and flipped it open to let Carvajal see the badge pinned in its fold. "If you can't make out my name, it's Long."

"A federal marshal?" Carvajal said, frowning. "In company

70

with *cacharros* of this kind? Why have you come here, Long? Is it that the federal government now comes to help these men steal the election from my people?"

"More likely the other way around!" Trent snorted. "It's you Mexicans and your bosses out at the Copper Queen that're fixing to steal votes from us!"

"Now, both of you shut up and listen to me!" Longarm grated. "Sheriff, I'm here to keep anybody from stealing anything. And I'll say the same thing to you, Trent! If I can help it, there won't be nothing but honest votes and an honest count."

"Why do you sit here and conspire with these men, then?" the sheriff demanded. "Why do you go to them before you come to me? You must not listen to these *mentirosos*!"

"Sheriff Carvajal," Longarm said quietly, "I'll listen to anybody that wants to tell me something. Whether or not I believe 'em is something else again."

Carvajal refused to be mollified. He drew himself up and said coldly, "This is not the time for me to talk further with you, Marshal. Or with you, either, Trent. Marshal Long, when you wish to know the truth of how it is here, you can come to me and I will tell it to you."

Spinning around on his bootheels, the sheriff stalked out of the saloon. For a moment, none of those at the table had anything to say.

Cross broke the silence. "Well, Marshal Long, you see the kind of damned fool them Mexicans elected sheriff. Carvajal's all blow and no go. Maybe you can understand now why some of us figure we better get rid of him."

"Yeah," Trent agreed. "That's why we try to keep them Mexes in their place. What you just seen sure oughta make you change you mind about coming in on our side, Long. How about it?"

"How many times have I got to tell you, Trent? I don't aim to be on anybody's side."

Naylor said softly, "If it's a matter of money, Long, we can match or beat whatever the Copper Queen's paying you."

"I ain't for sale, either, Naylor. Not to you or the Copper Queen or anybody else," Longarm said, holding his rising anger in check. "And I think I've heard about all I can stomach tonight. If any one of you's got anything you feel like telling me, you know where I'm staying."

Trent, Naylor, and Cross watched Longarm in silence while he picked up the bottle of rye and went to the bar. He put the bottle and a half eagle on the bar and waited for Corky to sidle away from the other customers, who'd been watching and listening to the argument as it blew hot and cool.

"Dig me out one of those full bottles you got in your storeroom, Corky," he told the barkeep. "I need another drink to cool me down, but I can't tolerate having it around those three jackasses. I'll take a bottle home with me where I can enjoy it. Not meaning you, Corky, but I don't like the company in this damn place!"

Chapter 7

As soon as Corky delivered the bottle of rye and gave him his change, Longarm left the saloon. He unhitched the Morgan from the rail and turned its head toward the mine. As he rode, he uncorked the bottle and tilted it up to let a satisfying swallow of the whiskey trickle down his throat. Dropping the bottle in the deep side pocket of his coat, he lighted a cheroot.

Now that was a fuss you'd have been smart to back off from, old son, he told himself as the horse moved along at an easy walking pace through the starlit night. But the way it come up so fast and all, there wasn't much way to stay out of it. And there's times when a man's got to stand up and have his say and not think about what it might do to him later on. Guess this was just one of those times. It's happened, and there wasn't much way you could keep it from happening, and now it's over and done with, so best just quit bothering about it and try to do better next time.

Try as he might to dismiss the saloon quarrel from his mind, the part he'd played in it was still chafing at Longarm's mind when he reined the Morgan in at the corral behind the cottage. He made quick work of unsaddling, looked to be sure there was fodder in the manger inside the open shed, and water in the trough. Then, carrying his rifle, saddlebags, and bedroll, he walked around the cottage to go in by the front door.

He'd noticed when he first came in sight of the house that a light was burning in the living room, and had reminded himself to remember in the morning to thank the young Mexican housekeeper for her thoughtfulness in saving him from stumbling around in a strange house, trying to find his way by lighting matches. He wasn't prepared to find her sitting in the living room, waiting for him to return.

"Now, you didn't have to wait up for me, Miss—" Longarm stopped short when he realized that Grady hadn't mentioned the housekeeper's last name.

She said, "If you're trying to remember my name, Mr. Long, it's Luz Parrejo. But I'd prefer you to call me Luz. It goes better with my position here."

"Well, that's fine with me, Luz." Longarm said. He saw that she'd undone the braided coronet in which she'd worn her black hair earlier, but still wore the scoop-necked peasant blouse and full skirt she'd had on that afternoon. He went on, "I sure didn't expect you'd go to the trouble of waiting up. If I had, I'd've started back sooner."

"It wasn't any trouble," Luz assured him. "I thought it might help you to feel settled, if I was here. And since you've been traveling, I wondered if you'd like to bathe."

"Now, a bath'd be right nice," Longarm told her.

"There's hot water on the stove, but you'll have to bathe in your bedroom or in the kitchen, in a washtub."

"Wouldn't be the first time. But you don't have to coddle me. I'm used to looking out for myself pretty much."

"I'm paid to serve guests of the Copper Queen," she said, smiling. "Perhaps you'd like some coffee? Or a bite to eat? Clarita left some cold food in the pantry, and there's a kerosene stove in the kitchen, so it would only take a minute to fix something."

"No." Longarm pulled the bottle of rye out of his pocket and put it on the table. "I'll just have another swallow out of this bottle that I bought in town. That's all the nightcap I generally take."

"You didn't have to buy whiskey. There's just about any kind of drink you'd care for in the liquor cabinet."

"No, thanks. Anyhow, I don't expect the Copper Queen to put me up and feed me and then buy my whiskey to boot," Longarm said. "Now, if you'll just show me where I'm going to sleep, I'll take this truck I'm carrying inside and get rid of it, then you can go off to bed. I can handle everything else myself."

"Thank you, Mr. Long, but if you're not going to bed right away, I'd like—" Luz stopped short and shook her head. "No. It'd be presumptuous of me to ask you."

"Ask me what?"

She took a deep breath and stood up, facing Longarm. "When you and Mr. Grady were talking this afternoon, I couldn't help overhearing what you said. About the election, and the way things are between the mine company and the town. Mr. Long, are you really going to keep the election an honest one?"

"That's what I was sent here to do. Mind if I ask why you're so interested?"

"Because my father-in-law is running against Raoul Carvajal. He's the sheriff now."

"I know Carvajal. Tell me about your father-in-law."

"It's hard for me to start trying to explain, things are so tangled up. He doesn't really want to run, but—"

"Just a minute," Longarm broke in. "If he don't want to run, why's he doing it?"

"To take my husband's place, Mr. Long. You see, my husband was going to run against Sheriff Carvajal, but he was one of the men those brutes in Mina Cobre murdered because they were afraid he might beat the man they're trying to elect."

Longarm stared at Luz, astonishment on his face. He said, "I didn't know about your husband, Luz. I knew there were two men shot, but nobody ever told me their names."

"There has been enough time since his death for the first ache to fade," she replied, shrugging. After a moment of silence, she went on, "Eusebio was the second one they killed. The other was the man who had persuaded Eusebio to run for sheriff. His name was Steve Carson. He was Mina Cobre's first constable, before the one who holds the office now was elected."

"Barney Trent? Yeah, I met him tonight," Longarm said. "We swapped a few hard words in the saloon. A couple of his cronies were with him, Cross and Naylor."

"Yes. They are not nice men, Mr. Long."

Longarm slid his saddlebags off his shoulder and put them in a corner of the room with his rifle. Luz watched him with a puzzled frown, but made no comment. He removed his hat and laid it on the table beside the bottle of Old Moore, then took off his coat and hung it over the back of the nearest chair.

He turned to Luz and said, "I guess you and me better have

that little talk you wanted to, Luz. I got a hunch there's some things you might be able to tell me."

"Yes, there are, Mr. Long."

"Look here, if I'm going to call you Luz, you better forget about this 'Mr. Long' stuff. I'd appreciate it if you'd just call me Longarm, and forget all this 'mister' business. It makes me sort of uncomfortable."

"It would make Mr. Grady angry, I'm afraid."

"You leave Grady to me, Luz. Now, if you'll find me a glass somewheres, we can sit down and talk while I have my nightcap."

Luz brought the glass and sat down, primly erect, in one of the straight chairs. Longarm stretched out in a lounge chair, a glass of whiskey in his hand.

"I guess we might as well start off with you telling me your side of this mess here," Longarm suggested.

"I don't know where to begin," she said, her brows drawing together. "I didn't really start doing anything until Eusebio was killed. Then Don Diego—his father—decided to take his place and try to get elected sheriff, and I've been trying to give him what help I can. But it hasn't been very much. You know, Longarm, our people don't believe a woman should be interested in what they consider to be men's affairs."

"Like who's going to be sheriff?"

"Among other things, yes."

"How come your husband was trying to beat out the fellow that's sheriff now? He's Mexican too."

"Raoul Carvajal? He is a clown! A fool! We need a real leader, not an actor. Carvajal thinks only of how he'll look to others, not what he can do to help the laborers in the mine."

"He seemed to be trying to do something in town tonight. He stood up pretty good to the constable, after Trent kicked out a Mexican who wanted to buy a drink at the saloon." Longarm gave Luz a condensed version of the incident. Her lips compressed now and then while she listened, and when Longarm had finished his story, she nodded slowly.

"You must understand why Carvajal did this, Longarm. He wants to be reelected more than he will let anyone see. He would not have bothered to do anything if he hadn't know the story would get back to the miners and make him appear brave."

76

"I figured that much out. But if there's two men from your bunch running for the same job, and that fellow Cross is running too, ain't it likely your votes will be split up, and Cross will walk off with the election?"

Luz shrugged. "That is what I asked Eusebio when he first began talking of running. He did not seem too worried, and he was sure that with work he would get the votes. Don Diego has a different way. He will not campaign for election. He's sure his name alone will get him the votes he needs."

Longarm refilled his glass and lighted a fresh cheroot. He knew he was smoking too much, but the rye really needed the smoke from a cheroot to bring out its finest flavor. He looked at Luz over the rim of his glass and asked her, "You mind if I ask you something personal, Luz?"

She shrugged. "You can ask. If it is too intimate, I will not promise to answer."

"That's fair enough. How did your family happen to come here to the mine to start with? You're not like the rest of the Mexican folks I've seen here."

"That I can answer, Longarm. My father and Eusebio's father had a large trading business with Mexico's northern colonies. It was a family business, you understand, three generations old. When your country took the colonies, California and New Mexico and Arizona, my grandfather moved from Mexico City to Guerrero, on the Rio Grande. Do you by any chance know of the place?"

"I've had some cases along the border down that way, but I can't say I ever heard of Guerrero. Where's it at?"

"Quite far south, a short distance above Nuevo Laredo. I'm afraid it's a shadow town, now. You see, after our war, when your country and mine were at peace again, Guerrero was built as a free zone, a place where neither country charged taxes or customs duties on merchandise that moved back and forth across the border. And the family's trade became centered more and more on Tucson and the mining towns just above the border."

"If you didn't have to pay taxes on the stuff you handled, business must've been pretty good."

"It was, until the free zone was abolished. Trade died then, of course. The people who had worked so many years for my

77

grandfather and father were suffering. We helped them, but our money was not all that much. Then, when mining began in this part of Arizona Territory, we emigrated here, still trying to hold together the people who had served us so well. Does that answer your question, Longarm?"

"Up to a point, I guess. But how about you, Luz? How come you're working in a job like this? You've had schooling, I can tell that. Ain't there something better you can do?"

Luz smiled, a mixture of sorrow and bitterness. "There are times when that is what I ask myself." For a moment she sat silently, then went on, "My grandfather had more wisdom than my father, I think." After a thoughtful pause she said, "But this is family talk, Longarm, not what you want me to tell you."

"Go on. It's all part of the story. What about your grand-father, Luz?"

"He was sure that your country would come to dominate Mexico sooner or later. After I had gone through convent school, he insisted that I go to Mills College in California. He wanted me to learn the ways of your people, and your language. He told me the day would come when I would need to know these things."

"Well, it turned out he was right, didn't it?"

"Yes. He did not live to see the day when our family would have no more money." She stopped again, shrugged, and added, "My costly education does me little good, as you can see."

"This don't look to me like it'd be a bad job."

"It's not. I don't have much to do. Clarita does all the cooking and most of the housework. I suppose I don't like it because I feel I ought to be doing something that would help my family and our people more. For someone like me, serving as a housekeeper—really, nothing more than a chambermaid— is not enough. But what can I do? That is all there is, here."

"So you began helping your father-in-law politicking?"

"When Eusebio was killed, I had to help him, Longarm. It isn't easy, of course. My people have had so many false promises held in front of them, they have no faith in men seeking office. I don't talk to the men, of course, they wouldn't listen to a woman. But their women do, and the women will

78

talk to the men—or at least that's what I'm hoping will happen."

"It usually does work out that way. I'd guess at what you're doing, Luz. You're telling them not to vote for Carvajal or Cross, ain't you?"

"Of course. There aren't a lot of votes, you know. I must get my people to forget about Carvajal. Cross will get all the town votes, of course, but if Carvajal doesn't get any votes from our people, Don Diego can still win."

"What about the Papagos on the other side of town? Who'll they vote for?"

Luz looked up, her dark eyes wide in surprise. "Why, the Papagos are Indians, Longarm! They don't get to vote!"

"They live here, don't they? Work here, too? Arizona Territory ain't like other places, where they put the Indians out on reservations, where they got their own government."

"No. But most of the Papagos work in town. There are only a few working for the Copper Queen."

"It'd seem to me that if the Papagos live here and work here, they'd have just as much right to vote as anybody else."

"I hadn't thought about it that way," Luz said thoughtfully. "You know, that might make a lot of difference in an election where there are so few votes."

"Well, you think about it a little bit. Maybe you'll get some ideas." Longarm reached for the bottle, then thought better of having another nightcap, and stood up. "It's getting pretty late, and I'm keeping you up a long time. You sleep on what we just talked about. And anytime you hear anything I ought to know about, I'd appreciate it if you'll pass it on to me."

"If it's something that will help Don Diego, I certainly will. And, Longarm . . ."

"You want to ask me something else?"

"No. I just wanted to thank you for listening to me and not laughing at me. Good night, Longarm."

Standing in front of the bureau mirror, with his balbriggans, pants, and boots on, Longarm pushed his mustache into its customary upward-sweeping curve. It was very early, the dawn light just creeping into the bedroom window. A cheroot was clamped between his teeth, and the first half of his eye-opener still tingled on his taste buds as he debated whether to dig into his saddlebag and get out his razor, or wait until he went into town and have a shave at the barbershop he'd seen there.

Before he could make up his mind, the murmur of voices coming from the back of the cottage, which had wakened him a few minutes earlier, suddenly erupted into an angry argument. He couldn't make out the words, but the volume and tone were unmistakable. He postponed making a decision about the shave and went to see what was wrong.

When the angry voices guided him to the kitchen, he saw Luz and another young woman, whom he took to be the cook, facing one another across the unpainted deal table that stood in the center of the room, hot words in Spanish filling the air between them. They saw Longarm and their voices died away into an embarrassed silence.

"Maybe if you'd tell me what you ladies are fussing about, I could help you settle things peaceful," he suggested.

"It is nothing," Luz said. "Clarita and I have a difference of opinion, that is all. I am sorry we woke you up, Longarm."

"Tell the *señor* why we are quarrel, Luz!" the other woman challenged. "Listen to what he say! Maybe you do not feel so smart when he tell you I know what of I talk!"

Luz started to speak, but Longarm turned to the second woman. At first glance, he'd taken Clarita to be older than Luz, but now he saw that she must be about the same age. She was a bit taller than Luz, darker in complexion, and instead of the thin aristocratic nose and narrow face with high cheekbones that bespoke Spanish blood, she had the broad nose and thick nostrils of those whose forebears were largely the Indians who had ruled before the Spanish conquest. Her figure was much fuller than Luz's, her breasts broader and more prominent, her body thicker.

Longarm asked her, "You'd be Clarita? The lady that does the cooking?"

"*Sí. Clarita Mendoza, sus ordenes, Señor Long.*"

"You talk any English?" Longarm asked her.

"*Seguro*, of sure I espeak. Too I talk Papago, Apache, an' Yaqui, Señor Long."

"English'll do fine, right now," Longarm told her. He looked from one of the women to the other. "If it ain't anything

80

too personal, you ladies want to tell me what the fussing's about?" When both of them tried to answer at once, he held up a hand and said, "One at a time. Luz, you go ahead."

"It is nothing," Luz said. "A difference of opinion. We will settle it ourselves, Longarm, you do not need to bother."

"Why, it's not any bother. Might be I can help you."

"Tell heem, Luz!" Clarita hissed. "He weel listen. He ees not like Señor Grady. My power is already tell me this."

Longarm frowned. "What kind of power you mean?"

"Ah!" Luz snorted. "Clarita claims she is a *bruja*—a witch. I have told her many times that this is Indian superstition, but she will not listen to me."

"A witch?"

Longarm looked questioningly at Clarita. Many years ago, in his West Virginia childhood, he'd known an old granny who was supposed to have been a witch, able to talk with the birds and animals and to see the future in tea leaves and cast spells that would bring on an illness or cure one. He'd seen the crone perhaps a half-dozen times, always at a distance, for mothers warned their children to stay away from her. That was as far as his experience with witches went.

He asked Clarita, "You mean you can cast spells? Look into the future? Things like that?"

"Pero sí, señor. Eet ees the owl of my people that show me these things I am to see and do to make the *hechizo."*

"You got an owl someplace that talks to you?" Longarm asked.

"Of course she hasn't!" Luz said. "She's talking about the owl-god the Papagos believe guides them and speaks to them."

Longarm felt that he was getting out of his depth. He tried to get back to his original intention of settling whatever argument had been going on between the two women.

"Is that what you two was fussing about?" he asked Luz.

"Clarita was telling me a foolish story about a warning she says she got from her owl-god last night."

"Ees true!" Clarita broke in hotly. "Ees to be beeg trouble, *horas turbulentas,* bad things to happen!"

"Foolishness!" Luz snorted.

"Wait a minute, Luz," Longarm told her. He asked Clarita, "What kind of trouble?"

"Lo más malo, señor," she replied somberly. "Men weel die."

"Nonsense!" Luz exclaimed.

Longarm looked at Luz and shook his head commandingly, and she said nothing more. He turned back to Clarita. "You still ain't said what kind of trouble."

She shrugged. "The owl ees not tell me this, *señor*. All I am know ees eet weel be soon and eet weel be bad. Very bad."

"We'll just have to wait and see if your owl was telling you the truth, then, won't we?" Longarm said.

"Is always tell true, the owl," Clarita replied. "You watch. Trouble weel come."

"Well, if it does or if it don't, we still got to get the day started, and the way I like to start mine is with a good hot breakfast," he said, looking from Clarita to Luz in turn. "Now why don't you ladies go ahead with what you're supposed to be doing, while I finish dressing."

Longarm went back to the bedroom and put on his shirt. He took another quick glance at his stubble and decided he'd wait for the barber in town to deal with it. Out of habit, he reached for his gunbelt, which hung in its usual position on the head of the iron bedstead, then realized he wasn't going to have to leave the house for breakfast. Leaving the holstered Colt hanging on the bedpost, he went in for breakfast.

Luz had the table set and a pot of coffee waiting. She came in from the kitchen when she heard him move the chair to sit down, and filled his coffee cup.

"Clarita's cooking your steak and potatoes now, Longarm," she told him. "They'll be ready in just a moment."

"Fine. Now, I aim to put in most of the day in town, so you won't have to fix anything for me at noon."

"You are going to arrest those men who killed Eusebio?"

Longarm put down his coffee cup and looked up at her. "Now, Luz, you're smart enough to know that I can't just walk into town and arrest people unless I got some evidence they killed your husband."

"But you are a federal officer, Longarm! In Mexico, the federal police do not wait for evidence!"

"So I found out, the few times I been there. You've been in this country long enough to know we don't do things that way."

"I know nothing about the laws of crime in America. I just assumed that in all countries the federal police have great powers that sheriffs and constables and the like do not."

"It'd sure make my job easier if we did, but that just ain't the way of it. Now, you be patient. Things have got a way of working out all right."

"There's not much else I can do but wait, is there?" Luz turned away, saying, "I'll get your breakfast."

Longarm watched her go into the kitchen. It don't seem to make much difference who women are and where they come from, he thought. They all got the same ideas that laws and justice are things you make up as you go along. And when they want a man to do something, they always want him to get it finished yesterday. There's times when it's a downright shame that a man can't get along without 'em!

Chapter 8

Clean-shaven again, surrounded by a strong scent of bay rum with an undertone of macassar oil, Longarm walked out of the barbershop. He swung into the saddle and set out to take a closer look at Mina Cobre than he'd had time for when he arrived the day before.

It was a nondescript town at best. The houses were sprawled out in the streetless area around the road that cut through the town and none of them bore any distinguishing identification. A stranger, he thought, would have a lot of trouble finding someone he was looking for, since all the houses seemed to have been built on the same general plan.

Details he'd missed in the cursory observation he'd been able to give the town on his arrival registered on his mind. The livestock that he'd seen wandering along the banks of the trickle that the creek became after it passed through town were not roaming loose, he saw. A brush-and-pole corral had been built in the quarter-mile wide strip that lay between the last of Mina Cobre's houses and the first reed huts of the Papago village. Horses, mules, milk cows, steers, goats, and sheep were intermingled inside the corral, more livestock than a Papago village would be apt to have. He decided the corral must be shared by the residents of Mina Cobre.

There was as little order to the Papago settlement as there was to the town; the Papago dwellings were also scattered at random. Some huts stood in the centers or at the edges of small garden plots; others were built so close together that they almost touched each other. There was much the same activity in the village as Longarm had noted the day before; it consisted chiefly of women carrying clay *ollas* back and forth from the stream to the gardens to pour water on the bushes of beans and

85

straggly stands of maize that seemed to be the only crops the Papagos grew.

Although he looked closely during the three-quarters of an hour that his inspection ride lasted, Longarm saw no signs of a city hall or courthouse. This surprised him not at all; in other towns as raw and young as Mina Cobre, he'd often found that a store or barbershop or saloon served as an unofficial town hall or courthouse until the residents found time to provide a building for local government offices.

Morning was merging into noon by the time Longarm's tour was finished. He reined in at the saloon and pushed through the batwings. Corky was standing behind the bar, cutting up lemons. He stopped and wiped his hands when he saw Longarm, and had the bottle of Tom Moore and a glass waiting for him when he reached the bar.

"Don't cutting them things up set your teeth on edge?" Longarm asked, indicating the lemons.

"I don't have to do it every day. There's a few customers who like lemon and salt for a tequila chaser, so I get a few now and then from the old mission up in the valley."

Longarm poured rye into his glass as he said, "I don't guess there was any more fireworks after I left last night."

"No fireworks, but a lot of cussing and discussing. You wasn't the most popular fellow in town when you walked out of here, you know. At least not with them three."

"If they've got any complaints, they won't have any trouble finding me." Longarm sipped the rye appreciatively.

"They're not quite ready to come looking for you yet," Corky said, smiling. "They'll want to see what you do before they make any kind of move."

"I don't expect to do much before election day," Longarm told Corky. "But your friends are welcome to watch me do it."

"They're no friends of mine," Corky said quickly. "Not all my customers are what I'd call friends. You think about it for a minute. Trent and Naylor and Cross have cost me a whole mint of money, not letting me have any Mexicans drinking in here. Dammit, I don't care what color skin a man's got. I want to see the color of his money."

Longarm smiled. "Now, I generally figure that's a pretty healthy way to look at things. And I recall Naylor said last night that he sells the Mexicans and Papagos whatever they want at his store. Seems to me you ought to have the same right."

"Them's my feelings too," Corky replied. "But I can't go against the three of 'em, you know. Trent's the law, and Naylor as good as runs the board of town selectmen. They could make things rough on me if they took a mind to."

"Maybe it's time I had a little talk with Naylor." He put a half-dollar on the bar. "See you after while, Corky."

Crossing the street, Longarm went into the general store. It was no different from other general stores he'd seen in similarly isolated small towns. There were shelves along the walls, tables of goods filled the floor, and such items as sides of bacon, hams, and harness and saddlery hung from the rafters. In spite of the generally cluttered interior, Naylor was immensely visible. His gross bulk overflowed the back corner in which he sat and seemed to dominate the store, its stock, and its fixtures. His reptilian eyes, hooded by his puffy eyebrows and fat cheeks, followed Longarm from the door to the corner where Naylor was sitting.

"Well, Marshal," he said, "I'm glad you decided to stop in and apologize for the unkind remarks you made last night."

"That ain't exactly why I'm here, Naylor." Longarm let the storekeeper wait while he took out a cheroot and lighted it. "I'm here to ask you what you've done about the election ballots."

He watched Naylor closely, waiting for him to react angrily, but the fat storekeeper's face remained expressionless. Longarm took the lack of an angry outburst to indicate that after he'd stalked out of the saloon last night, Naylor and his two friends had agreed to try to avoid rubbing him the wrong way.

"What about them?" Naylor asked.

"You being on the selectmen's board, I figured you'd know who's going to print 'em up, and when they'll be here, and how many of 'em you got, things like that."

"I see." Naylor kept his eyes fixed on Longarm. "You take your job seriously, don't you, Long?"

"I try to."

"Well, you can stop worrying about the ballots. They've already been printed, up in Tucson. There's enough for every

87

man in the county who's old enough to vote, with about two dozen extras in case some are spoiled. And they're locked up in the safe in my store here, where I intend for them to stay until election day."

"I guess they all got numbers on 'em?" Longarm asked.

For the first time, Naylor seemed uncomfortable. After a moment's hesitation he said, "No. As a matter of fact, they haven't. It seems the printer had some trouble with the dingus they use in printing shops to number things like ballots, so he had to leave the numbers off."

"But you're going to see they get numbered before election day, I guess?" Longarm asked guilelessly.

"I hadn't thought about it that much," the fat man replied. "Seems like a hell of a lot of trouble to take, when there's so few votes in the county."

Longarm puffed his cheroot and knocked the ash off it before he said, "Tell you what. Suppose I come in here some day before the election and count those ballots. If they ain't got numbers on 'em, it'd be awful easy for a few extras to get dropped in the ballot box." Then he added at once, "By mistake, of course."

"I don't see how anybody could object to that," Naylor told him. "If you think any of the candidates might want to do some counting, or watch you doing it, they can sit in. Carvajal, maybe, or that other greaser, Parrejo. They'd be the ones who'd feel like they couldn't trust us."

"That sounds fair enough," Longarm agreed. "If I can find out where Carvajal lives, I want to go see him after while. I looked around town a little bit, but didn't have much luck."

"He'll likely be at the Mex saloon down by the livery right after dinner. He's there most every afternoon."

"Thanks. That's where I'll look for him, then. And I'll take care of that little ballot-counting chore in a day or so."

"Whenever you feel like it. They'll still be here, all wrapped up just the way they were when they left the printer's."

"Don't guess we'll have any problems, in that case," Longarm said. "I'll stop in as soon as I take care of one or two more little jobs I got to tend to first."

"They'll still be in the safe," Naylor promised him.

Walking back across the street, Longarm felt tempted to

88

look over his shoulder; he could almost feel the fat store-keeper's eyes following him. He forked the Morgan and walked the horse the short distance to the restaurant.

That fat man's one to keep an eye on, old son, he told himself as he rode along the noon-quiet street. He's half again smarter than them other two he hangs out with. He was just too damned agreeable about me counting those ballots before the election. Now, if he's got in mind what it looks like he has, there's bound to be a way to handle it. And pennies'll get you peanuts that him and his bunch are going to try the oldest trick there is to steal votes. So all I got to do is figure a way to keep one jump ahead of him.

A dish of stew, more carrots and potatoes than meat, filled the emptiness of Longarm's stomach without satisfying his hunger. He waved away a second cup of coffee and went in search of Raoul Carvajal, at the Mexican saloon by the livery stable.

In contrast to Corky's place, the Mexican cantina was crowded. Longarm picked his way through a sea of straw sombreros to the bar. The swarthy barkeep looked at him suspiciously.

"Qué quiere, señor?" he asked.

Unless he was forced to do so by circumstances, Longarm seldom revealed his smattering of Spanish or of the few Indian languages with which he had some small familiarity. He said, "I'm looking for the sheriff. Raoul Carvajal."

"'Pues, no 'sta 'quí. Poco á poco viene."

"You mean he ain't here?" Longarm asked looking around.

"No, *señor*. Maybe pretty quick he is here."

"I'll wait, then. You got any rye whiskey?"

"De cuál?"

"Rye. Not bourbon."

With a shrug, the barkeep pointed to the shelves behind the bar. Most of the bottles bore no labels, but there were a few that identified the distillers of the tequila, aguardiente, mescal, habanero, or pulque they contained. Longarm pointed to a bottle of Sauza tequila.

"Pour me one from that bottle there." When he saw the man hesitate, Longarm pulled out a twenty-five-cent piece and put it on the bar. "That what you're worried about?"

A smile broke out on the barkeep's face. *"Es demasiado, señor. Tequila es solamente diez centavos."* He reached for the Sauza bottle, produced a somewhat streaked glass from below the bar, and filled it to the brim.

"Quieres limon y sal, señor?" he asked.

Longarm decided the words were close enough to English for him to understand. He nodded. "Sure, a slice of lemon and some salt goes good with tequila."

Telling himself it was part of his job, he sucked a few drops of lemon juice into his mouth, touched his tongue to the grains of salt he'd shaken into his palm, and tossed off half the *tequila*. Though the salt and lemon counteracted the somewhat oily taste of the liquor, Longarm knew he'd never be persuaded to switch from his favorite Maryland rye.

For as long as he could, Longarm nursed the tequila along and watched the crowd. From the appearance of their clothing, stained with streaks of the orange-hued soil that was common in the area of the Copper Queen, he deduced that most of the men worked at the mine. After the first few minutes, when he was the target of worried and suspicious glances, the men paid little attention to him. They seemed to accept the odd fact that the tall, pistol-wearing *gringo* had come into the cantina for no other reason than to have a drink of Mexico's native liquor.

Raoul Carvajal's arrival saved Longarm from having to consume a second glass of tequila. The sheriff had on the same cream-colored britches and white hat, the same silver-trimmed black leather accoutrements that he'd worn the evening before, but he'd changed his cerise shirt for one of vivid green. He recognized Longarm, and pushed through the crowd to greet him.

"I have been hoping I would see you today, Marshal," he said without preamble. "I have realize I was mistaken last night to think you might take part in a fraud, especially with men of the type of Trent and Cross and Naylor. My apologies."

"No offense taken, Sheriff," Longarm replied. "Sometimes a man gets riled up and says things he don't mean to."

Carvajal glanced at the glass in Longarm's hand. "You will have a *copita* with me, I hope? It will be my pleasure."

Longarm hesitated only long enough for his sense of duty to jog him. "Why sure, Sheriff, I'll drink with you."

90

Snapping his fingers at the barkeep, Carvajal said, *"Garcia! Otro lo mismo para el señor. Y que volvido, no tome su dinero, ponese a mi cuenta."* He explained to Longarm, "I have told Garcia that you are to be a guest of the house whenever you come in. It is a small courtesy he extends to me and my friends."

Longarm's glass was refilled quickly, and the barkeep handed Carvajal a bottle of aguardiente and an empty glass. The sheriff looked around the crowded room and motioned toward a table in the far corner; strangely, it was unoccupied in spite of the crowd in the cantina.

"We will go to my table," Carvajal told Longarm. "No one will disturb us there without permission."

A lane opened through the crowd as the sheriff led the way to the vacant table. He motioned Longarm to a chair and sat down with his own back against the wall, where he could look over the entire room. Filling his glass, he raised it to Longarm and took a swallow of the sugarcane brandy.

"Now, Marshal," Carvajal announced, "Let us talk together like sensible men."

"Anything special you want to talk about, outside of the election?" Longarm asked.

Carvajal smiled thinly. "You joke, of course. What other matter could be of interest to both of us?"

"Go ahead and talk, Sheriff. I'm listening."

Carvajal did not reply at once, but took another sip of the aguardiente. Then he said, "You saw last night what I must overcome in order to be reelected, Marshal Long. I am glad you will be here to watch the voting. There is more hidden below the surface in this election than those three men, though."

"I'll be interested in hearing what else is bothering you, Carvajal. Come on, out with it."

Again the sheriff played for time by sipping his brandy. At last he said, "You have perhaps noticed that the Copper Queen Mine employs many of the *gente*, Marshal." When Longarm nodded, he went on, "When I was elected sheriff, the owners of the mine gave me their support. They felt that a Mexican in this office I hold would help their workers to avoid trouble."

"Stands to reason," Longarm said. "After seeing the way

91

that poor devil got rousted last night in the saloon, I can't say I blame 'em."

"Yes. But now there is a problem. You must have found out even in the short while you have been here that I am not the only one of the *gente* who is running for sheriff this time."

"I heard something to that effect. Man named Parrejo's in the race too, ain't he?"

"Diego Parrejo, yes."

"What I heard was that Parrejo's running in place of his son, after the boy got backshot awhile back."

"Ah, that is what Don Diego says! But I think there is more to it than that, Marshal Long. I think the owners of the mine are secretly backing him, and will not now support me."

"Why would they want to do that?"

Carvajal shrugged expressively. *"Quién sabe?* This is something I cannot understand. I have asked Grady if he will support me or if he will help Parrejo, but he tells me nothing."

"Where do you figure I fit into this, Carvajal? It ain't my business to tell anybody who they can or can't push to get elected, as long as they do it honest, all open and aboveboard."

"Do you not think it is dishonest for the mine operators to take away the help they have given me and give it to someone who has had no experience in my job?" Carvajal demanded.

"Can't say I do. If they was to go out and buy votes or do something outright crooked to help him, that'd bother me a lot. But from what you just said, that ain't the way of it."

"I do not know yet that there is dishonesty involved, Marshal Long. But I strongly suspect . . ."

Longarm interrupted him. "Suspicions ain't good enough. You show me anything that's out of line, and I'll jump in. If you can't do that, I can't help you."

"But you can!" Carvajal insisted. "You can give me your personal support as a federal official, Marshal Long! The *gente* will listen if you tell them they must vote for me, instead of Parrejo or Cross!"

"Now that's something I can't do. It'd be sort of like a judge not bothering to hand down a verdict because he was on the prisoner's side. No, I'm sorry, Carvajal." Longarm stood up. "Looks like you're going to have to work this one out by yourself. But thanks for the drink, anyhow."

Outside the cantina, Longarm decided enough of the day was left for him to talk with the other two men on his list, Trent and Cross. He already had a good idea of what they'd say, but he was interested in watching their faces while they said it. He looked in Corky's saloon and in Naylor's store, and rode the length of the street twice from one end of Mina Cobre to the other, but neither of the two turned up. The idea of waiting in town and enduring another dish of stew at the cafe had no appeal for him. He headed the Morgan back to the Copper Queen.

Luz must have been watching for him, Longarm thought, for she opened the cottage door the moment he stepped onto the veranda. She said, "I didn't know when you'd be back, so I haven't had Clarita begin cooking supper yet. I hope you're not in a hurry."

"No hurry at all. I got a little chore that I need to do before supper, anyhow. Been moving around so much that I got a little bit behind."

"Is it something I can help you with?" Luz asked.

"I'll need some boiling water, if you got a kettle on the stove, or maybe you could boil a little bit for me while I'm having a little sip of rye."

"Of course, Will you want a cup or a bowl, too?"

"A bowl'd be handy to have. Just put 'em on the table."

His drink finished, Longarm went into the bedroom and rummaged through his saddlebags for the flannel cloths, oilcan, and short hickory rod that he always kept in them. When he got back to the living room, Luz had placed a steaming teakettle and an empty bowl on the table. He took out his Colt and ejected the cartridges from its cylinder, then removed the cylinder from the revolver's frame. Luz stood watching him.

"You're sure there isn't something else you'll need?" she asked.

"No, thanks, Luz. This job's something a man in my business has got to do for himself, and I been putting it off too long."

"I'll see to getting supper ready, then."

Longarm placed the Colt's cylinder on end in the bowl and poured boiling water into its chambers until the steaming water

93

ran down the cylinder's fluted sides. He held the gun's frame over the bowl at an angle and poured more water into the opening in the frame that the cylinder usually occupied, letting the hot liquid flow through the gun's barrel.

Selecting one of the pieces of flannel, which had dark stains that showed they had been used for this purpose before, he carefully wiped the cylinder dry and pulled the cloth through each chamber until his sharp eyes could detect no traces of burned powder residue clinging to the blued steel. When the cylinder was dry and shining, he used the cloth to rub the frame to a gleaming dryness. He passed the cloth through the barrel with the hickory rod until the spiraled rifling shone clean and sharp.

Finally, he applied a coat of the fine gun oil to all the parts of the weapon, wiping away as much of the oil as he could with a clean, dry piece of the cloth. Before returning the cylinder to the frame, he placed a scanty film of oil on the pawl and rachet, and wiped away the excess oil with the tip of his calloused forefinger. Cocking the Colt, he gave his attention to the hammer and trigger slots, using his fingertip to work the lightest possible film of oil into them.

Wiping the gun for a final time with the dry flannel, he reloaded five of the chambers and twirled the cylinder with the piece at half-cock. The cylinder spun silently and smoothly. Satisfied, Longarm laid the Colt on the table and was picking up the bowl and kettle to carry them back to the kitchen, when Luz came in. She looked at the Colt, gleaming against the dark wood of the tabletop.

"I am not fond of guns," she said, a trace of disapproval in her voice.

"Maybe that's because you don't know about 'em, Luz."

"I do not. Nor do I want to."

"Well, I've found out that most folks that don't like guns are the ones that don't understand about 'em. For the most part, people that use 'em regular respect guns, but they ain't afraid of 'em. And in my kind of job, they're just tools that you use to help you stay alive in a pinch or to keep some outlaw from hurting somebody else."

"Yes, I can understand that. It is the outlaws who should be denied them."

"I'll go along with that, but it'd be real hard to do. Maybe someday when the country's more civilized, as well as the people in it..."

"Perhaps you're right, Longarm." Luz reached for the bowl and pitcher. "Here, I will take these to the kitchen. Now put your gun away. Clarita has your supper ready."

Longarm ate supper in solitary splendor, with Luz serving him. Uncomfortable at the unaccustomed attention, he invited her to sit down and eat with him, but she shook her head.

"No. You spoke a moment ago about your job, Longarm. It is my job to attend to you, and I cannot do this if I am sitting at the table with you like a guest."

His meal finished, Longarm lighted a cheroot and took his second cup of coffee out to the cooler air of the veranda. The sun had set, but the sky in the west was still tinged with wide bands of red and orange. Kerosene lanterns and one or two carbide lights glowed in and around the buildings of the Copper Queen; as at most mining operations, work went on there by night as well as by day.

Longarm had drained his coffee cup and was thinking of going inside for a taste of rye, when a distant report broke the evening's silence. He cocked his head, listening, and stepped off the veranda to test the direction of the wind. It was blowing toward the mine from the town, and as he stood with his face turned up to the sky, a second report sounded.

He started toward the house, but stopped when a staccato rattle of distant gunfire reached his ears. Luz ran out on the veranda, with Clarita following her.

"Did you hear?" Luz asked Longarm.

"I sure did." Longarm paused as another volley sounded. "It's shooting, all right. Coming from town."

"Aha!" Clarita said triumphantly. "I say so thees morning, remember! *Horas turbulentas!* Is trouble, beeg trouble, at Mina Cobre!"

Chapter 9

"Sure sounds like it," Longarm agreed. He fixed Clarita's eyes with his. "What do you know about the trouble, Clarita?"

"Nada! Por Dios, Señor Long! Nada, nadamiente! I am *bruja, verdad,* but of what kind the trouble ees, I do not know. Thees the owl do not tell me!"

Longarm pushed past Luz and Clarita to the front door. Luz asked him, "Are you going to Mina Cobre to find out?"

"Of course I am! One or two shots, that'd mean a saloon fight or something like that. But that was more'n just a couple we heard. Sounded more like a dozen or so."

"Apaches!" Clarita exclaimed. *"O tal vez,* Yaquis."

"It might be." Longarm paused in the doorway. "Grady mentioned some roving bands that raided here once in a while, when I asked him about the guards at the mine. I'll find out soon enough." He disappeared into the house as another short, ragged burst, no more than three or four shots, sounded in the distance.

Longarm came out, rifle and saddlebags in his hands, and hurried to the corral. He resaddled the Morgan and poked his heels in its flanks to send it off at a smart canter. The sunset pink was fading fast, and the soft gray of twilight was beginning to shroud the land. Over the thudding of the Morgan's hooves on the baked trail, he heard one or two more shots as he rode, but the volleys that had sounded earlier were not repeated.

He rounded the shore of the lake and came to the Mexican settlement. A few men were trickling away from the adobe houses, most of them taking the more direct footpath instead of the trail. The village itself seemed to be maintaining its usual air of lazy placidity.

Beyond the Mexican houses and drawing closer to Mina

Cobre, Longarm found more lights shining through the gathering night than he'd though such a little town could muster. He saw why when he rounded the bend approaching the livery stable. Lights shone along the street, where the stores were open, as well as in the houses scattered around them.

Wherever he looked, there were open doors and unshaded windows. He could see women and a few children standing close to the houses, and every man in town seemed to be in the street. About half of them were carrying rifles or shotguns, and a few wore pistol belts.

Longarm pulled up before the Morgan crashed into the crowd and called to the man nearest him, "What in hell's going on? Who's doing the shooting?"

"Somebody said it's Apaches or Yaquis raiding the Papagos," the man replied. "Some says it's one, some says the other."

"What difference does it make, Apaches or Yaquis? That shooting started damn near a half-hour ago!" Longarm snapped. "Who's running things! Isn't anybody doing anything about it?"

"Damned if I know. We been waiting for somebody to take charge ever since the shooting begun, but nobody seems about to."

"Well, follow along with me," Longarm said. "We'd better find out pretty fast!"

With the Morgan high-stepping in and out among the men who darted underfoot, Longarm slowly made his way to the closest thing Mina Cobre had to a center, the saloon and store. In the saddle, he could look over the top of the batwings and see that the saloon was empty of customers. Across the street, the open doors of the store were clogged with men pushing to get inside.

Longarm began elbowing through the crowd. One of the men he pushed shoved back until he told the man, "I'll ask you to move aside. I'm a U.S. marshal, I need to get in there."

Immediately the man began calling, "Let him get through! He's a U.S. marshal! Now maybe we'll get some action!"

Reluctantly and with a bit more jostling on Longarm's part, the milling group opened long enough to let him get inside. Naylor apparently hadn't moved. The fat merchant was still sitting in the back corner where he'd been when Longarm had talked to him earlier. Cross was keeping the crowd away from the corner with a sawed-off shotgun. Between Cross and Naylor, Carvajal and Trent were standing. Longarm started toward them, and Cross raised the shotgun muzzle threateningly. Longarm brushed the twin barrels aside.

"Stop acting like a damned fool, Cross!" he said sharply. "You got about as much need for that thing as a bald man has for a hairbrush! Now get out of my way!"

Cross lowered the shotgun. A murmur began to rise from the crowd, and grew until it became a babble so loud that when Longarm first got past Cross, he couldn't hear the exchange going on between the constable and sheriff.

When he did get close enough to pick the constable's words out of the confusion of sound that filled the store, Trent was saying to Carvajal, "... won't tell none of the men from town to go! If you want to help them Papagos, take some of your Mexicans!"

"My people have few guns!" Carvajal protested. "If you will not help with men, then make Mr. Naylor let my *gente* have guns off his racks!"

Naylor said, "Look here, Carvajal, don't go putting ideas in Trent's head! Get it through your damned thick skulls that I don't hand out free guns to anybody! I won't do it for you, Trent and that goes double for any Mexican posse you put together, Carvajal!"

"What in hell are you fools doing?" Longarm burst out. "Standing here jawing about who's going to fight when you got a bunch of Apache raiders right in your backyard!"

"They ain't Apaches, they're Yaquis," Cross said over his shoulder. "And as long as we don't bother 'em while they get whatever grub they can steal from the Papagos, they won't bother the town."

"How the devil do you know that?" Longarm demanded.

"There ain't enough of 'em, for one thing," Trent said. "I don't imagine there's more than a dozen of 'em."

"What about the Papagos?" Longarm asked. "Didn't you ever figure that if the Yaquis get the idea you people here won't fight, they'll be back after while to raid *you?*"

"We got too many guns in town for the Yaquis to take us

99

on, and they know it. The Papagos ain't got three guns amongst 'em."

"More damn fool you, then, for not helping the Papagos!" Longarm told Trent angrily.

"No. Trent's right, Long," Naylor said. "The damned Papagos aren't worth helping. They don't spend ten dollars a month in town here, the whole tribe of 'em."

"How about you, Carvajal?" Longarm asked the sheriff. "You sounded like you wanted to do something to help those poor devils the Yaquis are robbing."

"I would lead my *gente* against them, but they have too few guns," Carvajal replied.

"How many of your people can you get to join a posse?" Longarm asked the sheriff.

Carvajal shrugged. "As many, perhaps, as eight. There are others who have weapons, but they will not join me." Then he added quickly, "For personal reasons."

Longarm suspected the personal reasons were really just the single reason Luz had given him, that many of the Mexicans thought the sheriff was a clumsy clown, but this was not the time to discuss it with him. He turned to Trent. "How many men can you call up in a hurry, Trent? As many as eight or ten?"

"About that many." Trent showed no interest in asking Longarm the reason for his question. His eyes widened when Longarm spoke next.

"Go get 'em, then."

"Hold on, Long! You're not going to try to force me to call up a posse! Being a federal man doesn't give you that kind of authority!"

Longarm moved a half-step closer to the constable. "I'll remind you of something, Trent. Those Papagos out there are wards of the United States government. That being the case, it's my duty to protect 'em."

His draw was dazzling. Before Trent realized what was happening, he found himself staring into the muzzle of the Colt.

Longarm said quietly, "And if I need more authority than my badge to protect 'em, I got it right here in my hand."

Naylor came to Trent's assistance. "You're not going to get away with this, Long!" Naylor blustered. "I won't let you! I've got friends in Washington!"

"Sure. Lots of folks have, Naylor. Now, we've wasted enough time. Trent, go get that posse together. Carvajal, can you get the men you're sure will join a posse and bring them to town inside of the next few minutes?"

"Of course, Marshal Long."

"Get your people here, then. Me and Trent will be waiting with his men. But get a move on! Those Yaquis ain't going to hang around all night!"

"Long, you're going to pay for this!" Naylor threatened. "By God, I'll have your badge before it's all over!"

"You're welcome to try," Longarm replied coolly. "You won't be the first one. Now shut up, or I'll shove that badge down your guzzle to keep you from butting in." He turned to Trent. "It's up to you whether you come along or not. Tell you what, though. If I was trying to get elected again, I'd sure be thinking about what people might say if you let Carvajal do all the work."

"Well..." Trent said, his face twisted with indecision, "if we're going to fight the damn Yaquis, I guess the town can't let the greasers claim all the credit. I'll see how many men I can get to join the posse."

Darkness was full and the moon was not yet up when Longarm and his motley posse edged past the last houses of Mina Cobre and down the trail to the Papago village. Longarm rode at the head of the straggling group of perhaps twenty-five men, of whom about half were from the Mexican village, the other half from the town. He, Carvajal, Trent, and three or four of the Mina Cobre men were mounted; the others were on foot.

There had been no further shooting from the Papago village during the time spent in getting the group organized, and as they moved into the darkness that closed down when the town's lights faded, Longarm could see fires flickering among the Papago huts, and dark figures moving around. In the darkness it was impossible to tell Papago from Yaqui, and Longarm knew that if a major fight broke out, the ill-assorted posse behind him would start shooting randomly at any figure that moved. He brought the posse to a halt.

"How many of you men done any fighting before?" he called.

Three voices replied. One said, "I was at the Wilderness." Another shouted, "I seen service at Cold Harbor." A third spoke up, "I was in the War, too." None of the three specified on which side they'd fought, and Longarm asked no questions.

He told Carvajal, "See if you got any veterans in your bunch."

"Quién hechan combate in algún guerra?" the sheriff asked.

This time there were only two responses: *"Lucho con Lerdo contra Diaz,"* and *"Tres veces combato los Yaquis en la fuerza de Felix Gomez."*

"You men come up front here, where I can get a look at you," Longarm called. He eyed them as well as he could in the darkness and decided they'd do. He told Carvajal, "Get two more men to go with these and send 'em across the crick to the far side of the Papago village. Tell 'em to hold their fire until they hear us cut loose from over here."

"Shall I go with them?" Carvajal asked.

"Hell, no! You got to keep the rest of your bunch in hand. I don't talk your lingo good enough." To the three veterans of the War Between the States, Longarm said, "You fellows pick out a man apiece to go with you. Sneak on past the village to that little rise. If the Yaquis start to run, they'll likely go that way, because that's the direction we're going to be pushing 'em."

"Where you want my boys, Long?" Trent asked.

"I want you and whoever else has got a horse to stay with me. The rest of 'em can string out along the trail here." Now Longarm raised his voice so all the men could hear him. "Pay attention, you men! There's Yaquis down in that place, and that's who we're after! There's a lot more Papagos, and there's going to be some of us down there, too. Now, I don't fancy gettin' shot any more'n the next man, so here's how it'll be. Those of us that's got horses are going to ride down there and let off a few shots in the air. You men up here and on the other side of the crick, you shoot too, but for God's sake don't shoot low enough to hit any of us."

102

"Dammit, I don't like that scheme!" Trent said. "We come out here to kill Yaquis, not to shoot off our guns at nothing!"

"Just wait'll I finish," Longarm told him. Raising his voice again, he went on, "After that first volley's let off, I'm figuring the Yaquis are going to get out of that place fast as they can. The way it looks to me, they had to circle around and come in from the north, because nobody in town or at the mine saw 'em. Likely they'll run the same way when they leave. Now, when they break and start running, we'll be able to tell the Yaquis from the Papagos, so you men on the rise, you can shoot at any Indian you see coming your way. But we'll be riding right behind those Yaquis, so be damn sure who you're shooting at! Now, has everybody got things straight?"

"Yeah, but I still don't like it," Trent said. "Shit, if we shoot a few Papagos by mistake, what difference is it going to make? I say we just cut loose from the trail and save all that messing around!"

Before any of the men had time to agree with the constable, Longarm said loudly, "Trent, you and your men can do what I tell you to, or you can get your asses back to town! Unless you can come up with a better plan, you might as well make up your mind that's the way it's going to be!"

There was a moment of uncomfortable silence while Longarm wondered if he was going to lose half of his fighting force.

Finally, Trent said grudgingly, "Well, I guess it could work out all right, if everybody just remembers what they're supposed to do. But I won't say I like your scheme any better than I did before, Long!"

"It's the only way I can see to get them Indians sorted out," Longarm said. "And it'll work if nobody gets too damned eager. Now let's all get in place before the Yaquis spot us milling around out here."

Following Carvajal's rapidfire instructions, the four men selected to cover the west side of the village set off to make their way across the creek. Longarm waited until they were well on their way, and dispatched the group chosen to man the ridge north of the Papago huts. Then, with himself and the other half-dozen riders in the vanguard, he led the remainder of the force along the trail toward the village.

They advanced until they were strung out along the trail

opposite the scattered fires that still burned around the mud-plastered reed dwellings before Longarm halted them. The trail was on high ground, the village in the shallow valley, spread on both sides of the creekbed. In the poor light, gazing into the fires, their vision was extremely limited. They could see the dark forms still moving between the huts, and an occasional scream from a woman or perhaps a child reached their ears.

"Sounds like them Yaquis is getting some Papago ass," Trent said to Longarm as they strained their eyes looking at the village. "Now'd be as good a time as any to start, I guess."

"Wait a minute," Longarm replied. "I think I spotted the Yaquis' horses, just past those last shanties, toward the rise. Looks like they rode in from the north, all right." He raised his voice and said, "You fellows follow me when we start. We'll head for their horses. If they get the idea they're likely to be cut off, they'll jump without thinking when we cut loose. And if you men can see their horses, bring down as many as you can!"

Longarm had no way of knowing when the other two groups were in position. He waited until the men around him began to get restless, then gave them the command.

"All right!" he shouted, pulling his Winchester from its boot and levering a round into its chamber. "Let's go!"

Hooves thundered on the baked earth as the half-dozen riders spurred forward. In the darkness they sounded like an entire cavalry troop. In the village, the Yaquis reacted instantly. Within a few seconds after the first sounds of the attack, the Indians were running toward their horses.

Gauging his aim by the shadowy forms he thought he'd seen, Longarm fired in the same direction in which the Yaquis were running. He let off three shots, then saved the rest of the magazine against a time when he'd have a certain target.

Most of the possemen, especially those afoot, were not as foresighted. Shots crackled and the red bursts of muzzle blasts flashed not only from the trail, but from the valley slope on the opposite side of the creek. The shrill yells of the Yaquis mingled with the hoarser shouts of the attackers and the thudding of hooves and the sharp barking of rifles. Now and then the duller boom of a shotgun sounded, as one of the posseman forgot his weapon's limited range and triggered a scattergun.

104

Above the rider's heads, the whistle of lead slugs cut the night. Most of the men shooting from the trail followed their instructions, and only an occasional whining bullet came too low for comfort. The shots whistling above their heads did little to slow the pace of the Yaquis' retreat. They were almost within reach of their horses before the posse's riders were close enough to loose accurate fire.

Longarm could barely see their shadowy forms in the starlight. He raised his rifle, but lowered it again before he shouldered it. The ridge was close ahead, and he could see that when the Yaquis reached its crest, they would be silhouetted against the sky.

So far the Yaquis had not fired a shot, but when they reached their horses, they realized the possemen would overtake them before they could get a good start. Rifles spat from the slope as the Yaquis whirled and fired. A horse belonging to one of the possemen with Longarm went down. The Yaquis had an advantage their attackers did not share. It was a negative advantage, but one of which they made the most. Their party was not split up, and they knew that any shadow they saw through the darkness was an enemy.

With bullets now singing around their ears, the posse's riders spread out and lost the advantage of massed firepower. Their rate of fire slowed as they maneuvered their mounts, trying to dodge Yaqui bullets. The impetus of their charge was lost, and the battle-wise Yaquis sensed it. Longarm shouted at his men to group closer, but his voice was lost in the almost constant fusillade of riflefire.

Making the most of their temporary respite, the Indians mounted and galloped up the slope. In the darkness, counting was impossible, but listening to the lighter hoofbeats of the unshod Indian ponies, Longarm guessed there were about fifteen in the Yaqui raiding party. He kneed the Morgan away from the Indians as they started up the slope, to be out of the line of fire that he knew should come very soon from the ridge.

Not knowing the exact location of the riflemen posted at the top of the slope, Longarm barely made it to a spot safely to one side of the rifleshots that came from the ridge. The three war-hardened possemen stationed there had instructed the novices well. After the first volley, which brought night-splitting screams from two or three of the Yaqui ponies, the half-dozen men on the crest kept the Indians under an even, withering fire.

Longarm, closer to the Yaquis than he really wanted to be at that point in the fight, saw at least one pony go down. He had his Winchester ready, and when the Indians crested the slope, he got off two quickly aimed shots. He was sure at least one of them went home, for one of the retreating raiders dropped from his pony as the animal disappeared over the top of the slope.

Though the Yaquis were out of Longarm's sight now, the possemen on the ridge turned and kept firing as the raiders continued their flight. Longarm shouted for the rest of the posse's horsemen to follow him, and nudged the Morgan to a gallop as he went over the ridge and continued after the Yaquis.

Perhaps the others did not hear him; perhaps Longarm's night vision was better than theirs; or perhaps the cavalry-trained Morgan was a faster and more surefooted mount than any of the posse had. Longarm galloped on, spurred by the sight of the fleeing Indians—dark, moving black shapes against the dun earth in the starlight. He had not ridden far before he found that he was pursuing the Yaquis alone.

Even when he realized that he was after eight or ten Yaquis by himself, Longarm did not think of turning back. He'd lost count of the number of shots he'd fired from the Winchester, and kept triggering the weapon each time he got an Indian in its sights, until the hammer clicked on an empty chamber. He was almost within pistol range of the last Yaqui rider now. He sheathed the Winchester in its saddle scabbard and kicked the racing Morgan in the flanks to get an extra bit of speed from the willing horse.

Though the Morgan was already going full out, it strained for the additional speed its rider demanded. Longarm closed the gap on the last Yaqui bit by bit. When he knew he was within range for his Colt, he drew the pistol and snap-shot two rounds, saving the three that were left in the cylinder. The Yaqui's horse screamed, a high-pitched, agonizing cry in the night. It broke gait, stumbled, and went down in a wild thrashing of legs.

Only a dozen yards had separated Longarm from his Yaqui target when he fired the shot that brought down the Indian's horse. In the gloom, the fallen man and his mount were a single shapeless form against the dun earth. Longarm tried to pierce the darkness with his eyes as the Morgan's gallop brought him to the spot where the downed horse lay struggling, but all he could see was a dark blur of movement.

He reined in hard, but the momentum of the Morgan's gallop was too great; the horse could neither stop nor veer away from the blur on the ground. Longarm looked for a target. He knew that if his shot had brought down the horse, it had not hit the rider. His eyes still had not separated Indian from horse as he swept up within a yard of the fallen Yaqui. Then a dark shape rose with surprising speed from the shadowy, formless sprawl, and the Yaqui launched himself at Longarm.

There was no time for Longarm to bring his Colt around and down to fire at the leaping Yaqui. He swung at the man in midair, using the pistol barrel as a club, but the blow glanced off the Indian's upstretched arms. Then the Yaqui was clinging somehow to Longarm, the impetus of his leap carrying Longarm out of his saddle. He barely had time to kick his feet out of the stirrups to avoid being caught and dragged, before the force of the Yaqui's leaping attack carried both men across the horse's back and to the ground.

They rolled together on the hard earth, both of them trying to breathe, to recapture the air that had been knocked out of their lungs when they crashed. Except for the straining gasps that rasped from their throats, they fought silently, neither man asking nor giving quarter.

Longarm felt the Yaqui's forearm stealing around his throat, trying for a stranglehold. He hit backward with an elbow, and could feel the Yaqui's jerk as the elbow landed in his belly. The Yaqui recovered before Longarm was able to use the momentary advantage, and tried again for the choke-hold.

As they lay momentarily on their sides, Longarm kicked up and back, bringing his booted heel up into the attacker's groin. The Yaqui grunted involuntarily, but he was desert-hardened and combat-tough. He used his spread legs like flippers, trying to roll Longarm facedown, to plant a knee in his back, all the while still trying to get his left forearm around

Longarm's throat in a throttling embrace.

Arching his back suddenly, Longarm managed to throw the Yaqui off and, in the same movement, rise to his feet. The Indian rolled as he tumbled free, and came to his feet. A knife in his hand glinted in the starshine. Longarm brought the barrel of his Colt around in a sweeping blow that landed on the Yaqui's temple. The Indian's knees sagged and he began to fold to the ground, but even as he was losing consciousness he carried through the slashing attack he'd started.

Longarm watched the Yaqui's slow fall carry the man to the ground, but at the same time he became aware that his shoulder was throbbing from a wound inflicted by the knife and that his blood was seeping out of the cut, wetting his shirt.

Chapter 10

Ignoring the sharp bite of the cut, Longarm holstered his Colt. He picked up the knife that lay beside the unconscious Yaqui and stepped over to the man's pony, a yard or two away. He cut the woven horsehair rope that had served the Indian rider as both halter and rein, and went back to where the unconscious Yaqui lay. Cutting a short length from the rope, he tied the man's wrists behind his back, pulling the loops tight and testing the double knot to make sure the lashing would hold.

Only when the Yaqui was securely tied did Longarm attend to his wound. Folding his bandanna into a long narrow pad, he opened his shirt and balbriggans and laid the pad over the knife slash, then gingerly pulled the fabric of his underwear and shirt down to hold the pad in place. It was a hell of a way to bandage a cut, but it would stop the blood until he could arrange a more permanent dressing.

At his feet, the Yaqui stirred and at once began struggling with his bound wrists, trying to free them. Longarm turned the man over with his boot toe and looked down at him. The Indian's broad, high-cheeked face was contorted with pain and hatred. He glared at Longarm, but did not speak. The two men exchanged stares until Longarm broke his eyes away and lighted a cheroot.

"You got a name?" he asked the Yaqui. The question brought no response; he tried repeating it in Spanish, asking, *"Qué es su nombre?"*

Repeating the question drew no response, either. Longarm did not try a third time. Ignoring the Indian, he drew his Colt, removed the spent shells from its cylinder, and replaced them with fresh loads. He leveled the weapon at the prone Yaqui's head. The Indian's face stayed impassive. He lay there, his obsidian eyes fixed on Longarm, waiting for the shot he fully expected. Longarm held the muzzle of the gun steady for almost a full minute before he gestured for the man to stand up. The Yaqui made no effort to obey.

Pressing the Colt's muzzle against his captive's forehead, Longarm fixed his free hand in the man's greasy coarse hair and lifted. The Yaqui resisted the upward strain for several moments before he reluctantly struggled to his feet. He stood without resisting while Longarm looped one end of the longer piece of rope around his neck.

In a voice as cold as the steel muzzle of the Colt he held firmly against the Indian's head, Longarm said, "I don't know whether you savvy what I'm telling you or not, but I'm going to get on my horse and you're going to walk alongside me while we go into town. You give me any trouble and you get shot or choked, and I don't give a damn which one it is."

A sharp whistle brought the Morgan to Longarm's side. He mounted, holding the end of the rope to which the Yaqui was tied, and started toward the Papago village. He allowed his captive little slack, but the man made no effort to run.

None of the possemen had remained on the crest, and when he reached it and looked down at the village, Longarm saw why. The fires that had been flickering out at the time of the attack on the Yaquis had been replenished. The possemen and the Papagos were gathered around the biggest blaze, in the center of the settlement.

Longarm guided the Morgan downslope toward the fire, and when those in the huddle around the blaze heard the slow clopping of the horse's hooves, they scattered to let him through. Trent pushed his way through the group and stopped in front of Longarm.

"We was wondering what become of you," the constable said. He looked at the Yaqui. "Where in hell did you pick him up?"

"I chased him down over the hump when the Yaquis took off. If some of you men had followed me, like you was supposed to, we might've caught a few more of 'em."

Trent noticed the blood on Longarm's shirt. "Hell! You're hurt! Bullet get you?"

"Knife. I had a little wrestling match with this fellow. It ain't but a scratch."

Trent jerked a thumb at the captured Yaqui. "You want me and my boys to get rid of him for you? Be glad to."

"Hell, no! I'll take him in and see if I can get anything out of him about where his tribe is holed up. I'll find a way to get him off my hands when I'm ready."

Trent shrugged. "I guess you got the right to keep him. You're the one that took him."

"Anybody else but me get hurt?" Longarm asked.

"One of my boys got a little crease, and a couple of the greasers got scratched. Nothing that needs doctoring. Oh, yeah, we lost a horse."

"We got off light. Night fights are that way, though, a lot of shooting and damn little hitting. How about the Indians?"

"Well, there's two dead Yaquis laying up on the slope, and they killed three Papago men and a woman before we got here. And I guess there's going to be a bunch of the squaws dropping half-Yaqui and half-Papago brats nine months from now."

"Looks like we done what we set out to, so we might as well pack it in," Longarm said. "Tell Carvajal, will you?"

Trent guffawed loudly. "Hell, him and the greasers started back as soon as the Yaquis run. They're halfway home by now."

"That's the place I'm heading for, too. I better get my shoulder tended to before it stiffens up."

"We'll be right behind you. All we was doing anyway was getting ready to go look for you."

Longarm had serious doubts that their search, if it had even begun, would have lasted long, but he saw no point in saying so. He nodded to Trent and wheeled the Morgan toward the trail to Mina Cobre.

In the short distance from the Papago village to the trail, Longarm saw that if he forced the prisoner to walk all the way, he'd spend half the night getting to the mine. Reining in, he used sign language to make the Yaqui understand that he was to get up on the horse's crupper and ride the rest of the way.

With his prisoner sitting ahead of the saddle, their bodies inches apart and occasionally touching, Longarm came close to gagging at the man's rank scent; it was a mingling of unwashed man-sweat, horse-sweat, smoke, grease, and dried blood. He almost changed his mind about letting the Yaqui ride, but decided that the speed he'd gain would make up for the nausea he was feeling. He lighted a fresh cheroot to mask the unpleasant odor and finished tying the prisoner.

He knotted the end of the rope to the saddle horn, leaving only an inch or two of slack. Then he indicated, by gesturing and tugging, that if the captive tried to jump off the horse, all he'd do was throttle himself. The Yaqui made no sign that he'd understood, but he gave Longarm no trouble as they skirted the town and picked up the trail to the Copper Queen on the far side of the Mexican settlement.

Lights were still burning in the cottage when it came in sight soon after he rounded the edge of the lake. The sound of the horse's hoofbeats reached the house some minutes before the Morgan and its load got to the corral. Luz and Clarita came running out. Luz carried a lantern. They stood in front of the corral, Luz holding the lantern as high as she could, watching Longarm's approach. He reined in, and as he started to swing out of the saddle he heard Clarita's voice raised in disgust.

"Yaqui!" the cook exclaimed. *"Qué hijo del Diablo! Carracador! Ladron! Por qué llevarse aquí?"*

"Hush, Clarita!" Luz exclaimed. "Longarm must have a reason for bringing the evil one here."

Longarm had swung out of the saddle by now and was— none too gently—helping the Yaqui off the horse. "Leave the animal standing," he said, when Luz stepped forward to take the Morgan's reins. "I want to go find Grady, soon as I get a drink inside of me and fix up this shoulder."

For the first time, Luz noticed the blood on his shirt. She exclaimed, "You're wounded! Let the Yaqui stay here while I attend to you, Longarm!"

"If I left him here by himself, he'd be long gone the minute we got out of sight. And don't go fretting about me, all I got was a little scratch. It's stopped bleeding and there's not any use in wasting time on it now."

"But it has bled so much!" Luz protested.

"Looks worse'n it is. Now, you did say something that makes sense. You mind going up to the bedroom and bringing me my handcuffs? I put 'em on the bureau when I turned out my pockets last night. The key's right by 'em."

"Of course. Here, Clarita. You hold the lantern, I won't need it."

Longarm inspected the corral posts until he found one to which the rails were solidly spiked. Luz returned with his handcuffs, and he led the Yaqui to the post. Untying the man's hands, he cuffed his wrists together with his arms pulled behind him, an arm on either side of the upright, the Indian's back against the sturdy post. The Yaqui glared at Longarm and the two women, but said nothing. After inspecting the post and crossrail again, Longarm led the women out of the corral.

"Now I got to go find Grady," he told Luz. "I need a place to lock that Yaqui up till I can get him started talking, and I don't know where it'd be, unless there's a closet or room in one of the mine buildings. Trouble is, I don't know where Grady lives. Never stopped to ask him yesterday before he left."

"Mr. Grady lives in a house that he built in a small canyon just off the lake. I can't describe to you how to find it in the dark, but I'll go and get him for you."

"You sure you don't mind doing that?" he asked.

"Of course not. I'll go as soon as I dress your shoulder."

"Better go right now," Longarm told her. "My shoulder's waited this long, it can wait a while longer."

"If that's what you wish," Luz nodded. She turned to Clarita. "Boil water while I am gone. And there are soft dishtowels that can be torn up for bandages."

Clarita nodded. "*No soy boba*, Luz. More cuts I have cared for than you have seen! Go, I weel do what is need to."

"Ride the Morgan," Longarm suggested. "It'll save time, he's already saddled up."

Luz smiled. "It's dark, no one will see me. I will do as I did when I was a small girl, ride my own pony bareback. Clarita, hold the lantern while I buckle on the bridle."

Followed by Clarita, Luz went into the corral and put a bridle on the pony. Longarm decided to take advantage of the lantern light; he led his horse in and started to unsaddle it. Luz mounted in a flurry of full skirts and rode out; Longarm lifted the saddle off the Morgan and started to swing it to the corral rail. In mid-lift, a pang tore through his wounded shoulder. He let the saddle fall and covered the knife wound with his hand.

"*Ay, caray!*" Clarita exclaimed. "*Portarse como necio!*

113

Come! I weel make good the *brazuelo. Adelante!*"

She shooed Longarm into the house as though he were a flock of chickens. Smiling despite the pain in his shoulder, he walked ahead of her flapping hands. She struck a match and lighted the burner of the kerosene range, on which a kettle was already sitting, then turned to Longarm and motioned him to a chair.

"Take eet off, *la camisa*," Clarita said. "I weel look at *su llaga*, the cut place, to see what must I do."

Longarm started to unbutton his shirt, but his left hand refused to behave as it should have. Clarita had begun rummaging on a shelf, examining dishtowels; she saw him fumbling with the buttons and came to help. She got Longarm's shirt off, then unbuttoned his balbriggans and pulled them off his arms. When she saw his much-scarred torso, she gasped but said nothing.

Gingerly, she tried to removed the padded bandanna that he'd placed over the wound, but the blood-caked cloth was dry and stuck to Longarm's skin. Clarita shook her head, frowning.

"Ees stuck, but I weel feex," she told him.

"I'm betting you just will," Longarm said. He sat quietly while Clarita soaked the bandanna off the wound and gently sponged away the caked blood that streaked his shoulder.

"Aha!" she exclaimed when she could see the wound clearly. "*No es tan malo.* I feex."

"It don't feel so bad," Longarm said. "Go ahead, Clarita. It won't bother me none. I been cut worse than this by a few barbers."

She frowned. "*Cómo?*"

"I said it ain't as bad as some of the things that's happened to me."

"*Ah, sí!* Thees I am tell." She traced the scar of an earlier knife wound with her fingertip; it ran around the bottom of Longarm's ribcage. Then she put her finger on one and then another of the puckered bullet-scars on his torso. "*Mucho hombre,*" she smiled. "*Las cicatrizas significan que tienes valor.*"

"I ain't so sure it's *valor*," Longarm told her. "Mostly they're my own fault. I just didn't move fast enough when I

114

was in a tight spot. Well, go on. I'm ready as I'll ever be."

"First theeng, I make to stop *infeccion*. Then I put on the *faja*, and eet ees all right." She walked across the room and fetched his whiskey bottle. *"Bebe."*

Longarm glanced down at his shoulder before tipping up the bottle. The wound was not deep. The Yaqui's knife had met his collarbone and slashed down. The blade had scored the flat layer of muscle that ran below the collarbone, slitting the skin above it, and then had bounced along his ribcage. A few drops of fresh bright blood were oozing from it. He drank, and waited for Clarita to finish stirring the purplish crystals she was mixing with hot water in a small pan.

"Hace picadura," she warned him as she brought the pan to the table. "Like you say, steeng."

"I been stung before. I won't yell. Go ahead."

Using a folded cloth as a sponge, Clarita swabbed the warm permanganate solution on the wound. It stung, but Longarm took another swallow of the rye. Slowly the bite of the anti-septic faded. Clarita stood watching him, strips of cloth torn from a dishtowel in her hands. When the permanganate was completely dry, and only the open area of the cut glistened in the lamplight, she applied the bandage. She worked quickly and with skill, crisscrossing the wound with a layer of over-lapped strips that were firm but not tight. Longarm recognized the skill of experience in her work.

"You done this before, ain't you?" he asked her.

"Seguro. I am go weeth my *novio* when he is fight for *El Plano de Palo Blanco.* Ees lot of small fights, then beeg one, Tecocac. *Lo mismo como otras lavanderas,* I take care from soldiers when they get hurt."

Longarm knew that *lavandera,* washerwoman, was the po-lite name given by Mexican soldiers to the women who fol-lowed the armies. The *lavanderas* not only did the washing for the troops, but cooked for them and slept with them. Some ministered to only one soldier and were reasonably faithful, but most of the women moved casually from one man to the next.

"What happened to your sweetheart?" he asked Clarita.

"Se muerte a Tecocac," Clarita said with a shrug that might

115

either have been an expression of long-ago sorrow or a reflection of her race's acceptance that death is life's inevitable end.

She stood up, and motioned for Longarm to do so too. He got to his feet and tried raising his left arm, experimented with moving it around and back and forth. The wound made its presence known each time he moved, and he knew that during the night his shoulder would grow stiff, but the pain of movement was not great enough to make the arm totally useless.

"It feels pretty good," he said. "Thanks a lot, Clarita. You're a right good nurse."

"*De nada*," she replied. Then, "Ees much hot water yet in kettle. You want *bano*, no?"

"I hadn't thought about it, but a bath'd go real good. Take some of the Yaqui stink off of me."

"*Bueno*. You go to bedroom, I feex."

Longarm picked up his bloodstained shirt and the whiskey bottle and went into his bedroom. He unbuckled his gunbelt and hung it on the bedpost in its usual position, and levered off his boots. He was still sitting on the side of the bed when Clarita came in carrying the same big zinc washtub in which he'd bathed the night before. She set the tub in the middle of the floor and went out, returning with the steaming teakettle in one hand and a pail of water in the other. She emptied both into the tub and put the empty pail and kettle on the floor. Longarm rose to his feet, thinking she would go, but she stood waiting, looking at him expectantly.

"Thanks, Clarita," he said. "I'll manage the rest of it."

Clarita shook her head. "No. Weeth sore arm, you weel need help. I am help you."

"Now, that ain't really necessary," Longarm protested. "I can take care of myself all right."

"*Es imposible.*" Clarita moved to his side and gestured to his belt buckle. "*Depone sus pantalones.*"

Longarm started to argue, but Clarita was already unbuttoning his fly. Before he could stop her, she had pulled his pants and balbriggans down to his thighs and was bending to lift one of his feet. Thrown off balance, Longarm instinctively raised his arms to keep from falling, but his wound prevented him from getting his left hand in synchronization with his right. He sat down heavily on the bed.

116

Clarita took hold of the ends of his trouser legs and yanked hard. His trousers and balbriggans slid off and she tossed them aside. She took his right hand and tugged to help him stand.

"Hurry to get into *el bano*," she urged, "Or eet weel be cold, the water."

"Now, damn it, I can walk by myself!" Longarm protested as Clarita pulled him toward the tub. "I'll do my own bathing!"

She paid no attention to his objections, but stood beside him, steadying him, while he stepped into the tub. Picking up the large square piece of the dishtowel that remained after she'd torn off the strips for bandaging, Clarita dipped the cloth in the warm water and sponged off his grimed cheeks.

Longarm studied Clarita's expression. Her broad face bore a small frown of concentration while she wet the cloth again, washed his uninjured shoulder and the exposed area of skin around his bandages, then began rubbing the cloth down his torso. He'd concluded that she intended to wash him, no matter what he said, and had philosophically abandoned his protests.

He watched while she rubbed the cloth over his stomach and down his hips, and saw her expression begin to change as she stopped to wet the cloth again before beginning to wash his groin. Her eyes opened wider and grew brighter and the frown of concentration turned slowly into a smile of anticipation.

Clarita let the cloth she'd been using drop into the tub. She knelt beside the tub, cupped her hands, filled them with water, brought them up to Longarm's abdomen, and spread her fingers to let the warm water trickle slowly through his pubic hair and down over his groin. She smoothed his wet skin with her fingers, spread her hands, and rubbed them slowly downward. The brushing became a caress. Her hands moved more and more slowly, and stopped completely when they reached his crotch.

For a moment or two, Clarita's fingers explored and fondled him, then she raised her head and looked up. She smiled when she saw that he was watching her.

"Me gusto," she said softly.

Longarm had felt himself stirring when Clarita's warm hands, slick with the water, had first touched him. Brief as her soft caress had been, its very unexpected nature had begun arousing him. He was still flaccid, but was making no effort

117

to retard the swelling that he felt starting in his groin.

"Es nabo silvestre magnifico," Clarita continued. *"Con permiso, quiero partir."*

"You mean, do I mind if you go on?" Longarm asked. He was sure he'd understood her meaning, even if he couldn't translate the words exactly. She nodded, and he said, "Do what you want to, Clarita. It feels pretty good to me too."

Clarita continued her caresses, devoting her full attention to arousing him. Longarm responded predictably. He began swelling and growing harder while her warm, moist fingers continued to stroke him, encircling him and squeezing softly. As Longarm's erection grew, she became more and more excited, her stroking and squeezing more vigorous. Finally she released him and, with quick, flashing movements of her hands, pulled the scooped neck of her loose peasant blouse down from her round brown shoulders to release her breasts.

"Quiero sentirse," she whispered.

Stretching upward, she pressed Longarm's erection into the soft warm valley between the bulging globes and squeezed their yielding flesh hard against him. She held him there, her face upturned, her eyes closed, her full red lips parted to show glistening white teeth.

Holding him passively did not satisfy Clarita for long. She grapsed him and traced his tip around the large rosettes of her breasts, moving from one to the other, until her nipples hardened and swelled and protruded from the pebbled surfaces like the ends of firm, dark fingers.

"No es bastante!" Clarita gasped after she had caressed her breasts with Longarm's tip for several moments. *"Dame su verga ahorita! Chíngame!"*

"There ain't a thing I'd like better'n to put it in you right now," Longarm said, trying to pull away from Clarita's clutching fingers. "But Luz and Grady are going to be back here in just a few minutes. We better stop this, Clarita, and wait till we can be by ourselves and take our time."

"No! Now! *Ahora!*" she insisted. *"Adelante, como esto!"*

Springing to her feet, Clarita raised her skirt. Longarm got a glimpse of firm-fleshed, full thighs and wide hips, with the wide triangle of her black pubic hair setting off soft brown skin before she whirled quickly and bent forward, her full-fleshed

118

buttocks spreading as she backed toward him. Her hand reached back to grasp him and slide his shaft within the rosy lips that shone moistly between her thighs.

Feeling himself already partly engulfed, Longarm abandoned caution and lunged into her hot wet depths.

"Ay, que bueno!" Clarita gasped breathlessly. *"Dámelo, bien arrigado! Pronto! Pronto!"*

Grasping her hips, Longarm began stroking, going into her in deep, hard-driving lunges that brought a sigh each time his hips met Clarita's fleshy buttocks. He had made perhaps a dozen such deep thrusts when the sound of hoofbeats outside the cottage reached his ears.

"That's Luz and Grady," Longarm said. He hesitated, wanting go to on, but knowing there was no time.

Swiftly the hoofbeats grew loud enough to cut through Clarita's sensual haze. She cried out, a throaty dismayed grunt, and stepped forward.

"I weel tell them you are make the *bano*," she said as she quickly smoothed her skirt and pulled her blouse back over her shoulders. "Then you weel have time to put on the clothes." She started for the door and, before reaching it, said to him over her shoulder, *"Retienes su vergeza*. We weel have time later, after they have gone."

Chapter 11

Longarm stepped out of the tub and made a few quick passes over his wet skin with a towel. In the adjoining room he could hear Clarita telling Luz and Grady that he was just finishing his bath. After taking a quick look at his bloody balbriggans and shirt, he decided not to bother with either of them and hurriedly pulled on his pants. He went into the living room. Grady and Luz were standing in the center of the room, Clarita beside the kitchen door. She paid no attention to Longarm, gave no sign of the intimate situation the newcomers had interrupted.

"Luz said you'd been hurt fighting off a bunch of Yaqui raiders," Grady said when he saw Longarm. "That was the first I'd heard about it. My house sits down in the bottom of a canyon and I guess my wife and I didn't hear the shooting. What the devil happened, anyhow?"

"Yaquis raided the Papago village, and I went with a bunch of men from town to chase 'em off. Can't figure why they'd bother with those poor devils. Papagos don't have anything worth stealing. It'd make more sense for the Yaquis to raid the Copper Queen or the town, but maybe they figured to get by without too much of a fight."

"From what I've seen and heard about Yaquis, they don't give much of a damn who they take on, or where," Grady said. "But my guess is that there are too many men with guns at the mine and in the town for them to tackle with a small party."

Luz added, "The Yaquis don't raise crops, Longarm. They've always gotten beans and maize by raiding the Papagos."

Grady indicated Longarm's bandaged shoulder and said with a frown, "I hope you're not hurt too bad. The nearest doctor's the army surgeon at Fort Huachuca, and that's a good long ride."

"It's only a little cut, not such a much," Longarm told the mine superintendent. "Clarita fixed it up fine. It'll heal all right without any more doctoring."

"Are you sure, Longarm?" Luz asked.

"I been cut before, Luz," Longarm replied. "Now stop fretting about me." He turned to Grady. "Guess Luz told you, I got one of those Yaqui raiders handcuffed to a corral post out in back. You got some kind of place at the Copper Queen where I can lock him up safe for a day or two?"

"Well . . ." Grady knitted his brows thoughtfully. "There are a couple of sheds where we keep the acids and a few kegs of blasting powder. They're pretty solidly built, and they're always locked. I suppose you can put him in one of them."

Longarm nodded. "Sounds like just about what I got in mind."

"Why do you want to keep the Yaqui, anyhow?" Grady asked. "The army ought to have him. We're supposed to hand prisoners over to the nearest post, so we do it, even if the army's let us know unofficially that they'd just as soon not be bothered with them. Not that there's all that many prisoners taken in raids. I can have a couple of the mine guards take him to Huachuca in the morning, if you say the word."

"Oh, I'll see the army gets him," Longarm said. "But I want to ask him a few questions first. If I can find somebody that talks his lingo, that is."

"There might be no need to question him in Yaqui, Longarm," Luz suggested. "Most of the Indians in Mexico speak Spanish. I can try—"

Clarita spoke for the first time. She broke in on Luz to say, "A leetle Yaqui I talk. *No mucho, pero tal vez bastante que ayudale.*"

"Looks like you've got the help you need right here," Grady told Longarm. "I wouldn't count on getting too much out of your prisoner, though. From what I've seen of Yaquis since I've been here, they're a pretty tough breed of redskin."

"It's still worth a try," Longarm told the mine superintendent. "You'd like to stop worrying about raids on the Copper Queen, wouldn't you?"

"Of course. We've fought off five or six raids since we've been in operation, and every one of them has cost us a guard or two wounded and has closed us down for a while because of damage to our equipment and livestock killed. Sure, I'd like to see them stopped! But that's not the job you came here to do, is it? I thought all you're interested in is the election."

"That's still a little time ahead, Grady. As long as I'm here, I figure I might as well kill two birds with one stone, if I can. Won't cost the taxpayers any more money, and might save you folks a lot of trouble later on."

Grady nodded. "It would, at that. Well, is there anything more you want me to do? If there's not, I'll go on to the mine and arrange to have a couple of my men come get the Yaqui and lock him up in one of those sheds."

"Don't send 'em too soon. Give me a little while tonight to try asking him a few things. He's still all keyed up right now, mad and a mite shook up."

"You're not in shape to do much more tonight, Long," Grady objected. "Why not wait until tomorrow?"

Longarm shook his head. "Tonight's the best time, while he's still off balance from the fight and being captured. Give him time to settle down, he'll toughen up considerable, I'd imagine."

Grady nodded. "Whatever you say. I'll tell the guards to pick him up sometime after daylight."

"That'll be fine."

"I'll be on my way, then, if you're sure you're all right," Grady said. "If you need anything else, just let me know."

"Sure. And if I get anything interesting out of that Yaqui, I'll stop by and tell you about it."

Grady left, and in a moment they heard the hoofbeats of his horse fading in the distance. Longarm asked Clarita, "You sure you know enough Yaqui to talk to that one out at the corral?"

"*Creo que sí*. Ees not hard to learn, the Yaqui talk."

"If you ain't too tired, then, let's take the lantern and go out and see what he's got to say."

"*Seguro. Siempre que quiere,*" she shrugged.

"It might take us a while to get him started talking," Longarm cautioned her. "If you get tired, say so, and we'll quit and

123

start in again at daylight. But I'd rather try him now, like I told Grady, while he's still all riled up."

"Ees not make matter how much time we take," Clarita said. "I weel stay so long as you want."

"I'm going too," Luz said. "I don't know whether I can help much, but I intend to be there."

"Come along, then," Longarm told her, strapping on his gunbelt. "If it gets too rough, you can always come back inside."

"You sound like you're going to torture the Yaqui," Luz said to Longarm as the three of them walked to the corral. "Are you?"

"I don't know what I might have to do, Luz," Longarm replied. "I don't know all that much about Yaquis, but I've heard they're meaner than Apaches or Comanches, so whatever cards I get handed, I'll just have to play the way they fall."

Longarm's effort to stare down the Yaqui before beginning to question him was not a success. The Indian met Longarm's gunmetal-blue eyes squarely, unblinking, and their gazes locked while the seconds ticked away, until Longarm realized he was wasting time and turned to Clarita.

"See if he'll tell you his name," he suggested.

Clarita rattled off the question in a language that was composed mostly of gutturals and grunts, though an occasional word with a Spanish root was understandable by Longarm. Most of the questions, though, came through with inflections, accents, and elisions unlike any tongue Longarm had heard before. The Yaqui listened expressionlessly, as though he were deaf. After she had repeated the question several times in slightly different form, Clarita shook her head.

"He ees not to talk," she said.

"Ask where his camp is," Longarm suggested.

No answer was forthcoming to the second question, or to any other inquiry that Clarita made in response to Longarm's prompting. Finally, Clarita shrugged and said, "*Es como preguntando à un sordomudo*. He ees not to talk to me."

Throughout the time that Clarita was relaying Longarm's questions, the Yaqui had kept his eyes fixed on the darkness beyond the circle of lantern light, where he'd focused them after he and Longarm had first locked stares. He stood firmly erect, his back pressed against the corral post, showing in his face none of the strain that having his arms pulled back around the corral post must be causing him.

"Guess we'll have to try something he'll savvy better, then," Longarm said. He turned to Luz and told her, "Maybe you better go back inside. I'd send Clarita too, but I'll need her here if I get him started talking. But it's going to take more than words to open his mouth, and you might not want to watch."

"I'll stay," she replied firmly. "I'm not a child, Longarm, you don't have to protect me from anything. Go ahead with whatever you intend to do."

When he handcuffed the Yaqui, Longarm had taken off the horsehair rope with which he'd tied the man originally and hung it over the top corral pole. He reached for the rope now, and cut it into two lengths. He stabbed the point of the knife into the corral post and looped one piece of the rope around it.

With the other length in his hand, he stepped over to the Yaqui and lashed one end of the rope around an ankle. Then he pulled the man's leg as far as he could force it to stretch away from the post to which he was handcuffed.

When the Yaqui realized what Longarm intended to do, he resisted for the first time. Under the stretched fabric of his cotton trousers, his muscles corded as he tried to keep his leg from being pulled to one side.

He could not match the force which Longarm could bring to bear. The man's foot slid across the hard soil until it extended at an angle from his hip. Longarm looped the rope around the bottom corral pole and pulled on it. Slowly the Yaqui's knee bent, the leg came up, and when his ankle reached the pole, Longarm tied it there firmly.

Taking the second length of rope, Longarm lashed an end to the man's free ankle and pulled it away from the post in the direction opposite from the other leg. The Yaqui fought against the rope with all his strength, but his backstretched arms slowly slid down the post as Longarm pulled the remaining ankle along the ground. When he had stretched the leg as far as he could force it, he brought it up and bound the ankle to the pole.

125

Longarm stepped in front of the spread-eagled prisoner. The Yaqui was now dangling in midair. His knees did not touch the ground, his thighs were pulled back at an angle that made his torso bend forward. His position kept him from using the muscles in his arms and thighs, and the sinews in his shoulders and chest knotted under the strain as he struggled to hold his body erect. The effort failed and he let his body sag, but when Longarm stopped in front of him he lifted his head and unflinchingly returned Longarm's stare.

Behind him, Longarm heard Luz gasp. Over his shoulder, he said, "Luz, I'll tell you this one more time. You might not want to see what comes next."

"Go ahead," she said between clenched teeth. "I will not go back to the house!"

Longarm nodded and said to Clarita, "Ask him if he's figured out what I'm going to do to him."

Clarita repeated Longarm's question in a rapid string of guttural, explosive Yaqui. The prisoner ignored her. He did respond, in a way, by spitting on the ground at Longarm's feet.

Reaching for the knife that he'd jabbed into the corral pole, Longarm pulled it free. He moved in front of the Yaqui and bent forward. Grasping the waistband of the man's trousers, he cut it, and the trousers dropped to the Yaqui's knees, exposing his genitals.

Placing the knife blade against them, Longarm said, without taking his eyes off the Yaqui's face, "Clarita! Tell him that if he don't start talking, I'll dock him like a steer!"

Clarita relayed Longarm's words, but the Yaqui did not show any signs of breaking until Longarm grasped his genitals and, without applying enough pressure to cut, rasped the knife edge on the man's scanty pubic hair. Then the Yaqui let go with a short burst of angry words. Longarm looked questioningly at Clarita.

"He say keel him, only not to take hees *machismo*," she interpreted.

"Tell him I'll start cutting if he don't start talking!" Longarm said, keeping his voice coldly threatening.

Clarita repeated the threat. For a moment the Yaqui's inner struggle was apparent, but at last his fear of being emasculated overcame his fierce tribal pride. He nodded and said a few words. Some of the fire had left his eyes, but not enough to hide his hatred of Longarm and the others who'd witnessed his humiliation.

"He weel say to what you ask heem," Clarita told Longarm.

"Find out his name first."

Clarita asked the Yaqui a short question, two words, and he replied with the longest string of words he'd uttered so far. Clarita said to Longarm, her brow furrowed, "Eet ees foolish what he say."

"What did he say?"

"He ees not have one name, he ees have *tres*. He ees not say all of them, only hees war name. Eet ees El Griego."

"El Griego!" Luz exclaimed, "The Greek! That's what they call the Yaqui chief everybody on the border is afraid of! He's the leader of a band of renegade Yaquis who have killed God knows how many in the last few years!"

Clarita nodded. *"Es lo mismo."*

"He can't be!" Luz insisted. "My father says there's no such person as El Griego. He says it's just a name used by the Yaquis to scare us with."

"You think he's lying, then?" Longarm asked her.

Before Luz could reply, Clarita said, "He ees tell me true."

"How do you know, Clarita?" Longarm asked.

"Do not forget, I am *bruja*. I know when I hear lie."

"Bruja!" Luz said angrily. "Bah!"

"Be quiet a minute, Luz!" Longarm told her. He said to Clarita, "Tell him we don't believe him. Tell him you're a witch and you'll know if he's lying. Go ahead and talk to him, don't stop every few words to tell me. That'd give him time to think up lies. Go on now, see what else you can get out of him."

For the next few moments, Clarita talked with the Yaqui. He seemed more willing to speak, now that he'd taken the major step of breaking his stubborn silence. When their conversation reached the point where the Yaqui began shaking his head, refusing to reply to her questions, Clarita shrugged and turned back to Longarm.

"Well?" he asked her. "What'd you find out?"

"He ees say same theeng over and over. He swear *por la*

sangre de la Virgen he ees El Griego, he say he ees only one call El Griego *y no hay más.*"

"You believe him, Clarita?" Longarm asked.

Clarita nodded, her face very sober. *"Sí, ya lo creo.* I am see he ees fear me after I tell him I am *bruja.* I do not theenk he ees lie."

"You two talked a pretty good spell. He must've said something else besides just claiming he's El Griego."

"Sí." A smile flicked across Clarita's full lips. "He ees say you are *cabrón y hijo de cabrón."* The tiny smile vanished and her features grew sober once again. "He ees say eef you do not let heem go, hees tribe weel get other Yaquis to join them and weel come to keel us all, *todos,* all een mine, een Mina Cobre, all Papagos too, and set heem free. He ees very mad weeth you, I theenk."

"And that's all?" Longarm tried to keep his disappointment from showing. He'd hoped to find out the number of fighting men the Yaquis could muster and where they had their main camp.

Clarita nodded. *"Sí. Es todo que dice."*

Suddenly and surprisingly, El Griego began shouting. Longarm, Luz, and Clarita stood staring at him, too startled by the unexpected outburst to move. The prisoner spoke in his own tongue, and his shouts lasted for only a few moments. When he stopped, the Yaqui pressed his lips close together and his face took on its earlier impassiveness.

"What'd he say?" Longarm asked Clarita.

She shook her head, a puzzled frown on her broad face. "Ees funny. Ees like he talk to somebody ees not here."

"But what did he say?" Longarm repeated.

"He is say to get all Yaqui *batalladores* and breeng them here to keel us and make heem free," Clarita said slowly. "Ees like what he ees tell me *ahorita.* I do not—"

"Be quiet!" Longarm snapped. "Listen!"

Distantly, they heard the thud of hoofbeats on the hard earth. As they listened, the drumming sound faded steadily.

"Do you think that could've been—" Luz began.

"I'm real damn sure it was!" Longarm interrupted her. "One of El Griego's Yaquis must've trailed me. Skulked around and tried to get him loose, but couldn't open the handcuffs. El

128

Griego had him wait, in case we didn't turn him loose, and all that yelling was to tell him what to do!" He started on a run for the stable, calling over his shoulder, "Luz, you and Clarita get indoors! Get my rifle out of the bedroom and shoot anybody you hear prowling around!"

"Where are you going?" Luz called.

Longarm was leading the Morgan out of the corral, feeling thankful that he hadn't found time to unsaddle the horse earlier. He said, "I'm going after that Yaqui!"

"No!" Luz called. "You have no chance of catching him! He has too much start!"

"Start or no start, he's carrying El Griego's orders back to his main camp," Longarm replied. "And if I don't stop him, there's going to be hell to pay around here in a day or two!"

Kicking the Morgan to a run, Longarm turned the horse's head southwest. The lake lay northwest of the cottage, the trail to Mina Cobre ran north, the mine was almost due south; he was sure the fleeing Yaqui would avoid these directions. He kept the Morgan at an all-out gallop until he reached the broken country beyond the lake, then reined in.

While he'd been questioning El Griego, the moon had come up to flood the countryside with silver, and he could see for a reasonable distance through the night. Wherever he looked, there was no sign of movement. A few yucca clumps shot their spears into the air, casting black shadows on the light-colored soil around them. A saguaro loomed tall in the distance, and everywhere there were small canyons seaming the bare earth, jagged black gaps on the moonlit terrain.

There was not a sound to break the stillness. Longarm kept a light pressure on the reins. He was fairly sure that when he'd begun to catch up, the Yaqui he was after had heard the hoof-beats of his pursuit, and had taken cover in one of the canyons. The Indian's strategy was obvious. Hidden in a canyon, he could follow Longarm's progress by listening to the Morgan's hoofbeats. He'd wait until Longarm came close, and dash out of his hiding place for a quick rifle shot that could end the chase.

If he don't hear you, old son, he's got to come out and look for you, Longarm told himself, scanning the area ahead of him for any signs of movement. And if you hadn't taken your rifle in the house like a damn fool, instead of leaving it in the scabbard, you might even have a chance of knocking him down instead of chasing him till you get in pistol range.

Longarm set himself to be as patient as he knew the lurking Yaqui would be. He kept his eyes in constant motion, knowing he must avoid the mistake made by novices at night pursuit, of fixing their gaze on a stationary object and holding their eyes on it until the object seemed to be moving. With quick flicks of his eyes, turning his head constantly, he managed to keep the area ahead of him under close observation.

In spite of his precautions, he did not see the Yaqui when he first came out of hiding. Not until a rifle shot broke the quiet and a lead slug whistled past him did he actually see his quarry. Even then he did not see the Indian; the man himself was hidden by the muzzle blast of his rifle.

Longarm did not return the man's fire; to have done so at the distance the Yaqui was from him would not only have been wasteful, it would have told his antagonist that Longarm was armed only with a pistol. He gave the reins a quick twist and the Morgan stepped quickly to one side. The movement was just enough to cause the Yaqui's second shot to miss, and it was this shot for which Longarm had been waiting. He let himself fall forward in the saddle and roll off the horse's back.

He'd been careful to fall in the shadow cast by the Morgan in the moonlight. Pressing his ear to the ground, he waited as seconds and then minutes ticked away. Then his patience was rewarded. The scraping of movement and the slow, soft, thudding hoofbeats of an unshod horse being led told him the Yaqui was coming to investigate.

Taking no chances, Longarm slid his Colt from its holster. The sounds grew louder, then suddenly stopped. Time stretched taut and still the noises did not resume. From where he lay, Longarm could not see the approaching Yaqui. He did not know whether the man had stopped as a precaution, or because he'd caught some hint of movement when Longarm had drawn the gun.

His time was running out, Longarm knew. If he'd spooked the Yaqui, the man would end the chase by shooting the Morgan. It was a risk Longarm did not want to take. He rolled out of the shadow that had hidden him, Colt ready. The Yaqui was standing beside his horse a far pistol shot away.

Longarm fired, but the range was too great. The only effect of his shot was to draw the Yaqui's return fire; the bullet was aimed at the Morgan, but the slug only plowed up the dirt between the horse's forefeet. Longarm loosed another shot, knowing it was nothing but a gesture, but counting on it to do what it did, force the Yaqui to swing onto his pony's back and gallop away.

Once again, Longarm took up the chase. Now he had a visible quarry in the moonlight ahead of him, and he pressed the Morgan to its best speed. He was closing the gap when the Yaqui veered off the straight course he'd been taking and headed for a wide canyon that lay to one side of them. Longarm turned the Morgan at a tangent, racing to cut off the Indian before he reached the canyon's mouth, but the Yaqui's start had been too great. Rider and pony disappeared into the black opening that yawned in a swath a quarter-mile wide across the desert soil. Longarm reined in. Time was of no consequence now.

Don't go acting like a jackass, he advised himself silently, looking at the canyon mouth. It's a coppered bet the Yaqui knows that canyon like you know your face in the mirror. All he wants is for you to go breezing in there looking for him, and once he gets you close enough, you're a dead man.

He studied the canyon mouth for a long moment, and shook his head. Stay out of that trap, old son, he thought. There's times it pays to take a chance, and you've took your share of 'em, but this ain't that kind of time. You got a pretty fair idea of where that Yaqui camp must lay. At least you know the way he was headed. And if they're going to pull a big raid, like El Griego told 'em to, they won't be moving out tomorrow or the next day. You be smart and hyper on back to the Copper Queen. There ain't any reason at all to get yourself killed tonight.

Swinging the Morgan around, Longarm rode back in the direction of the cottage.

Chapter 12

Dawn's first gray tinges were showing in the east when Longarm got back to the cottage. As he rode past the corral he saw that the women had untied El Griego's feet from the corral rail, allowing him to stand erect. The Yaqui looked stolidly at him, his obsidian eyes glittering, his face impassive. There were still lights burning in the house. Longarm rode up to the back door and called, "Luz! Clarita!" and the two women came out.

"Did you catch up with the Yaqui?" Luz asked.

"No. He ducked into a canyon and give me the slip. But if I'm right, the main Yaqui camp's to the southeast someplace."

Luz nodded. "Yes, it would be in that direction, across the border in Mexico, I imagine."

"It ought not be too hard to find, if it's any size. If I'd had my rifle and a shirt on and a full canteen, I might've had a try, but I wouldn't've got far, the way I was, out there."

"Did you come back for your gear so you can go look for it?"

"Not right this minute, Luz. Later, maybe."

"Then what do we do now?"

"I don't know what you're going to do, but I'm aiming to have a good big tot of Maryland rye and eat about a ton of breakfast. Then I'll get on a shirt, so the sun don't fry me, and ride over to the Copper Queen and have a talk with Grady. After that, I ain't so sure."

"You'd better get some rest, Longarm. You're wounded, and you've been up all night."

"Rest can wait. I ain't all that tired. Did anybody come noseying around the house while I was gone?"

"No. Clarita and I took turns sleeping and watching, but we didn't hear anything."

"Good." He asked Clarita, "You think you can rassle me up some breakfast while I unsaddle my horse and get him fed and watered?"

"*Seguro*. You like *bistec* and *patatas fritas, lo mismo como ayer*?"

"That'd suit me fine. I'll be back in a minute or so."

At the stable-shed, Longarm ignored El Griego as studiously as the Yaqui chief ignored him. He unsaddled the Morgan and saw that there was plenty of feed and water, then walked back to the house. The smell of frying steak greeted him at the door and reminded him how hungry he was, and a healthy slug of rye only whetted his appetite. Luz came in, carrying his breakfast on a platter.

"Do you mind if I sit with you while you eat?" she asked.

"Sit down and have your breakfast too," he invited.

"No. Clarita and I ate a little while ago. Watching and waiting is a hungry thing." She smiled and waited until Longarm had swallowed a few bites of food, then asked, "What will you do after you talk to Mr. Grady, Longarm?"

"That'll depend a lot on Grady. I got an idea El Griego wasn't bluffing when he said what he did."

"About his men getting others, and then coming to free him?"

"Yes. I don't know how many men he can muster, but from the way them fellows from Mina Cobre done last night, they ain't fit to put up much of a fight against a good-sized bunch of Yaquis."

"I don't know how big a tribe the Yaquis are." Luz frowned thoughtfully. "I do know they fight as fiercely as the Apaches, maybe even more so. Until Mr. Grady started keeping guards with rifles on duty, the Yaquis were constantly harassing the mine."

Clarita came in carrying a steaming coffeepot. She set it on the table and went back into the kitchen without looking at Longarm and Luz.

Luz asked him, "Do you think she's really a *bruja*, Longarm? A witch?"

"That's something I don't know too much about." Longarm pushed his empty platter aside and filled his coffee cup. "She sure seemed to make *El Griego* believe she is, though."

"I don't believe it myself," Luz said. "Why would she be doing a servant's work here if she can really work magic?"

"Well, that's something else I wouldn't know." Longarm stood up, lighting a cheroot. "Now, I'll go dig up some duds and get on my way. If I'm right about those Yaquis, we won't have much time to fool around. There's a lot of things to do, and we ain't sure how much time we'll have to do 'em."

At the Copper Queen, Grady listened thoughtfully while Longarm gave him a condensed account of the night's events. He said, "That's not very good news, Long. Even that little raid last night put a lot of my men into a panic. About a third of them didn't show up this morning. It's going to take me a few days to get production back to normal. If I lose much tonnage, I'll have my bosses from Boston on my neck."

"Does that mean you can't lock the Yaqui up for me?"

"Of course not. I haven't sent the guards for him yet, because you said you wanted to talk to him again this morning."

"Well, you can have your men go get him anytime now. The sooner he's put in a safe place, the better I'll like it."

"Have you made up your mind about turning him over to the army?" Grady asked.

"Oh, I'll do that sooner or later. Maybe sooner, if we can get a troop of cavalry sent over here from Fort Huachuca to be on hand in case those Yaquis do come after him."

"It's worth a try. I don't know how many men they've got on duty there now, but protecting the mine and the town's part of their job."

"How far is Huachuca, anyhow?"

"A little over eighty miles. A long, dry ride."

"It'd be two days, maybe three, before they could get here," Longarm said, after doing a little mental arithmetic. "I'd say we got that much time. You got a man you can send?"

"Not today, I haven't. I need every man I can muster. But you'll surely be able to find somebody in Mina Cobre to go."

"It's worth a try. I'll let you know how I come out."

• • •

On the way from the Copper Queen to Mina Cobre, Longarm stopped off at the cottage to replenish his supply of cheroots. He saw Carlita at the back of the house, her elbows deep in a washtub of suds, and inside found Luz busy sweeping and dusting.

"What did you and Mr. Grady decide to do?" she asked.

"Grady can't do much of anything. Half his hands didn't show up today. I'm on my way into town now to find somebody who'll ride to Fort Huachuca and get some troops in here."

With surprisingly little bitterness in her voice, Luz said, "It's a pity Eusebio was killed. He was such a fine horseman. He'd have ridden to Huachuca in a minute for you, and he'd have been someone you could trust."

"Oh, I'll find a man to take on the job. Trent or Carvajal will be bound to know—"

Luz interrupted him. "Longarm, why can't I go?"

"To town? Why, sure you can, and welcome too."

"Not to Mina Cobre. To Fort Huachuca."

"You know I can't send you all that long way, Luz. It's got to be a fast ride, to the fort and turn around and come right back. It ain't a woman's job."

"I've ridden it three or four times, with Eusebio. I know the trail, where the water holes are, everything."

Longarm shook his head. "You ain't going to talk me into it, so you might as well give over. Now, I'm going on in to town. I'll find somebody there to go to the fort."

Longarm's first stop was at the saloon. At that hour of the morning he'd expected it to be deserted, but there were still a few customers—left over from the night before, judging by their bedraggled appearance.

Corky set the rye bottle and a glass in front of Longarm. He asked, "Where'd you get off to, last night? I wanted to buy you a few drinks. You done a good job of getting rid of them Yaquis. I figure the town owes you."

"Well, if I got any credit, I'm about to cash it in. Who's a good rider that's got a good horse, Corky?"

Corky pointed to three men slouched down in their chairs

136

at a table. "You're looking at three of 'em. That one on this side of the table's Caleb Purdy. He's got a roan gelding that'll outrun any horse around here. Fellow on his right's Ed Weeks, he's damn near as good, but he can't beat Caleb. Other one's Jeff Talley. He's all right too. Why?"

"I'll tell you later." Longarm carried his glass over to the table where Purdy and his companions sat. He asked, "Mind if I set down with you for a minute?"

"Hell, take a chair." Purdy stared up at Longarm. "Sure, I know you. You're the U.S. marshal that helped us run off them Yaquis last night."

"Set, marshal," Talley invited.

Longarm sat down. "How you feeling about now, Purdy?"

"Like a buzzard puked in my liquor. But we sure had a hell of a night, didn't we?"

"We done right well," Longarm agreed. "But we still got a ways to go. Those Yaquis are going to come back and try to get even with us for clearing 'em out last night."

"That don't surprise me," Weeks said. "Well, hell, let 'em come ahead. We'll give 'em what-for next time, too."

"I guess we can try." Longarm looked at Purdy. "Can you and me talk private for a minute?"

"What about?"

"Now, if I wanted to spout off in front of your friends here, I wouldn't've asked you to talk private, would I?"

"I ain't got no secrets from nobody," Purdy said. "Go ahead and spout, Marshal. Jeff and Weeks is my best friends, I ain't got no secrets from them."

Longarm saw that he wasn't going to be able to persuade Purdy to leave his friends. He said, "Corky tells me you got the best horse in town. Says you're a bang-up rider too."

"Hell, anybody'll tell you that. What about it?

"Hold on," Weeks said. "Not everybody says Caleb's the best. What're you up to, Marshal? Getting up a race? If you are, me and Jeff wants to know about it."

"Not a race. I'm looking for a man I can deputize to do a little riding for me. He'll draw special deputy's pay, a dollar a day and feed for the horse."

"I'd like to oblige you, Marshal," Caleb said. "But Strawberry pulled a muscle in that ruckus last night. Be a while before I'd want to ride him, even around town."

"Suppose I get you a horse from the livery stable," Longarm suggested. "Will you go then?"

"Hell, no! First reason is, the livery's got no horses to rent, all they do is board nags for folks in town who ain't got barns. But the big reason is that I'm running for constable against Barney Trent, and I got to spend my time getting all the votes I can muster up in the next few days."

"How about me for the job?" Weeks demanded. "Tell me more about what this special deputy's got to do."

"First off, he's got to ride to Fort Huachuca. You know that Yaqui prisoner I brought in? Well, I want to hand him over to the army."

Weeks shook his head. "No, sir! That kinda ride ain't for me. I got a festering boil big as a hen's egg on my butt, and I ain't going to set no two days in the saddle for nobody, not even for Uncle Sam."

"How about you, Talley?" Longarm asked.

"Well, I'd like to, but my old woman's about due, and I'm damned if I'll go kiting off on a two-day ride with my kid about to pop out."

Longarm had never seen interest evaporate quite so fast as this. He asked, "Well, do any of you men know somebody with a good horse that'd be interested?"

"You been out to the town corral this morning, Marshal?" Purdy asked.

"That's the brush corral between here and the Papago village?" Longarm asked. When Weeks nodded, he shook his head. "I ain't been out there since I left with the Yaqui."

"Well, we didn't know about it till daylight, but them Yaqui bastards must've sent some of their bunch off with the horses that they stole before we jumped 'em," Purdy said.

Talley added, "We rode out for a look-see this morning, and there ain't a hoss left. Nothing but the mules and goats and sheep. Hell, Marshal, outside of our nags and the ones Trent and that greaser sheriff was riding, there ain't a hoss worth calling a hoss in this town today!"

"There sure ain't one that'll make a fast ride to the fort and back," Weeks volunteered. "That showy nag Carvajal rides,

138

hell, it's spavined. It'd make maybe ten miles if you walked it all the way."

Purdy spoke up again. "I lent Barney my brood mare to ride last night, but I wouldn't lend her for a ride like you're talking about. Looks like if you want somebody to go to the fort, it'll have to be you, Marshal."

"Oh, I'll find a man," Longarm told them, with a confidence he didn't feel. "If one of you changes his mind, you'll find me around town."

Longarm considered the options remaining to him as he rode back through Mina Cobre from the saloon. There wasn't a man except himself that he felt he could trust to organize and lead a defense of the town, the Papago and Mexican villages, and the mine, more or less simultaneously.

Grady's guards could be relied on to do their jobs at the mine, unless things got too bad, but if a couple of hundred savage Yaquis bent on revenge were to swoop down, they could chew up the three settlements one at a time and then concentrate on the Copper Queen. From what he'd seen of Trent and Carvajal, neither of them commanded the amount of respect that would make men follow their orders in a battle. He had a pretty definite idea that neither of them had the ability to organize the kind of defenses that would be needed in a major fight.

And this ain't one you can turn your back on, either, he reminded himself. If it hadn't been for you grabbing off that El Griego last night, this mess never would've been stirred up. So, since you're to blame for the mess, you damn well have got to clean it up, and you ain't got time to set around and stew, trying to figure an easy way to do it.

By the time he reached the cottage, Longarm had debated the odds that his last alternative would succeed, and had reluctantly decided that he'd better take it while he had the chance. At the corral, he noticed that El Griego was no longer handcuffed to the post; apparently, Grady's men had come for the Yaqui. He dismounted and went inside. Luz was sitting in the kitchen, mending his shirt and balbriggans where El Griego's knife had slashed through them.

"I see Grady's guards came and got the Yaqui," Longarm said, dropping his stetson on the table and pouring a glass of rye from the bottle that stood waiting. He sipped the whiskey gratefully before taking off his gunbelt and putting it on the table beside the hat.

"Yes. They came quite soon after you left." Luz snipped the thread of the seam she'd sewed in the underwear and picked up the shirt. Her voice very casual, she asked, "Did you get someone to ride to Fort Huachuca?"

"Not so's you'd notice." He tossed off the remainder of the rye and lighted a cheroot. "It wasn't because I didn't try. There just wasn't anybody to take on the job."

"Except me?"

"Well, I ain't forgot you offered, Luz. But I don't feel right about asking you to make a ride like that by yourself, with Yaquis running around all over the place."

"They're not going to be all over the place. They've gone back south of the border by now, into Sonora. And there aren't going to be any Yaquis to the east, Longarm. That's not Yaqui country, it's Apache country."

"Which is just about as bad," he reminded her.

"But the Apaches are north of Fort Huachuca. They're superstitious about that part of the territory. They've avoided it since the massacre in seventy-one."

"What massacre would that be? I can't recall hearing about Apaches ever being massacred, not anyplace."

"They were at Fort Grant. Almost a hundred and fifty of them got penned up in a church there and killed."

"By Yaquis? Or by the army?"

"Neither one. By the Papagos."

"Papagos killing Apaches? Now, Luz, you know the Papagos don't fight nobody."

"They did that time. And since then, the Apaches have been afraid to go anywhere near there."

"You ain't afraid to make the ride, then?"

"Not a bit. I've been sitting here hoping I could do something useful, instead of just looking after a house that belongs to somebody else. When do you want me to start?"

"If you're going to go, I guess it better be sooner than later. You think maybe in the morning early—"

140

"I think maybe right now, Longarm. If I leave this minute, I can be at Fort Huachuca before midnight."

"Do nearly half the ride at night?" Longarm shook his head. "I don't like that idea one little bit."

"It doesn't bother me. I know the trail and the water holes, I told you that this morning. And I'm ready to leave. I went home and got Eusebio's rifle. I've got food in my saddlebags, and a full canteen. I don't see any reason to put off starting."

"Well," Longarm said, "I never knew a woman yet that couldn't get her way if she set her mind to it. All right, Luz, start out whenever you're ready. We can sure use a company of troopers, or even a squad, if those Yaquis come back."

"Clarita will look after you all right," Luz said, putting aside her mending. "You'll just have to tell her what to do."

"She knows that as long as I get steak and spuds and plenty of coffee, I don't ask for much else."

Luz had slipped on the light jacket that had been hanging on the back of her chair. She started for the door, Longarm following her. They walked to the corral. He was surprised to see her pony saddled and fitted for the trip.

"If I didn't know better, I'd swear I told you this morning to get ready to ride to Fort Huachuca," he told her. "But I know I said different."

"You didn't tell me," Luz said. She swung into her saddle and looked soberly at Longarm, then added, "But Clarita did."

Longarm's jaw dropped open. "Clarita?"

"Yes. Oh, I know, I never did believe what she says about being a *bruja*. Not until now. She came in after you'd gone to Mina Cobre this morning and told me I'd better get ready to ride to the fort. I laughed at her, but she kept telling me to do it, so I did. I guess she really is a witch of some kind, Longarm."

"Or a real good guesser. Well, if you're going to make the fort by midnight, you'd better go."

He removed the corral poles and Luz rode off. She turned to wave at him, then headed due east across the trackless desert. For a few moments, Longarm stood and watched her figure growing smaller in the distance, then went back into the cottage. To his surprise, Clarita was sitting in the chair Luz had vacated. She had taken up the mending that Luz had laid aside, and was busy completing the job of sewing up the rip in his shirt.

"I got another shirt, Clarita," he told her. "You don't have to finish mending that one unless you ain't got anything better to do with your time."

"I do not have, unteel now." Clarita put the shirt down and stood up. "All last night you have not sleep. Is time now you rest. Come. I help you."

Clarita took Longarm's uninjured right arm and led him into the bedroom. The bed had been freshly spread, he noticed.

"You sure all you got in mind is me resting?" Longarm asked her, smiling.

"Ees not all. We have sometheeng between us we are start and not feenish."

"I ain't forgot that, Clarita."

"Is very bad luck for man and woman, they do not feenish what they have begin."

"Well, now's as good a time as any to finish up, I guess."

"*Sí.* Weeth man like you, *especialmente.*"

Clarita was shrugging out of her low-cut blouse as she spoke. She tossed it aside and slid her skirt over her hips. She wore nothing beneath it. Longarm looked at her tawny body, a mature woman's body, generously fleshed, with flaring hips and swelling thighs, a scanty but wide pubic triangle of deep black. In spite of her full figure, or perhaps because of it, her skin was baby-smooth. She was quick to notice the bulge swelling at his groin and came over to him.

"*Su verga me gusto,*" she said, running her fingers over his beginning erection. "*Desnudese, no? Lo mismo conmigo.*"

While Longarm levered his boots off, Clarita was unbuttoning his trousers. She moved casually, unhurriedly, as though it were something she did every day. Longarm could not ignore her full breasts, so close to him that their tips brushed his biceps each time she moved.

He let her continue to undress him while he stroked her breasts with his calloused fingertips, and bent to take their nipples between his lips. Clarita inhaled gustily as he continued his caresses, and when she finally got his balbriggans off, she wrapped her hands around his erection, full and upstanding now.

142

"Qué tronchudo hermoso!" she sighed, tucking him between her thighs and bringing them together to hold him firmly. *"Tome a la cama, soy ascua!"*

With a strength that surprised him, Clarita whirled him around and pulled him down on the bed, on top of her. She opened her thighs and placed him, and raised her hips to meet him as he lunged and buried himself to his full length in her eager body.

Longarm began stroking, and after a moment Clarita grew accustomed to his rhythm. She began responding with fierce upward oscillations of her hips that brought them together at the end of each lunge with a pounding collision of his hard hips against her soft fleshy thighs.

"Dámelo más presteza!" Clarita gasped. She was writhing now under Longarm's lusty, deep penetrations. *"Siente cuando toca mí panza! Tu chingas como ariete! Pero más presteza, más y más!"*

"I'm giving you all I can, Clarita," Longarm panted. "And as fast as I can, too."

"Después, sostuvelo! Sostuvelo hasta que"—her voice broke and her gasps became a constant rasping from deep in her throat—*hasta que . . . hasta que . . . Ay, ahorita, ahorita!"*

Clarita's writhing turned into quick, jerking spasms that shook her full body again and again until her head arched back on the pillow and she grew rigid for a moment before Longarm felt her muscles relax and her flesh soften around him. He slowed the tempo of his thrusts. Now he went into her with a slow, steady stroke that he maintained without pausing until she sighed happily and began to respond to him again.

"No aún acabas?" she asked, surprise in her voice. *"Vaminos otra vez inmediatamente?"*

"Sure. It takes me a while, Clarita. You ain't tired yet, are you?" he asked. *"Cansada?"*

"De ningún modo! Adelante! Más y más!"

Longarm stroked more slowly now, building to his own climax, knowing that Clarita would be ready when he was. He felt himself reaching a peak and sped up, holding back to bring Clarita to readiness. She tightened her legs around him and began riding with him, rising to meet his lunges, her breath coming faster, her body beginning to quiver now and then.

143

Soon she was writhing as before, gasping with pleasure, and when Longarm felt the quick jerks of her spasm beginning, he speeded up. She started to tremble and Longarm let himself go, holding himself buried until he was spent and drained and her body grew quiet again beneath his.

"Ay, qué bueno!" she sighed after her breathing calmed. *"Tu es sin par! Hombre igual para bruja!"*

Longarm looked down at Clarita's smiling face, and asked the question he'd been wanting to since he'd first heard of her reputed witchcraft. "Are you really a witch, Clarita? *Bruja verdadera?*"

"Sí. I am truly *bruja.* You do not believe thees, I am know, but I weel show you."

"How?"

"Paciencia! You are tire now. Me, I am a leetle bit tire, too. Better we sleep for now. *Más tarde,* later, I weel show you I am really *bruja.*"

Longarm was not inclined to argue. He'd been more than thirty-six hours without sleep, and the strenuous activity in which he and Clarita had been engaged, combined with the fast pace of those other hours, were taking their toll of even his toughened frame. He knew he was tired. For one of the few times he could remember, sleep appealed to him more than the idea of having a postcoital drink of rye accompanied by a cheroot.

"Maybe that ain't such a bad idea," he yawned. "A little nap would go real good right now." He stretched hugely and said, "Just be sure to wake me up in time for supper."

Then, snuggling up to Clarita's soft, full body, Longarm went to sleep.

Chapter 13

Sundown was near when Longarm woke up hungry. He was alone in the bed, and from the kitchen, over the clattering of pots and pans, he heard Clarita humming the light, happy strains of the *venadito* song: *"Lo que digo que hay in día..."* He rolled off the bed and padded barefoot and naked into the living room, where the bottle of Old Moore stood waiting, and cheroots and matches were in the pockets of his vest, which hung over a chair.

With a cheroot clamped in his teeth and a tot of rye in the glass he was holding, Longarm stepped to the kitchen door. Clarita looked at him from the stove and smiled. Unlike him, she had dressed when she left the bed, but she paid no attention to his nakedness.

"Hace su cena," she said in a matter-of-fact voice, indicating the pan of steak frying on the stove. *"Poco á poco se comes."*

"Tell me something, Clarita," Longarm said. "There's times when you talk pretty good English, but there's times when you act like you don't know a word that ain't Spanish. Why's that?"

She shrugged. "Eef I get in hurry, *estimulado*, I am not theenk of word I need to say."

"Well, that figures. But maybe if you'd talk English more with Luz, when you two are working around here—"

"Basta con Luz!" she interrupted. "Luz ees *gachupine*. Me, I am *indio*. I am not espeak so good like her. She ees make me sound like *estupida* when I talk while she ees here."

"There ain't all that much wrong with the way you talk English. All you need to do is talk it more."

"Ees no need. You got no trouble to onderstan' me, no?"

"No. And it ain't none of my business anyhow."

145

"I have tell you what you ask me," Clarita said. "Now, you tell me what I ask you, *sí*?"

"Sure. Ask away."

"You are name Long, *sí*?"

"That's right."

"Then why ees Luz call you Longarm? I have the afraid to say your name, because maybe I am wrong, and you get mad."

"Oh, that's just a sort of nickname my friends call me. Nobody much uses my regular name."

"Neekname? *Cómo apodo*?"

"If that's how you say it in your language."

"Then you weel not be mad eef I call you Longarm too?"

"Of course not. And while we're answering questions, don't forget you promised me you'd show me you're really a *bruja*."

"I am not forget. But ees better I do thees later, after you have eat. *Venga, sientese*, Longarm. Ees supper."

A healthy meal finished the job of restoring Longarm that sleep had begun. He moved to sit in one of the easy chairs while Clarita was clearing the table. As he puffed lazily on a cheroot, he wondered how Luz was progressing on her ride to Fort Huachuca.

"Ees have no trouble, Luz," Clarita said. "Ees make *bien viaje*. So, ees no to worry."

"How'd you know I was thinking about Luz?"

"I am know theengs. *Soy bruja*."

"Damned if I ain't beginning to believe it," Longarm said. "I never put much store in witches, though. You still got to prove you're one."

"I am promise I weel do thees for you, so I do eet," Clarita replied. She came to the easy chair and stood facing Longarm. "You are enjoy *tiempo atrás*, no? When we make *cortejando*?"

"Sure I did. And you acted like you did too."

"I like, *sí*. *Muchisimo*. So we go back to bed, no? Ees best place for show you."

"You sure all you want to show me is that you're a witch?"

"No." Clarita smiled. "Ees not all."

She pushed her skirt down over her flared hips, and as it slid to the floor she pulled the loose neck of her blouse down and shrugged out of it. She stepped out of the little heap of clothing and stood with her feet apart. Standing naked in front of him, she spread her arms, the twin spheres of her breasts growing taut and quivering with her movements.

"I am show you I am woman who ees want man. Ees woman and *bruja* both for you. You want them, Longarm, no?"

Longarm stood up. He took Clarita in his arms and bent to kiss her. She met his kiss with her full lips already parted, her tongue thrusting into his mouth, and slid her hand down between their bodies to grasp him. Longarm tightened his embrace, her breasts flattening like warm, soft pillows against his chest. Without breaking their embrace, they moved slowly into the bedroom.

Clarita's urgency, the frenzy that had ruled her earlier, had not yet returned. She held Longarm close as they lowered themselves to lie side by side on the bed, caressing him as he stiffened and swelled, rubbing his shaft gently against the wiry curls of her pubic brush. When they broke their kiss, Longarm bent his head to tongue her breasts, tracing their pebbled surface and closing his lips over her protruding nipples.

"*Ahorita su verga encenarse,*" she told him softly. "*Dámelo, Longarm. Dámelo despacio, con dulzura.*"

Pulling Longarm gently with her, Clarita rolled onto her back and opened her thighs, guiding him into her. He started to go in with a deep, hard thrust, but she pressed her hands against his hips to stop his thrust, and then relaxed their pressure so that he sank into her slowly. As he went in deeper, Clarita spread her thighs wider, and in the final instant of his penetration she clasped her legs around him to trap and hold him.

At the same time, Longarm felt her inner muscles close around him. Other women had grasped him this way, but none of them had closed as firmly around him as did Clarita. He felt his erection being squeezed as though it were entrapped by a giant hand, which unexpectedly began to massage him with a rippling that he could feel progress in subtle pressures that moved from tip to base and back, only to be repeated again and again.

Longarm levered himself up on his elbows to look down at Clarita's face, but suddenly he was not seeing Clarita; the pale face he saw on the pillow was the of blond Annie Dawkins, whom he'd known in Mormon country. Before he'd recovered from his surprise at seeing Annie, he found himself gazing into

147

the dark eyes of treacherous Rosie O'Brien, but Rosie suddenly became Nalin, the Mescalero Apache girl from Lincoln County in New Mexico Territory, and after the fleeting instant when Longarm recognized Nalin, he saw that he was looking at Vivian Montgomery, who'd been Silverheels, in Leadville.

Bewildered by the transitions he'd been watching, the sudden shifts that sent his mind stumbling back into the past, Longarm closed his eyes. When he opened them again and looked once more at Clarita's face a few inches below his own, Longarm did not know how much time had passed since the first change he'd seen. He did know in an instant the sensation he now felt. The squeezing and rippling of her inner muscles had brought him close to an orgasm.

He moved his hips to lunge into Clarita again, and felt the pressure that had been gripping him relax. Clarita was smiling up at him, and Longarm collected himself enough to thrust hard into her, and before he passed the point of no return, he felt her body stiffen and quiver and saw her eyes close and her lips pull back as he let go and their bodies trembled together for moment after moment until once more they lay relaxed and spent.

"Damned if you ain't a real *bruja*, Clarita," Longarm said when his breath returned. "How in the hell did you know about those women you turned into, one right after the other?"

She shook her head, her black hair rippling on the pillow. "I am not know how. Only I know that I am *bruja*."

"Can you see things that're going to happen? All I saw was some women I used to know."

"I see notheeng only what the owl is let me see. Eet is not me, the woman, who do thees. Are you understand, Longarm?"

"Not a bit. Which I guess ain't too odd, seeing as you don't seem to, either."

"Then you are satisfy?" she asked.

"I got to admit you proved what you been saying."

"*Bueno*. Now I have show you, I weel be *bruja* no more tonight, Longarm. But I am woman too." Clarita's hand sought Longarm's shaft once more. She went on, "And you are *mucho hombre*. Now, you be *hombre con tronchado magnifico*, and I weel be woman for as long as you weesh."

148

• • •

In midmorning, Longarm rode into Mina Cobre once again. He stopped first at the barbershop, not only because he needed a shave, but because barbers hear as many confessions as a prient or a doctor, and are much less reticent about passing them on. He was a bit disappointed that the shop was empty, but took his place in the chair after hanging up his hat and coat. He'd learned from past experience not to remove his vest and gunbelt.

With a dexterity born of practice, the barber whipped the cloth around Longarm's shoulders and lapped it tight around his neck, then picked up a shaving mug and began churning up lather with the brush.

"Didn't know who you was when I shaved you before," he said as he began to lather Longarm's cheeks. "U.S. marshal, ain't you? Name of Long?"

"Yes."

"Come to see if you can keep the election honest, I hear."

"Not much use in having elections if they ain't run fair and square."

"Well, there's those in Mina Cobre wouldn't agree with you, but I guess you're used to that."

"I've run into it before."

"What I hear is, you're sorta tromping on everybody's toes, too. Or was, till you showed 'em how to whip them Yaquis the other night."

"I ain't so sure the Yaquis are going to stay whipped."

"Meaning what?" the barber asked, pulling the brush away from Longarm's face, leaving only half of it lathered.

"Well, the folks here in Mina Cobre handed 'em a whipping, and from what I hear about Yaquis, they don't stand for being whipped. They might pull out if they get set back, but it ain't long before they're back to get revenge."

"You telling me they might raid the town next time, not just them Papago shacks?" the barber demanded.

"I hear that's the way they do things. Now, will you finish my shave, friend? I got business that needs tending to."

Though the barber tried to get him talking again, Longarm

remained obstinately silent until he'd been shaved and bay-rummed, his mustache trimmed, and his hair smoothed down with macassar oil. He paid the barber the fifteen cents that the knight of the razor requested and left the shop, confident that the seed he'd so carefully planted would send roots of rumor throughout the town within a matter of a few hours. Mounting the Morgan, he rode to the saloon and went inside.

Corky was quick with the rye bottle, as usual. As soon as Longarm had put away half of his first drink, the barkeep asked, "You ever find the man you was looking for yesterday? One who'd make that ride to Fort Huachuca?"

Longarm lighted a cheroot before answering the barkeep's question with the literal truth. He said, "Do you know, Corky, there wasn't a man I talked to who'd take on that job? Damned shame, too. Turns out that Yaqui I captured the other night's one of their main chiefs, fellow called El Griego."

Corky's mouth gaped open. "El Griego! Godamighty, Longarm! You know he's about the meanest, toughest Yaqui there is?"

"I heard something to that effect, but you know how a bad reputation like he's got gets blowed up beyond common sense."

"Not this time! Why, that El Griego has dealt misery to this part of the territory ever since the first settlers hit here! I don't blame you for wanting to hand him over to the army! Why, as long as he's anywhere nearby, them Yaquis of his is going to come after him for sure!"

"Oh, I know that's what El Griego says they'll do, but who's going to believe a renegade Indian?"

"I am, for one! Why, he can raise two or three hundred Yaquis to fight on his side! If a bunch that size ever sets out to raid a little place like this, they'd put up more of a fight than this town could handle!"

"Well, I'd like to get him away from the town, but I don't rightly know how to go about it," Longarm said casually, refilling his glass. "Of course, if you got any ideas..."

"I haven't got any right now, but I'm sure going to try to come up with some." Corky's brow knitted thoughtfully for a moment, then he said, "I've got one idea already."

"Oh? What's that?"

"Just as soon as my swampie gets here, the first thing I'm

going to do is to step across to the store and get me a few boxes of fresh ammunition. Dammit, this saloon's all I got, and I'm going to keep it from getting looted and maybe burned down, if them damned Yaquis raid us!"

"Why, Corky, if you don't want to wait for your swampie, I'll be right glad to stay while you go over there."

"You will? You wouldn't have to do anything but tell whoever comes in to wait. It'll only take me a minute."

"Sure. I can't get behind the bar and tend it for you, but I'll just take my bottle over to that table by the door and set there and tell your customers you'll be right back."

"You do that, then, Longarm. And whatever drinks you take while you're waiting are on the house!"

Longarm watched the barkeep hurrying across the road. He smiled as he sat down at the table beside the door. There goes the closest thing to a newspaper headline this little place has got, he told himself. Between what that barber passes on to his customers, and the talk Corky can stir up across the bar, there ain't going to be a man or woman in Mina Cobre that'll go to sleep tonight without looking under the bed. By this time tomorrow, it ain't going to be no job at all to find men that'll join up in a posse to keep watch and fight, when the time comes.

As he'd promised, Corky returned within a few minutes, before any customers had come in. He carried three boxes of shotgun shells, which he put on one of the shelves behind the bar.

"And the first job that damn swampie gets when he comes in is going to be to get my gun out of the storeroom and clean it up!" he promised Longarm.

"See you do that, Corky," Longarm replied soberly. "Time a man spends taking care of his guns never is time wasted. Now, I had breakfast early, and it's getting on toward noon. I'd better move along, if I want to get to the cafe before they start watering down the stew."

During a leisurely meal, topped off with a slab of pie and two cups of coffee, Longarm watched the seeds he'd planted beginning to sprout. At the short counter and at the tables, wherever two men sat, they kept their heads together in whispered conversation, many of them looking around apprehensively when a new customer entered the restaurant, as though it might be El Griego himself coming through the door. The word, Longarm thought with satisfaction, was spreading faster than he'd hoped.

Although he wasn't sure he'd be a welcome visitor, Longarm rode from the cafe up to Naylor's store. The fat proprietor was sitting back in his usual corner, munching alternately on cheese and crackers and halves of peaches from an open airtight that stood on a chair beside him. Naylor looked at Longarm, but made no acknowledgement of his presence. Longarm went to the counter, and a straw-haired clerk came up to wait on him.

"I need a handful of cigars," Longarm said. "Just like the one I'm smoking."

Turning to the shelves, the clerk selected one of the cedar boxes that held cigars and put it on the counter in front of Longarm, raising its lid. Longarm scooped up a handful of the slim cigars and put money on the counter. The clerk counted the cigars and gave Longarm change from the till. Tucking the cheroots into his pocket, Longarm walked back to where Naylor was sitting. The obese storekeeper stared at him, but gave him no greeting.

"I been trying to find time to get in here and tell you I ain't forgot about counting them ballots. I been just a mite crowded for time since that ruckus out at the Papago village," he told the merchant.

"There's not any rush," Naylor grunted. "I didn't think we'd be lucky enough to be rid of you after that dust-up."

"Oh, I don't aim to go anyplace until the election's over."

"You know, Long, we ought not have to put up with you snooping around and making trouble. Damned government's getting nosier every day. A man can't call—" Naylor broke off and looked up as a clatter of footsteps reached them.

Longarm turned, following Naylor's eyes. Barney Trent had come hurrying through the door and was rushing almost at a run to the corner. He saw Longarm and skidded to a halt. The constable hesitated, then turned to Naylor.

"By God, Ed, if you got the pull you say you have in Washington, you better use it to get this fellow here out of our way! He's got this town into one hell of a big mess!"

"If you got any complaints to make about something I done, Trent, make 'em to me," Longarm said sharply. "Or hadn't you noticed I'm standing right here in front of you?"

"Talking to you is like talking to a stone wall, Long. You only listen to what you want to," Trent retorted.

"Oh, I can be reasonable sometimes. I'm right here now, and ready to listen to you. You might try telling me what's on your mind, unless you've got to wait until your boss here tells you what he wants you to do."

"Wait a minute, Marshal," Naylor protested. "Just because Barney happens to come to me for advice now and then doesn't mean I boss him or give him orders!"

"If that's the way of it, Naylor, suppose you just stay out of whatever talk Trent wants to have with me, and let him do his own talking," Longarm suggested. He returned his attention to the constable. "Well, Trent, what's on your mind? Come on out with it."

"How come you didn't tell me the other night that Yaqui you took out at the Papago village was El Griego?"

"Mainly because I didn't know it myself," Longarm replied. "I didn't know El Griego from Adam's off-ox until he told me himself who he was, and even after he told me, it didn't mean a damn thing, seeing as I never heard his name before."

Trent asked skeptically, "You never heard about the biggest renegade Yaqui in Arizona Territory?"

"Hell, Trent!" Longarm said, making no effort to hide his disgust. "Renegade redskins are a dime a dozen in any territory I can name you! Fifty miles from where they live, nobody's ever heard of most of 'em. Now, I'll grant you this El Griego sounds like he might be a little bit worse'n some, but—"

"Worse!" the constable broke in. "The son of a bitch is a killer, and the bunch of renegades he's head of is all just about as bad as he is!"

"Oh, I ain't arguing with you," Longarm said quietly. "But I don't see what in hell you're getting so riled up at *me* for."

"Because we were getting along just fine here in Mina Cobre until you stuck your nose into our business!" Trent said hotly. "Now everything's upset and a lot of people are leaving town because they're afraid of the Yaquis, and there's more talking

153

about going. And I blame that on you, Long!"

"You ain't making much sense," Longarm said quietly. "Those Yaquis were bound to hit your town sooner or later. The way it turns out, looks like you'll be on notice and have time to get ready for 'em."

"Get ready with what?" Trent demanded.

"With whatever you got!" Longarm retorted. "I'll tell it to you straight. What rubs your fur backward is me being here at all, and the reason that I'm here for. Now let's forget about elections and talk about Yaquis. Seems like you've forgot we whipped El Griego's men the other night, when he was leading 'em himself."

"Shitamighty!" Trent snorted. "That little bunch we chased off wasn't but part of his outfit, Long. There's a couple of hundred more just like 'em down below the border, in Sonora, and as soon as the word spreads that El Griego's being held prisoner up here, they'll get together and go through Mina Cobre faster than Grant took Richmond!"

"So far you ain't asked me for advice, Trent," Longarm said. "But I'll give you a word or two, for whatever it's worth. You and Carvajal better settle whatever differences you got between you, and start getting the men here in town ready to fight the Yaquis, if you're so damn sure they're going make trouble."

"Your advice is worth about as much as a dried-up horse turd, Long. Now, I'll tell you what I want you to do. Take El Griego out in the desert, give him a horse, and let him loose. That way we'll settle this mess without no more trouble."

Longarm looked at Trent for a moment before he answered, then he said quietly, "That won't settle one damned thing, Trent. I caught that Yaqui, and I aim to keep him until I can hand him over to the army. And if you want to turn him loose, you'll have to take him away from me. And I don't suspicion you've got the guts to do it!"

154

Chapter 14

For a moment, Longarm thought that Trent was going to take up the challenge he'd thrown. The constable's eyes slitted, his mouth contorted, and he dropped his right arm, swinging it gently at his side, his hand curved as though he were going to draw.

Longarm ignored the movement of Trent's hand. He kept his eyes on the constable's face, and when he saw the slitted eyes begin to widen and a red flush stain Trent's face, he knew the critical moments had passed, those few quick-ticking instants when a man's heartbeat speeds up and draws blood from his brain to his muscles, leaving his face white. Those, Longarm knew, were the seconds when a man commits himself to gunplay. He saw the signs that they'd passed, and let his vigilance relax, certain that there'd be no guns drawn.

He gave the angry constable a few moments longer to think things over, then asked in a level voice, "Well? You going to take my advice, Trent? I could see you didn't figure it was worth much a few minutes ago, but if you think about it a mite longer, it might look better."

From his seat in the corner, Naylor said, "Listen to what the marshal says, Barney." The store owner looked at Longarm and added, "I still don't like the idea of you being in town, Long, but you do talk sense where the Yaquis are concerned."

"Maybe it's a good thing there's something we agree on," Longarm said curtly. "You'll just have to put up with what you don't like about me, because I aim to stay around."

Addressing Trent as much as Longarm, Naylor said, "I suppose I've got more money tied up in this town than anybody else who lives here. I don't propose to lose what I've got by letting a bunch of goddamn Yaqui savages loot my store, and maybe burn it up to boot!"

"I'd say you ain't the only one in town who'll feel that way, Naylor," Longarm told the fat man. "You give most folks a reason to stand up and defend what's theirs, they'll generally do it. Now, I got other business to take care of. Maybe you can talk some sense into Trent. You said he takes your advice, and I can't think of a time when he needs advice more. *Good* advice."

Longarm crossed the street to the saloon and started to go in when, peering inside above the batwings, he saw that the place was crowded. A solid line of men stood at the bar, with Corky talking to them. Now and then, the barkeep emphasized his words by pounding the top of the bar with his fist. Longarm grinned. He didn't need to hear Corky's words to know what he was saying. Turning away from the batwings, Longarm swung into the saddle and walked the Morgan down the street to the cantina.

As he had expected, Raoul Carvajal was holding court at the table in the center of the crowded saloon. He saw Longarm and waved him over. Today the sheriff wore an indigo-blue shirt with his fawn-colored trousers, creamy hat, and silver-trimmed black leather accessories.

"*Bienvenido*, Marshal," Carvajal said. "You will drink with me today?"

"A little bit later on, Carvajal. Right now, we got to have a serious talk."

"So. We will talk seriously, and then"—the sheriff smiled—"we will have a *copita* and discuss more pleasant things. Now what is this so serious matter you wish to speak of?"

"A Yaqui renegade called El Griego."

Carvajal's smile vanished. "That is indeed serious. I have thought several times since our great victory over the Yaqui raiders a few evenings past that we were fortunate they were not of El Griego's band."

"That," Longarm said patiently, "is what I'm trying to tell you. It was El Griego that pulled off that raid."

When Carvajal had first mentioned the Yaqui's name, those nearest the table where he and Longarm sat had grown silent. When Longarm made his announcement, the silence spread over the entire cantina, to be broken by a buzz of whispering voices.

156

Carvajal stared wide-eyed at Longarm. "You mean this? Those were the Yaquis of El Griego we fought?"

"They sure as hell were. And if you want the rest of the story without any frills on it, he was leading the raid himself. He's the Yaqui I chased down and captured. You'd gone when I got back with him, and I didn't find out who he was until last night or thereabouts."

Incredulously, the sheriff gasped, "You captured El Griego? And you are still holding him prisoner?"

"That's about the way of it," Longarm nodded.

"What will you do with him?"

"Why, I aim to hold him till I can get around to handing him over to the army," Longarm replied casually.

Like his earlier announcement of the Yaqui's capture, this news, too, traveled almost instantly to the corners of the room.

Carvajal frowned. "This is indeed a serious thing. Do you realize, Marshal Long, that El Griego commands scores—*ay, caray*, more than scores!—he leads hundreds of Yaqui renegades!"

"So I've been told, by just about everybody I talked to since I found out who El Griego is."

"His men will surely attack Mina Cobre if they find out El Griego is here!" Carvajal said vehemently, slapping the table with his palm. "*Seguro*! I see what we must do, Marshal Long! We must send at once to Fort Huachuca for soldiers to defend us!"

"I've already done that," Longarm assured the nervous sheriff. "There ought to be some troops here tomorrow or the next day."

"How many will they send?" Carvajal asked. "There must be enough to guard the homes of my *gente* as well as the town!"

"I ain't got any more of an idea than you have how many men they'll be able to spare from the fort. Which means that you're going to have to make up a posse from your people, like we done the other night. The army might not be able to spare us enough soldiers to go around."

"But they must!" Carvajal exclaimed. "There may be hundreds of Yaquis attacking us! We must have the soldiers, or we die!"

"Well, anytime men shoot at each other, somebody's likely

157

to die," Longarm pointed out calmly. "Thing is, we just got to kill more Yaquis than they kill of our men." When Carvajal did not reply to what Longarm considered a common-sense observation, he went on, "Now, as long as you're the sheriff, it's up to you to get your people to do what's got to be done. I'll just leave that part of it for you to work out with Barney Trent."

"Trent!" Carvajal exploded. "How can I work with him, Marshal Long? You saw what he thinks of the *gente*."

"I'd say a pretty good way to make Trent change his mind about your people is for him to fight with 'em side by side. You think it over, Carvajal. We got maybe a day or two or three before El Griego's Yaqui crew is apt to show up."

"A day or two!" Carvajal gasped. "So soon?"

"Oh, I'll grant you we ain't got much time to waste, but it does give us time to work things out. Now, I got a little bit of other business to take care of, so I'll just hold off on that drink we were going to have until the next time we get together."

Longarm rose and saluted Carvajal with an uplifted forefinger and walked to the door. The cantina was much quieter when he left than it had been when he came in. He took the Morgan's reins from the hitch rail and mounted and was about to turn the horse toward the Copper Queen when he noticed about a half-dozen or so men standing in front of Naylor's store. On the generally somnolent street that ran through Mina Cobre, a gathering of that size was unusual enough to justify a closer look. He turned the horse's head in that direction instead.

As he came within earshot of the men, he could see that they were arguing among themselves. It was a peaceful rather than an angry discussion, and their voices were pitched too low for him to hear what they were saying. Tossing the reins across the hitch rail, Longarm went into the store.

There was another, louder argument going on inside, centered around the corner Naylor used as his office. The merchant himself was hidden by a semicircle of men whose voices filled the store with a sharp, angry babble of sound and made it impossible to understand what any one of them was saying.

Longarm started pushing through the group. They pushed

back until one of them said, "Let him get by, fellows. He's a U.S. marshal. Maybe Naylor'll listen to him."

Longarm recognized the speaker as Caleb Purdy, the man who was running against Trent for constable, and who'd refused to go to Fort Huachuca to get help. The men in front of him stepped aside, and now Longarm could see Naylor, who was leaning back in his chair, which had been pushed as far into the corner as it would go. His shoulders were pressed against the corners of the wall, his legs stuck out in front of him. Longarm had never seen a hippopotamus outside of a circus, but it struck him that the storekeeper, with his enormously swollen belly and bulging arms and legs, and the three chins covering his collar, was what a hippopotamus at bay might look like.

"Seems to me you're having a mite of trouble, Naylor," Longarm said calmly.

"I am, damm it! And Barney Trent's right, you're to blame for most of it, Long!" the fat merchant snapped.

"Supposing you tell me how and why."

"You got the town all stirred up about the Yaquis going to jump us! Don't try to deny it, because I heard what you told Barney not more than a couple of hours ago! And you got Corky from across the street all hottened up, I found that out from people who've come in here from the saloon!"

"Well, I never tried to make a secret about what El Griego's Yaqui renegades are likely to do, Naylor," Longarm said. "I figured the folks here have got a right to know, so's they can get ready. You'll recall that was what I was telling Barney. You heard us talking about it yourself."

"Yes, dammit! I heard you! But what I didn't know was that you'd spread the damn story all over the place!"

"Now it wouldn't help a bit to try to keep it secret, would it? But you still ain't told me what these men here are so mad about. Maybe you better get around to that."

"These men all want to buy guns, but they don't want to pay my price! They want me to let 'em have them for nothing!" Naylor explained, his voice quivering with either fear or anger.

"That's a damn lie!" one of the men exclaimed. "He's put up the prices of his guns since noontime!"

"And that's gospel truth," Purdy affirmed. "I was in here

day afore yestiddy, after that ruckus out at the Papago shacks put me in mind to buy a new rifle. Well, I put it off, and when I made up my mind today and come in to buy it, this damn swindler'd raised the ante on it by twenty dollars!"

"That right, Naylor?" Longarm asked. Naylor did not reply. More sharply, Longarm went on, "Did you do what these men say you did? Dammit, I want an answer!"

"Well, if I did raise the price a little bit, it's only because of the law of supply and demand," the storekeeper replied defensively. "I guess you've heard about that law, Mr. Federal Marshal? I've got the only guns for sale in Mina Cobre, and when things get scarce, their prices go up. Now that's the kind of law businessmen go by."

"His prices are too high on everything, the way it is!" one of the men grumbled. "He's a damn bloodsucker."

"If you don't want to pay my honest prices, take your trade somewhere else!" Naylor said hotly. Ignoring the grumbles that rose from the men in front of him, he added, "By the time I pay a teamster to haul my merchandise from Tucson, I'm lucky if I make a dime on anything I sell!"

"Let's get back to those guns," Longarm suggested. "Seems to me I recall something you said when I was in here this morning, something about you not going to let El Griego's Yaquis loot your store and maybe burn it. You remember saying that?"

"Yes," Naylor replied hesitantly. "I guess I did make some kind of remark to that effect."

"Now let me ask you something," Longarm went on. "You think these men don't value their houses and what's inside 'em as much as you do your store? If they fight El Griego's renegades, you don't think they'll be doing it for your sake, do you?"

Reluctantly, after a long pause, Naylor admitted, "No. I don't guess they'd be worrying much about me."

"But you're trying to make 'em pay for the guns they need to fight the Yaquis." Longarm did not try to keep the disgust out of his voice. When Naylor did not reply, he asked harshly, "Ain't that exactly what you're doing to 'em, Naylor?"

"Well, if you put it that way . . ."

"You know any other way to put it?" Longarm demanded.

160

One of the men in the crowd said, "I don't know who you are, mister, but I hope you've come here to stay. We need somebody like you to keep leeches like him in their place!"

"I'm a deputy U.S. marshal," Longarm told the man. "Name's Long. And I didn't come here to help you people fight Yaquis, but I'm making it my business because it's partly my fault if they do raid your town."

"By God! You're the one that caught El Griego!" the man exclaimed. "Sure. I heard about you."

Longarm turned back to Naylor. "Well, you've had time to think about what you want to do. There ain't any way I can make you sell your merchandise at a fair price, but if it was me—"

"All right, damn it, Long!" Naylor broke in. "I'll put the guns back to the price I had on them to begin with, if that'll satisfy you!"

Before Longarm could reply, a murmur of approval began swelling from the men. He said, "I guess that's your answer, Naylor. But you know, if it was up to me, I'd sort of take the sting away from what you tried to pull by throwing in at least a box of shells with every gun one of these men buys."

"Long, do you know what rifle cartridges cost me, hauled out here from Tucson?" Naylor asked. "I don't—" He became aware of the eyes fixed on him, and the silence that had settled over his potential customers, and said hastily, "I don't see how it'd hurt me to do that. Anybody who buys a gun gets a box of shells free!"

Longarm turned to the waiting men. "Now I don't want none of you to get any wrong ideas. I'm going to expect every man who's got a gun to use it, if the Yaquis jump the town."

"If we didn't intend to use 'em, we wouldn't be buying 'em, Marshal," a man in the group called. "You say the word, and we'll be there!"

When the men had trooped over to the gun rack, Longarm asked Naylor, "Where's your friend Cross, Naylor? I missed seeing him around for the past day or two. I thought you and him was pretty thick."

"Oh, Jim's around town somewhere. Come to think of it, I haven't seen him myself since sometime yesterday. Which isn't too uncommon. We're friends, but we don't live in each

161

other's back pockets, Long. Why're you asking, anyhow?"

"Oh, just curious. No real reason." Longarm took out a cheroot and touched a match to it. "Well, I think you done the right thing a minute ago, if that makes you feel any better. Now I better be on my way. It's close to suppertime, and I'm getting hungry."

Through the last touches of a crimson desert sunset, Longarm rode back to the cottage. Clarita greeted him with a happy smile. "Ees good you come back when you do, Longarm. For you tonight, I am cook *mole de pava*. Ees *herve con dolzura* seence all day. You like?"

"I don't know whether I do or not, Clarita. Can't say I ever tasted mo-lay before. What's in it?"

"Ees *pavo*—like you say, torkee—all cook with *salsa especial* unteel it so tender like *cucharro de un chiquirritin*. I theenk you like. You eat, anyhow. Ees no more *bistec*."

"Well, if that's what we're having, I'll eat it and like it, I guess," Longarm said. "But you wait till I've had a little sip of rye and set for a minute before you dish it up."

"*Seguro*. You seet down. I feex."

Longarm remembered when he tasted the *mole* that he'd had the dish before, on one of the cases that had taken him to Mexico. On that occasion, though, he'd just been starting to work on a case, and had paid so little attention to what he was eating that he hadn't known exactly what the dish was called.

Even if Clarita hadn't told him, he was sure he'd have recognized the meat as turkey; he'd brought in many a turkey to the family larder as a West Virginia boy. He wasn't so sure about the sauce. He could tell there were tomatoes in it, but he couldn't figure out what gave the smooth, creamy mixture a flavor that was piquant, peppery, bland, and slightly bittersweet, all at the same time.

It was a filling meal, though, and one he'd needed to restore his peace of mind after the day of maneuvering he'd spent in Mina Cobre. He complimented Clarita on her fine cooking and stretched out in an easy chair in the cottage parlor while she was washing the supper dishes. There was a cup of steaming coffee on the table by the chair, and he had a smoldering cheroot clamped between his strong teeth.

He heard the tattoo of hoofbeats approaching the cottage, and wondered briefly if it might be Luz returning. Instantly he realized that there'd be more than a single horse if she was coming back with a squad of cavalry from Fort Huachuca.

Then, because it was part of his business to be ready for surprise visitors who might have unfriendly ideas, he got up and stood by the table with a hand resting near his Colt while the hoofbeats stopped outside the door and he waited for the visitor to knock.

There was no knock. Clark Grady burst into the room, his lips compressed with anger. Without any preliminaries, he burst out, "Long, what in hell are you trying to do to the Copper Queen? Close me down completely?"

Longarm stared with surprise at the mine superintendent. He said, "Hold on, Grady. I ain't been around your mine since the other day, and far as I know, I ain't seen or talked to any of your men. Why, I didn't even see the guards you sent to pick up the Yaqui."

"That's where my trouble is," Grady said. "If I'd known my men were so panicked at the idea of that damned Indian being anywhere within a hundred miles of them, I never would've offered to keep him in that shed!"

"You mean to say your crews are too scared to put in a good day's work just because El Griego's locked up out there?"

"I mean they're so afraid they won't even *come* to work! I had just enough men to see me through the day, and I'm betting I won't get even half enough tomorrow to keep on schedule. And that's not all I want to talk to you about. There's a—"

"Now hold on a minute." Longarm indicated one of the easy chairs and said, "I don't see any use in us being uncomfortable, Grady. Sit down and have some coffee or a drink while you and me do some talking about all this."

Grady's initial outburst seemed to have relieved him, at least temporarily. He sat down and controlled his obvious impatience while Longarm called Clarita and asked her to bring coffee. As soon as she'd served the coffee and returned to the kitchen, he began, "Now, that other matter I want to talk to you about is these damn rumors you've been starting in Mina Cobre. Ed Naylor came over to my house this evening, which

163

is why I came all the way back out here. He's—"

"I know what he told you," Longarm interrupted. "He said I've been spreading stories around the town that the Yaquis are going to raid the place."

Grady nodded. "That's right. I told him you didn't seem to me to be the kind of man who'd pass around a lot of idle talk, but Naylor swears you've got that town standing on its head, seeing Yaqui renegades in every shadow, and generally getting the people stirred up."

Longarm grinned. "Well, I wouldn't put Naylor real high on my list of friends. Come down to it, he'd be way below the bottom. But this time he was telling the truth for a change. Sure, Grady. I dropped a few hints here and there while I was in town today, about El Griego and his Yaquis."

"You must be out of your mind, Long! Dammit, as soon as I started putting two and two together, I realized those rumors you spread are going to keep a lot of my men from reporting to work tomorrow! And I've told you how important it is for me to maintain production at the Copper Queen!"

"Now just pour yourself a drink of whisky and lean back a minute, Grady, while I explain what I'm doing, and maybe tell you a few things you don't know yet."

"Your explanation had better be a good one, Long," Grady warned. "It's going to have to pass my bosses, if they come down on me for losing tonnage."

"If they get mad, just ask 'em if they'd rather have the Copper Queen lose a little production, or not have any Copper Queen at all," Longarm suggested.

Grady sat upright, his drink forgotten. He said, "Do you really mean there's a chance of those Yaqui renegades wrecking the mine?"

"Once they find out their chief was locked up out there, I wouldn't put it past 'em. Now hold on," Longarm said quickly as Grady started to speak. "I admit that's my fault. I didn't know how many men that damned El Griego had in his bunch when I asked you to keep him safe. Hell, I didn't know he's got him an army of his own, enough men to take over six towns the size of Mina Cobre. And I started doing something about it the minute I saw what could happen. First of all, I sent Luz for help."

"A woman?" Grady asked, startled.

"Couldn't find a man for the job, and she wanted to do it. I couldn't see any danger. It'll be a while before the Yaquis can get their men all mustered together."

"She's gone to Fort Huachuca, I suppose?"

Longarm nodded. "Ought to be back with some cavalrymen late tonight or sometime tomorrow. I don't know how many men she'll bring back, maybe a squad, maybe a troop."

"All right. I feel a lot better already. What about the talk you've gotten started in town?"

Longarm took a swallow of rye and lighted a fresh cheroot before continuing. He said, "You hire a lot of men, Grady, so you ought to know how cussed human nature can be." When the mine superintendent nodded, he went on, "If I'd gone into Mina Cobre and flashed my badge and told everybody I was going to make 'em turn to and fight off a bunch of Yaquis, about half of the men in town would've told me to go to hell, and half of 'em would've had to be dragged into helping. You agree that's a pretty fair split?"

"Yes," Grady said. "I've learned that when you try to order a man to do a job, he bucks. If you ask him to, or let him just go ahead and see there's something to be done and do it, you get a lot better results. I think I'm beginning to see what you've been doing, Long."

"Well, I figured if the men there in town sort of stirred themselves up, they'd be a lot more willing. So I dropped a word here and there, and now I think things are starting to move. If I take care of the town, can you handle the Yaquis if they jump the Copper Queen?"

"I can if I don't lose any more of my guards, even without looking to the army for help. We've got all the rifles and ammunition we need."

"Let's leave it that way, then, if it suits you."

Grady nodded. "I'll settle for that, as long as you're sure you can handle your end."

"Don't worry. I'll manage."

"Then I'll go back home. I feel like I can get some sleep now. If I hadn't found out you know what you're doing, I don't think I could have."

After Grady had gone, Clarita came in from the kitchen.

"I am hear what you and Señor Grady are say. Eet will be all right, no, Longarm?"

"I'd imagine it will. Your owl give you any ideas about how this is all going to turn out, Clarita?"

She shook her head. "No. I have tell you before, ees not all time I know what ees to happen, even eef I am *bruja*." She looked at Longarm and added, "You are need to theenk, no? I weel go feex *la cama*. I wait, you come when you are ready."

Longarm sat quietly thinking while he had another drink and smoked a cheroot down to a stub. When he'd decided there was nothing more he could do until morning, he stood up, stretched, and was bending over the lamp chimney to blow out the light when once again he heard hoofbeats outside the cottage.

He remained standing by the table, his hand close to the butt of his Colt. The hoofbeats halted and footsteps sounded on the porch. Again, there was no knock. This time, though, it was Luz who came through the door.

She showed the strain of her long ride. Her face was sunburned and drawn, and tendrils of windblown hair straggled from beneath the wide brim of her hat. Her riding crop was still dangling from her wrist.

"You're tired," Longarm said quickly. "Sit down and drink some coffee, or a glass of whiskey, if you'd rather."

"Whiskey, I think," she replied. "But don't worry about me, Longarm. I'm tired, but I'm all right."

"I wasn't looking for you back tonight," he told her. "You made a real quick trip." He realized then what was lacking, and frowned. "I didn't hear but one horse. Where are the soldiers?"

"They decided to bivouac down by the lake, where there's plenty of room and water for their horses." Luz replied, sipping the whiskey he'd poured for her.

"If they need all that much room and water, there must be a good bunch of 'em," Longarm said, filling his own glass. "How many come back with you? A troop, I hope."

"No. Not a troop."

"A squad, then? Well, that'll sure be better'n nothing."

"I brought back half of the Fort Huachuca garrison," Luz told him. "Every man the fort commandant felt he could spare."

166

"Well, now!" Longarm smiled. "You done real good, I'd say. How many men in all, Luz?"

"I . . . I'm afraid you're going to be disappointed, Longarm."

Something in Luz's manner brought a frown to replace the smile on Longarm's face. He asked again. "How many men?"

"Six."

Chapter 15

Longarm stared at Luz, his mouth falling open. "Six? I thought you said you'd brought back half the Fort Huachuca garrison with you!"

"I did." Luz smiled sadly. "Fort Huachuca's been abandoned by the War Department, Longarm. The commandant— a very young lieutenant just out of West Point—showed me the orders. The last of the regulars moved two weeks ago, to forts up in the northern part of the territory. All that's left there is a clean-up detail. The lieutenant let me have half of them."

"Any of them ever do any fighting?"

"Two of them have. The others are just new recruits."

"At least they got guns, I hope. And ammunition."

"Oh, they've got carbines and cartridges and sabers. But if I were you, I wouldn't count too heavily on them."

"It's sort of hard to count on six men to be much use."

"Well, at least there'll be some uniformed cavalary. That ought to make the people in Mina Cobre feel that they're not by themselves in fighting El Griego."

"I reckon it will. And it sure ain't your fault the army didn't do better. I feel bad about sending you on that long ride for just six men, though."

"Don't. You didn't know, nobody knew. And it's not as if I came back without any soldiers at all."

"Six is sure better than none, all right."

A yawn caught Luz by surprise. She tried to bring up her hand to cover it, but didn't quite succeed. She said, "I guess it must be the whiskey making me sleepy."

"I'd be surprised if you weren't sleepy. Go on to bed. We'll go down to the lake first thing in the morning and I'll see what the soldiers look like."

"Yes. They're willing, and as you said, six are better than none. Good night, Longarm."

For a moment after Luz left, Longarm stood by the table, not sure whether he wanted to stay awake and think out a new plan to replace the one he'd schemed up such a short time ago, or whether bed was more appealing. He was still debating when Clarita padded on bare feet from the bedroom.

"Ees not good we make *cortejando* tonight, I theenk," she told him. "Weel be other times, Longarm. I sleep een my own room, no?"

"I reckon you better, Clarita. I'll see you tomorrow."

Longarm picked up his gunbelt, blew out the lamp, and went into the bedroom. He undressed in the dark and stretched out. He'd had another full day, but now felt not at all sleepy. He lighted a cheroot and lay in bed puffing it, each inhalation bringing its coal to a glow that shed a faint illumination over the room.

He tapped the ash off the cigar into the spittoon that stood beside the bed and puffed deeply, then sat upright, his hand going to the Colt that hung in its holster on the bedstead before he realized that the shimmering white form revealed in the doorway by the cheroot's glow was Luz. Releasing the huge quantity of smoke he'd inhaled involuntarily, he let his hand drop away from the pistol butt.

"I'm sorry I startled you," Luz said softly. "I...well, I guess you'd have to say I sneaked in barefoot, because I didn't want Clarita to hear me."

"It's all right. You want me to get up and light a lamp?"

"No," she said quickly. "I...I couldn't sleep. I suppose I'm too tired. I...well...I don't know how to say it..."

"Don't try to say anything, then," Longarm told her. "If you got a miserable sort of all-alone feeling, I know all about that. Just come lay down by me, if that's what you want to do."

Luz moved silently to the bed. She stood at its side and hesitated for a moment, then lay down beside Longarm. He made no move toward her. After a moment or so of silence, she said, "I thought about you a lot while I was riding to Fort Huachuca." He made no reply, and she went on after a long pause, "I don't know what there is about you, but...well, you

170

know, it's hard for a woman who's been married to get used to being without a man."

"Sure it is," he assured her.

Leaning over the edge of the bed, he stubbed out the butt of his cheroot in the spittoon. With the faint glow of the cheroot extinguished, the darkness in the room was almost total. Longarm was aware of the warmth of Luz's body next to him but not quite touching him. He could see dark blurs where her hair flowed over the pillow, and smaller blurs that were her eyes and lips, but that was all.

"I needed to be with someone. Not like the troopers I rode with from the fort, but somebody I felt I could talk to."

"Nobody likes to be alone all the time, Luz," he said. "Now, you stay here as long as you want to. If I doze off, don't let it bother you."

After a moment of silence, Luz whispered, "It's not just company I want, Longarm. It's something more."

"If you're sure about it," he said.

"Yes. I'm sure."

Longarm felt Luz stir and turned his head to look at her. He could see enough in the darkness to follow her motions. She was sitting up, her arms above her head, taking off her gown. He felt her hand, soft on his arm, as it traveled to his shoulder to finger his bandages.

"Your shoulder's not too sore?" she asked.

"It's all right. Anyhow, that ain't what you came in to ask me about, is it, Luz?"

"No. But I wondered."

"It's fine," Longarm said, turning on his side.

His head was level with Luz's breasts and he kissed the rosettes softly before trailing a line of kisses up the softness of her shoulders and across her cheek until his lips found hers. She did not open her mouth to him, but her lips were alive under his, moving and twisting.

Their bodies were touching now. Luz's hand rested for a moment on Longarm's chest and trailed slowly, almost hesitantly, down his side to rest on his hip. Her hand moved still more hesitantly across his body until he felt her touching him, her touch as soft as his flaccid member.

She turned her head to break their kiss and whispered,

171

"You're very big, aren't you? Even soft, you're big."

"Does it bother you?"

"No," she replied, a hint of doubt in her voice.

Her hand had closed around him now, and was feeling him swell in its warmth. Longarm was kissing Luz's neck now, his tongue tracing the soft, throbbing pulse he found in the hollow where her neck and shoulder joined.

She shivered softly and her hand tightened around him. He felt her muscles grow taut as she shifted her body, then felt the soft smoothness of her inner thigh as she slid it along his leg up to his hip. He turned toward her, and she began to push against him, to let him slide into her. He brought his hips forward to go in deeper, and Luz gasped with a sudden inhalation as he kept pressing forward.

"No, wait," she said, before he'd penetrated her fully. "I have to spread more to take all of you, you're so big."

"I don't want to hurt you," he told her.

"You're not. Oh, a little bit, maybe, because I've been empty a terribly long time. Even when it hurts it feels good, but I'm not used to such a big man. Put me underneath you, Longarm, so I can spread my legs wider."

Longarm lifted his hips, and Luz squirmed to lie below him. He waited until she'd brought her thighs high, along his sides, and then began to go into her again.

"Oh, that's wonderful!" she sighed. "I can feel you where it does me the most good now, so it doesn't bother me anymore that you're so long and big around."

Longarm completed his penetration with a short swift lunge, and Luz sighed even more deeply when he started to stroke, slowly and gently for fear of hurting her, until she began to move up to meet his thrusts and the sighs became a continuing moan until her muscles contracted around him and he started driving faster. Then suddenly she shook and twisted her hips, grinding them into his groin, and she was shaking, pulling herself against him, and laughing while she cried. Longarm stopped stroking and held himself against her until she'd passed through the last throes of her orgasm. He waited a moment, then began lunging once more.

"Again?" Luz whispered. "So soon?" Then the realization reached her and she asked, "You didn't finish, did you?"

"Not quite. But unless you want me to stop—"

"Stop! Of course not! Now I'm wet and slick, and it feels better to me now than it did before. Go on, Longarm! I want you to go on! Please! As deep as you can!"

Longarm began to drive again, and this time Luz responded sooner, bracing her feet beside her hips and clasping her ankles with her hands to bounce up eagerly against his sudden downward lunges, joyous bubbling laughter escaping from her throat each time their bodies met. Her sheer pleasure was contagious, and Longarm responded to it. He built far more swiftly to his own climax and was almost ready when Luz began to shudder and push her hips up to meet his with a harder, swifter rise.

When Longarm felt her beginning spasms he drove faster to hasten his, and then they were shaking in a last outburst of quivering while their final sighs of satisfaction died in the still night air and Luz flung her arms around him and pulled him with her as she sank down limply to the bed.

After they'd lain for a while, still intertwined, Luz stirred and Longarm rolled away. Her voice soft, Luz said, "I'm going to have to go back to my own room, Longarm. I want to stay here with you, but I don't dare. I can sleep now, and I'd better be in my own bed when I drop off."

"There'll be some more nights," he told her. "And both of us need to get some rest. Those troopers are used to getting up at daybreak, and I want to be waiting down there at the lake when they wake up."

A quick kiss, and Luz was gone. Longarm stretched luxuriously, and reached over to the chair for a cheroot. Before his hand found his vest, he realized how sleepy he was. He turned on his back and in three breaths was fast asleep.

Neither Luz nor Clarita was awake when Longarm left for his dawn inspection of the troopers. He slipped quietly out of the cottage and saddled the Morgan, then walked the horse from the corral and around the shore in the red-streaked beginning day. He saw the horses first, on staked tethers close to the water. Six humpy bedrolls in a relatively neat line at the lake's edge told him that the troopers were not yet awake. There was no sentry. Reining in, he lighted a cheroot and waited.

One of the men sat up and looked in every direction except

173

behind him, where Longarm was sitting on the Morgan. Still in his blankets, the trooper called, "Hey, Sarge! It's daylight, hadn't we oughta get up and stir up some grub?" There was no reply to the question, but another head popped up above the blankets, then a third, and in a moment or two all six of the men were sitting up, gazing across the quiet surface of the water.

Eventually, one of the men looked around and saw Longarm. He called, "Hey, mister, where can we find the man we're supposed to report to? If you live around here, you'd know him. He's a U.S. marshal, and there ain't likely to be more'n one of them around. His name's Long."

"I'm the one you're looking for," Longarm replied. He toed the Morgan forward, stopped by the bivouac, and swung out of his saddle. He said nothing for a moment while he eyed the group. Four of the troopers were little more than pink-cheeked boys, one was in his middle twenties and already looked like a hardcase, the third was on the way to fifty, his face tanned the hue of cordovan leather. None of the men had on shirts, so Longarm had no way of knowing which was the ranker. He asked, "Which one of you men's commanding this bunch?"

"Oi'm the CO, sor," the oldest of the men said. His brogue and his face gave away his origin even before he went on, "Timothy O'Rourke, sergeant, Fourteenth Cavalry, U.S.A., sor."

Longarm nodded. "Maybe you better start out by acquainting me with your men, Sergeant O'Rourke."

"Yes, sor." O'Rourke pointed to the oldest of the others. "Curtin, sor. He's got no rank, but he's next in service time to me, so Oi guess ye'd say he's second in command. An' there's Sloan, he's Boyd, that's Martin, and the other's Wimberly, sor."

"Combat?" Longarm asked next.

"Meself, sor," O'Rourke replied. "In the real warr an' a few scrapes with Indians. Sloan, he's fought Comanches an' Utes. Oi'm afraid the ithers are a bit raw, sor. Recruits, just joined the troop these few months past."

"You know why you're here, I guess?" Longarm asked.

"Yaquis, we were told, sor," O'Rourke answered for all of them. "And the lady told us a bit more, on the way."

"All right, you men get dressed," Longarm told them. "Then saddle up and give me a quick look at your weapons. We'll ride into town after that, and have breakfast. Save your rations for when you might need them more."

Hunkering down, Longarm lighted a cheroot and watched the men dress. O'Rourke and Sloan made quick work of getting ready; they were dressed, their bedrolls secured and their horses saddled, long before the recruits, who seemed to have a bit of trouble with almost every item of their gear. Finally the six stood by their horses, while Longarm gave their guns a quick look. O'Rourke and Sloan had Spencer carbines, while the recruits were equipped with older Ballard breech-loaders.

All the guns had been converted to metal cartridges, in .44 caliber to match the ammunition used in their Dragoon Colt revolvers. Longarm released a deep breath, almost a sigh of relief, when he found that the guns all used the same ammunition. In addition to their firearms, each man carried one of the new short sabers on his saddle pommel.

"I hope you've learned how to use that, son," Longarm told Wimberly, the youngest of the recruits, as he handed his carbine back to him. "You ever shoot at a man?"

"Well . . . no, sir," the pink-cheeked lad replied. "But I don't guess it's any different from shooting at a target."

"Just two ways, Wimberly. Targets don't shoot first, and they don't shoot back. You remember that, and you'll be all right, I hope."

"Ah, now," O'Rourke said stoutly, "they'll be all right, these boys will, sor. Oi've had the trainin' of 'em meself. They'll do what they've been taught when the toim comes, sor. You'll see."

Longarm nodded without comment; he was already planning the best way to use the six men. They were the only disciplined force he had, the only men he was reasonably sure could be depended on to stay on duty as long as O'Rourke commanded them to do so.

He completed his plans while the men ate, the only customers in the restaurant at that hour, while Mina Cobre was just waking up.

After they'd eaten he led them west of the town, to the open

175

area between the Mexicans' adobe houses and the lake, and told them to dismount. From the slight elevation, they had a clear view to the west, and could look back on the town and the huts of the Papago village in Sonoita Draw.

"We'll put Sloan here," he told O'Rourke. "The Yaquis rode in from the west last time, and I'm guessing they'll do the same thing again." He pointed to a hillock between the town and the Papago huts. "Martin will stand duty there, and we'll station Boyd on that rise past the Papagos. Wimberly can cover the east side of the draw, by the corral, and that leaves the hump just past the road on the east side, opposite to Sloan, for Curtin."

"Beggin' your pardon, Marshal Long, but what about me, sor?" O'Rourke asked.

"Your job's to patrol," Longarm replied. "Start beyond the mine and ride a quarter-mile out from your men, all around the place. Don't hurry. Watch the west, mostly, and keep an eye on your sentries to be sure they're where they're supposed to be."

"And at noight, sor?" O'Rourke frowned.

"Night and day's going to have to be the same to us for a while, Sergeant. Oh, I'll have some of the men from town come out and bring you grub and spell you for a while around noon, and somebody to stand night watch while you sleep. But those places I just showed you are going to be your home till this Yaqui thing's all settled."

"Only one thing bothers me," Sloan said gruffly. "The lady that came to Huachuca after us said you was looking for a lot of Yaquis to raid this place. You mind telling me how many Yaquis is a lot, Marshal?"

"Even if I knew the answer to that, Sloan, I ain't so sure I'd tell you. It just happens that I don't know how many we can look for. Some of the men in town allow there might be up to a hundred or more." Quickly, before the figure buffaloed the young recruits, Longarm added, "But you'll have help. When and if any of you sees the Yaquis coming, let off a shot. There'll be men in town ready to come to whichever post the shot's fired from."

"Enough to handle a hundred Yaquis?" Boyd asked nervously.

"There better be," Longarm told him, his voice grim. "If there ain't, we're all in trouble." He waited for a moment, but none of the other troopers had anything to say, so he continued, "Now, if everybody knows what to do, let's ride around and you men can take your posts."

As Longarm and O'Rourke were leaving the last post, the sergeant asked, "Where'll you be, sor, if Oi moight need to ask you a question, or somethin' of the sort?"

"I'm going to town and make sure you and your squad will be fed, Sergeant. Then I'm going to find the constable and sheriff and get your reliefs fixed up. After that... well, after that, I aim to scout to the southwest a ways, just sort of sashay a few miles out that way and see if I can smell anything that stinks like a Yaqui."

Passing the cantina on his way into Mina Cobre, Longarm saw Carvajal's horse standing at the hitch rail. He reined up and went inside. The sheriff came rushing up to him the instant he shoved through the batwings. Today, Carvajal's shirt was the color of an overripe orange.

"Marshal!" Carvajal exclaimed. "Is it true what I have heard?"

"Depends on what you heard and who told you, I'd imagine. Just what'd you hear?"

"That the soldiers you promised would be here to protect us from the Yaquis are only six! And that there will be no more!"

"Well, six is better'n none, Carvajal."

"But the Yaquis, there will be hundreds of them!"

"All the more reason why you better get as many of your *gente* together as you can. You get every man you know who's got a gun, and tell him he's going to help the soldiers when the Yaquis get here."

"How can I persuade my *gente* to fight against such odds?" the sheriff demanded.

"Mainly by telling 'em what'll happen if they *don't* fight. Now, your people are damn good fighters, I've fought along-side 'em more than once. And one way you're going to get the rest of this town to respect you is to hold up your end of this thing. Otherwise, you're going to see men like Barney

177

Trent kicking their asses all up and down the street. You make 'em see that, and you won't have any trouble."

Leaving the sheriff staring at his retreating back, Longarm walked out of the cantina.

As he'd expected, he found Barney Trent in Naylor's store. The constable, the storekeeper, and Jim Cross had their heads together back in Naylor's private corner. They looked up as Longarm approached them.

"Damned if you're not the biggest fraud I ever saw, Long!" Naylor greeted him. "Promise us soldiers and give us six! From the way you've been talking, all you had to do was crook your finger and the army'd come running! Well, what're you going to do now?"

"Just about what I figured to do all along, Naylor. Get the men in this town together and be ready to fight if El Griego's Yaquis come riding in."

"Oh, they'll come in, all right," Cross said. "Mainly because you've got El Griego tucked away someplace and they want to get him loose. Why don't you be smart, Long? Let the Yaqui son of a bitch go, and save a lot of trouble for everybody."

"*Make* a lot of trouble for everybody is what you're saying, Cross," Longarm replied. "If you think letting El Griego go is going to keep the Yaquis from raiding Mina Cobre, now or any other time, then you must've been hiding behind your mama's petticoats when the brains were passed out. They're going to keep raiding until you beat the shit out of 'em."

"That sounds fine, Long," Trent said. "Now tell us the rest of it. How're we going to whip a couple of hundred Yaquis with what few men we got to fight 'em?"

"It ain't how many men we got. It's how good their guns are," Longarm told the constable. "Most of the renegades' guns are old Mexican Army smooth-bores that won't carry fifty yards, or hit the side of a barn. Most of our men got good repeaters with two or three times that much range." He turned to Naylor. "And if you want to keep the Yaquis from burning you out, you'll see the men from town have got all the ammunition they need."

"Who's going to pay for it?" Naylor asked.

"Just pass out the cartridges and worry about getting paid

for 'em later," Longarm replied. "Now, Trent, here's what I want you to do."

Quickly, Longarm sketched the jobs the men from Mina Cobre would be expected to handle, supplementing the cavalrymen at the sentry posts, and keeping themselves ready to rush to whatever point the Yaquis attacked. Grudgingly, Trent agreed to see that the citizens would carry their share of the load.

"Looks to me like you got a job for everybody but yourself, Long," Cross said skeptically when the planning was completed. "What're you going to be doing, if you don't mind telling us?"

Longarm repeated what he'd told O'Rourke. "I'll be scouting around six or eight miles to the southwest. If we know which way El Griego's bunch is coming from, and when, we'll be able to put our men where they need to be. We do that, and half the fight's won before the first shot gets fired."

Wish I felt as sure about this fight as I let those men think I was Longarm told himself as he rode around the lake toward the cottage after leaving Mina Cobre. It'd be a lot different if I could trust Trent and Carvajal to do their jobs right, because if either one of 'em don't hold up their end of the deal, this town's going to be up shit creek without a paddle. But I'm doing about as good as I can with what little bit I got, and if a man plays his best cards and adds a little bluff to his calls, he's got a good chance to rake in the pot, when all the chips are down.

Longarm felt a glacial atmosphere in the cottage the instant he stepped inside. Luz was dusting the parlor furniture. She greeted him with a cool "hello" tossed over her shoulder, and kept on with her work as though he was not in the room.

Ignoring the chill in her voice, but guessing the reason for it, he asked, "Where's Clarita?"

"In the kitchen, where she belongs," Luz answered without turning around to look at him.

Going to the kitchen door, Longarm saw Clarita stirring some sort of mixture at the table. He said, "Clarita?"

"Qué quiere, Señor Long?" she asked, keeping her eyes on the bowl she held.

179

"I want to talk to you and Luz. Come on in the parlor."

"Es imposible. Es necesario que cuidar a mí trabajo," she said. Like Luz, she did not look up at him.

"Clarita," Longarm said sternly, "get in the parlor right this minute! I don't care what you're doing!"

Her lips pressed into a thin line, Clarita brushed past him without looking at him and stopped just inside the parlor door. She did not appear to see Luz, and Luz ignored her.

"Now, I don't care what kind of fuss you two've been having," Longarm told them. "Whatever it is, you can work it out later on."

"We do not need your help to settle anything," Luz said with a vein of ice in her voice. "It is between Clarita and me."

"Fine. I'll leave it that way," Longarm told her. "Right now, I want both of you to get out of here. This place ain't safe for you, and won't be till we've beat off the Yaquis. Grady told me you've got places to go to in town, so start for 'em this minute. And don't come back here till I say you can."

Both Luz and Clarita looked as though they were about to protest, but both remembered in time that they were not on speaking terms with him. They exchanged cool looks, then Luz left by the front door, Clarita by the back.

A few moments later, Longarm stood by the corral, watching them on their way to town—Luz on her pony, Clarita on the burro. He shook his head and grinned. Then his face grew grim, and he swung into the saddle and headed the Morgan southwest to go and look for Yaquis.

Chapter 16

A man on horseback in the desert has a horizon seven miles distant; in flat country with no high vantage points, this is the limit of his vision at any given instant. Longarm had ridden south from the Copper Queen until the top of the big Eclipse railroad windmill was no longer visible, then had gone an additional three or four miles before turning the Morgan's head west. He'd ridden through the afternoon without seeing any signs of Yaquis, seeing nothing move except an occasional lizard scurrying for a shady spot at the edge of a rock, a buzzard soaring on solitary high patrol in the bright, cloudless sky, and a tarantula or two legging it across a patch of bare soil.

He had not pushed the Morgan, but had let the horse set its own pace. Only occasionally did he touch the reins to angle its course toward a canyon mouth or around a mesa or one of the high sandstone formations that might be used as cover by an advancing raiding force.

Before beginning his ride, Longarm had stopped for a brief visit with Grady, to make sure the mine's defenses were in order, and to check on El Griego. He'd wasted no time trying to talk to the Yaqui renegade, but had unlocked the small sheet-metal shed that was being used as a prison and glanced inside. El Griego had been sitting on the floor, leaning against the shed's back wall, his knees drawn up to his chin. He'd said nothing to Longarm, but the glare of hatred that flashed from his obsidian eyes had carried its own message.

With the first hint of sunset now staining the western sky in wide, faint streaks of orange-yellow between sun and earth, Longarm decided the time had come to turn back. The wide, shallow arc he'd covered extended from five or six miles south of the Copper Queen, into the desert for perhaps an additional

181

five miles at the extreme edge of its curve, and northeast until he reached the stretch of broken country seven or eight miles west of Mina Cobre.

At the beginning of the leached-out stretch of desert, cut by ridges and seamed by arroyos, he'd decided that not even a Yaqui force would spend the time required to cross it, and had reversed his course, heading southeast parallel to his earlier path but some five or six miles beyond it, to widen the arc he was scouting.

His military maps were of little help; most of the landmarks it showed were marked simply "mesa" or "canyon," and in the desert one canyon looked like the next; one mesa could not be distinguished from another. By his rough reckoning, Longarm was now perhaps fifteen miles from Mina Cobre in a crow's-flight line, and twenty if he included the detours he'd been forced to make in order to avoid the canyons and isolated, towering mesas that lay between him and the town.

Though he had not covered every square foot of the area, he'd seen no signs of a fresh trail that would have been left by a large group of Yaqui fighting men. If El Griego's followers were indeed on their way to rescue their chief, he was sure they had not gotten close enough for an immediate strike.

Reining in, Longarm stood up in the stirrups to extend his range of vision while he picked the best route back to town. He noted the areas offering the smoothest ground, picked his path, and was settling down into the saddle when he glanced behind him. He blinked and took a second look. Three or four miles away, short of the rim of the horizon, he saw a flicker of movement between the mesas.

Still standing in the stirrups, Longarm turned the Morgan with a few quick jabs of his boot toe in the animal's belly. He stared at the spot where he'd seen the momentary motion, wondering if his fleeting glimpse had been an illusion. For all he'd been able to tell during the few seconds when the movement caught his eyes, it could have been the rising of a buzzard from feeding or the low, ground-hugging swoop of a little cactus-dwelling elf owl darting down on a mouse or desert shrew.

Several hundred yards away, the hard-baked soil humped to form a low hillock. Longarm settled down and headed for it. When the Morgan reached its rounded top, he stood up again to look. He'd almost decided that what he'd seen had been a bird when the rim of the horizon was suddenly broken, and the jagged forms he saw against the sunset in silhouette became the unmistakable outlines of horsemen.

Longarm watched them through slitted eyes. There was no other large band of horsemen, except El Griego's Yaquis, that could have been riding toward Mina Cobre.

If there had been any room for doubt in his mind, it was banished in the next few seconds when the scout whose movements had first caught his attention came into full view around the base of the mesa the man had been circling.

Longarm and the scout saw one another at the same time. The man was far out of rifle range and Longarm did not waste time or a bullet on him, but as he turned the Morgan's head north, he heard the Yaqui's rifle bark, a signal to the main band.

For the next two or three miles, Longarm devoted his full attention to the terrain ahead, then he looked back to get an idea of the number of his pursuers. He guessed there were at least a hundred and fifty horsemen riding after him, more than double the number of defenders that Mina Cobre could muster.

He was turning his head away after his quick count when he saw the Yaquis splitting into two groups, a maneuver designed to trap him in a crossfire. Within the next quarter-hour he learned that this had not been the Yaquis' only purpose. Less than a mile away, the horizon split in two. The irregular edge of a long ridge lay just ahead and formed a false horizon. Beyond it the real horizon stretched to the end of his vision.

You been outfoxed, old son, Longarm told himself. Those damn Yaquis know this country better'n you do. They knew about that drop-off, and now they're herding you like a steer to a place where they can turn you into dead meat.

Risking a trade of distance and time for knowledge, Longarm rode to the very edge of the ridge and looked along it in both directions. Below the rim, the face of the cliff was almost vertical as far as he could see, and neither to right nor left could he see an end to the ridgeline.

There was no choice of direction and no time left to waste. Stopping at the edge of the cliff had already cost him half the lead he'd had on his pursuers. Longarm made the best of a bad bargain. He pulled the reins to send the Morgan on a long slanting course to the left, and heeled the Morgan's flanks to bring its pace to a full gallop as he began trying to outrace the Yaquis on that side to the rim.

His course set, Longarm looked back again. The Yaquis now flanked him on both sides. While he watched, the two straggling columns of horsemen changed their course to follow the new direction in which he was moving. He widened the angle at which he was approaching the ridge, but even as he changed direction he could see that the odds were in favor of the Yaquis.

Though the Morgan was already going at an all-out gallop, Longarm tried to urge a bit more speed from the animal. He knew most horses of the breed could outrun anything except a quarter horse for short distances, but knew also that it could sustain a full gallop for a relatively short while. The horse was still breathing well, showing no signs of strain, but Mina Cobre was still more than ten miles away, and Longarm did not need to remind himself that his life depended on the Morgan's ability to cover the full distance.

Looking ahead, he saw that the Yaqui band had turned toward him. The Indians had begun to string out now, the faster ponies outrunning the slower ones as they raced to cut across his course at right angles, before he could gallop between them and the rim of the ridge.

Still farther ahead, the ridge line stretched as far as Longarm could see. He glanced over his shoulder; the Yaquis coming from that direction were within rifle shot of the ridge, effectively preventing him from doubling back.

A quarter of a mile now separated Longarm from the drop-off on his right. He edged closer to the rim, hoping he'd see a slope down which the Morgan might slide, but nowhere did he see a slope or any spot where the drop-off was not vertical.

Having no other choice, Longarm kept galloping straight ahead along the edge of the drop-off. He pulled his Winchester from its saddle scabbard as he drew closer to the Yaquis in front of him, gauged the range, and let off a round at the Indians.

He shot low, aiming at the horses instead of the men. It

was not mercy that guided his aim; one dead Yaqui out of so many would not hold up their chase, but a horse dropped in the Indian line could cause three or four of the Yaquis behind it to fall, and create confusion and delay.

With his second shot, Longarm brought down a horse, and the three riders behind it could not swerve in time to avoid the falling beast. They piled up in a thrashing of flying hooves, and the Yaquis behind them lost time as they were forced to swing wide off their straight-line course to avoid the tangle.

Encouraged, Longarm fired again. It took him three shots this time to drop another horse, but the resulting collisons and falls were worth the shells expended. Now he shifted his aim to the Yaquis at the head of the band. Two shots dropped one of the leading horses, but the Indians had fanned out by now, and the falling animal brought down only one other with it.

Suddenly the Morgan shied, almost throwing Longarm. He'd been paying no attention to the terrain ahead. Now he looked and saw a narrow crevasse, wide enough to jump, but not wide enough to accommodate a rider, running in the direction of the rim.

It was an outside chance, but the only chance he had. He dropped from the saddle and led the Morgan to the crack. The horse planted its forefeet on the edge of the opening and refused to step into it. Pulling off his hat, Longarm brought it down in a series of wide swings against the Morgan's rump, while he yelled at the top of his voice for the horse to go.

For another moment the horse refused to move, then it took the plunge and let itself into the gully. Longarm watched as it started a neighing slide down the little arroyo, before turning his attention back to the Yaquis.

By now they'd gotten close enough for Longarm to be within range of their outdated rifles. Lead began singing around him, but the antiquated rifles of the Indians were far outranged by Longarm's flat-shooting Winchester. The Yaquis were still firing from the saddle, while Longarm was standing with his feet planted on solid ground, getting off aimed, accurate shots that set the Indian mounts to milling as one and then another went down.

Longarm waited until he'd brought down one more Indian pony, then followed the Morgan down the crevasse. His legs

185

spraddled wide, one foot on either side of the narrow arroyo's walls, Longarm half-ran, half-skidded to the bottom. The Morgan was standing at the base of the ridge. Its legs were shaking and it had a few chafed spots on its rump, but as far as Longarm could tell, it had not really been hurt during its sliding plunge.

With the Yaquis' yells now reaching his ears, Longarm swung on the Morgan's back and beelined away from the cliff. The Yaquis got to the rim in time to pepper the air around him with lead slugs, but within a few minutes he'd galloped out of range. He pulled the Morgan's pace down to a steady canter and turned its head toward Mina Cobre just as the top rim of the sun vanished under the horizon and the long desert twilight began.

Sloan's sentry station, between the town and the lake, was the closest to the route Longarm took back. He reached the edge of the lake as dusk was deepening, and rode up the gentle slope where the cavalryman sat staring across the desert.

"I was pretty damned sure that was you on the Morgan that I seen streaking this way, but I couldn't be sure in the bad light," Sloan said as Longarm dismounted. "You run into anything on your scout, or was you just in a hurry to get back in time for supper?"

"A little bit of both. We'd all better have an early supper tonight, because there's about a hundred or so of El Griego's Yaquis heading this way. They're still ten miles or so out on the desert, but they'll be here in the next couple of hours."

"You want me to give the signal?" Sloan asked.

"I reckon you better. The sooner our men get in place, the better shape we'll be in to stand 'em off."

Sloan picked up his carbine and fired a shot into the air. "I hope them civilians ain't forgot what that means," he said.

"We'll know pretty soon."

Longarm lighted a cheroot and hunkered down to wait. The cavalryman joined him after a moment, and together they stared out across the desert while the last traces of daylight faded away.

"You expect them Yaquis to start shooting as soon as they get here?" he asked Longarm.

"They didn't come all this way just for the ride."

"Most redskins don't like to fight in the dark. Superstitious or something. Comanches, now, they don't even like to *move* at night. Say it's bad medicine. What about the Yaquis?"

"They didn't mind the dark when they raided the Papagos a little while ago," Longarm said. "Of course, they didn't do a hell of a lot of harm, either, for all the lead they used up."

"Well, I been waiting all day for something to happen," Sloan said. "Looks like it's finally about to."

A shout broke the darkness behind them. Sloan answered and in a moment Tim O'Rourke rode up. "Oi hope ye meant that signal shot ye let off, Sloan," the sergeant said. "The civilians are on their way from town. They'll be moighty mad if ye got 'em up here on a woild-goose chase."

"It wasn't a fool's shot, O'Rourke," Longarm said. "I just rode in maybe ten miles ahead of the Yaquis."

"If that's the way of it, sor, then Oi'd better go on to the ither posts, and tell the men to be ready."

Longarm nodded. "You do that, Sergeant. And tell 'em the Yaquis will be coming in from the southwest. Remind 'em to aim a bit in front of the Yaqui's muzzle blasts if they don't want to be just wasting lead."

"Yes, sor Oi'll do that. And Oi'll be puttin' meself in whatever place Oi'm needed most, after the foightin' starts."

Five men from Mina Cobre, all strangers to Longarm, arrived soon after O'Rourke had left. Only one of the newcomers had seen any military service, and Longarm and Sloan shared the job of telling the others what to expect, what to do and what not to do, when and if the Yaquis attacked. They were still giving the novices bits of good advice when the drumming of many hoofbeats broke the stillness of the night and grew to a loud rumble.

"By God, they're here!" Sloan said. "Sounds like a damn big bunch of 'em, too!"

"There's enough," Longarm replied absently. He was peering through the gloom, looking for a target. "Remember, they most likely don't know we're waiting for 'em. Watch the sky, and when you see something come between you and the stars, shoot!"

For a few tense minutes the little party waited, lying prone on the slight rise of Sonoita Draw. The heavy drumming of hoofbeats died away, but there were still sounds of riders moving about in the darkness on the flat in front of them. Following his own advice, Longarm watched the sky. He saw a dark outline against it, aimed quickly, and fired. Immediately the silence and the darkness were broken by a ragged volley of rifle fire and the red flare of muzzle blasts.

Longarm had rolled away from the spot where he'd been lying when he fired. He waited for a muzzle blast to flash in front of him, saw one, and let off a round on either side of the spot where it had cut the night. On both sides of him, Sloan and the civilians were firing too. Ahead, the Yaqui guns kept up a broken crackle of shots in a line that extended from the lake to beyond the Papago village.

Whether it was the effect of finding the town ready to meet what the Yaqui renegades had planned as a surprise attack, or whether the defenders' shooting had been effective, Longarm was never to know. The Yaqui rifles spoke at less frequent intervals and soon died away altogether. The hoofbeats no longer thudded from the flat, and silence returned to the night.

"By God, we druv 'em off," one of the Mina Cobre men said, huge satisfaction bulging in his voice. "I bet if we could see out on the flat, there'd be a whole damn pile of dead Yaquis!"

"You're just about right, Tom," one of the other novices agreed. "Them renegades is running for the border right now like a bunch of whupped puppies!"

"I don't aim to start no arguments with you men," Longarm said quietly, "but I been in fights like this before. It's my bet there's maybe a half-dozen Yaquis been hit, and maybe three or four killed. Night shooting's chancey at best, and that's what fools a lot of folks."

"You think that's right, Perk?" the man who'd spoken first appealed to the civilian who'd seen battle. "Or is the marshal just trying to flamboozle us?"

"My money's on the marshal," Frank replied. "I seen a few night brushes myself, and it's just about the way he says it is. But I don't reckon we'll know, because if these Yaquis is like other redskins, they'll haul away the ones that's got hurt or killed."

"You men might as well figure on staying here the rest of

188

the night," Sloan put in. "What I know about Yaquis ain't much, but you can bet on one thing. Even if they lost a few, they ain't going to give up this easy. Just don't get happy too soon. Chances are, they'll try again after a while."

After a while the Yaquis did try again, but with smaller forces. Gunfire crackling from the east side of the town told the defenders the reason; Mina Cobre, the Papago village, and the Mexican settlement were now encircled, and the Yaqui forces were spread thinner than they'd been during the first attack.

"Sounds like they got us ringed in," Sloan commented, cocking an expert's ear at the sounds of the rifles barking in the darkness.

"Sure. They'll wait till day light now, and then try a rush or two," Longarm predicted.

For the first time, the men from the town seemed worried. One of them asked, "You think we can hold 'em off? Far as I know, there's only about sixty of us."

"We'll hold 'em off," Longarm assured him. "There ain't but a few Yaquis that's got what you'd call good rifles. Our guns outrange 'em, and unless somebody along the line pulls a fool stunt, they won't get near enough to do all that much damage."

"You'd think them bastards up at the Copper Queen would be here helping us," a Mina Cobre man complained. "They got all the guards and rifles they need up there, I guess, and they don't give much of a shit about us."

"They'll be doing well enough if they keep the Yaquis away from the mine," Longarm said quietly. "And I'd imagine there's a little ruckus going on up there too, right about now."

"Just the same, they oughta be giving us some help."

"They're helping us just by being there," Longarm reminded him. "If the Yaquis hadn't had to split up, there'd be enough of 'em down here to give us real trouble."

Slowly the firing died down, except for an occasional nervous shot from somewhere around the perimeter of the ragged line the men from town were holding. When an hour or more had passed without another mass attack, Longarm stood up.

"Looks like it's settling down," he told the others. "They might try another rush in an hour or so, when the moon comes up, but not much is apt to happen till then. You men better get some sleep while things are quiet."

"What're you going to do, Marshal?" Sloan asked.

"As long as things stay this way, you men can hold this place without me. I'll just take a little sashay around and see if I can find out what's happening."

There was very little happening anywhere he looked. He walked the Morgan slowly, moving behind the firing line. In the dense darkness he could occasionally see one of the defenders, sitting or lying on the ground. The Yaquis were invisible, but a random shot came from their position now and then, which the defenders seldom bothered to answer.

Until the shooting dwindled away, Longarm had not thought of either food or a cheroot. Now he quickly became aware of the distress signals his stomach was sending out. Rummaging in his saddlebags, he pulled out a stick of jerky and chewed it as he rode. His stomach had quit growling by the time his slow progress brought him to the Papago village, but he kept his hands away from the pocket where he carried his cheroots. The cigar's glowing tip might draw fire, and he reminded himself that he'd been intending to quit for maybe the tenth time this year, anyhow.

Above the Papago village he splashed across the narrow stream that ran down the center of the draw, and had almost reached the road to Mina Cobre when he heard the slow hoofbeats of another rider coming toward him. Reining in, Longarm waited.

"That you, Marshal?" O'Rourke's voice reached him from the darkness just as the sergeant became visible in front of him.

"It's me, O'Rourke."

"Thought it moight be, sor." O'Rourke pulled up his horse as he came abreast. "Couldn't think of anybody else who'd be patrolling around."

"Figured it's as good a time as any for a look-see. There likely won't be anything happen until moonrise."

"So Oi was thinking meself. It's when there's loight enough to shoot by that the redskins will be savin' their powder for."

"What's it like, the way you've come from?" Longarm asked. "Anybody get hurt?"

190

"There was a man killed at Wimberly's post, sor. That was when the fight first started. And three wounded, but not too bad. The ladies from town are takin' care of them in the saloon." O'Rourke looked at the sky, brightening now, though the moon had not yet shown above the horizon. "Oi'm thinkin' we moight not be that lucky after it loightens up, though."

"Afraid you're right. Well, there's no use me covering the rest of the line, if you've just come along it. I'll stop at the saloon for a look and a drink and then get back to the others before moonrise."

"Oi've had my tot, so Oi'll be movin' along. At least to have a look at Boyd and Martin. Sloan's no recruit, he won't be needin' me to cheer him up."

Longarm reached the road and turned onto it, toward town. Mina Cobre was dark except for a faint light coming from the saloon. He tossed the Morgan's reins over the hitch rail and went inside. He blinked with astonishment. Luz was sitting at one of the tables, two other women with her. Along the wall, the three wounded men lay on quilts spread on the floor. All of them were sleeping.

"Luz!" Longarm said. "I didn't look to find you here."

"It is Eusebio's father, Don Diego. He is wounded. They sent word to me, and I came to care for him. He is not a young man. I worried about him."

"I hope he ain't hurt bad."

"He isn't. A flesh wound in the arm. In a day or two he will be recovered." She gestured toward the batwings. "What is happening out there, Longarm? We have heard almost no shooting for more than an hour."

"It's just been too dark for shooting. We can't see the Yaquis, they can't see us."

Longarm went behind the bar and took down the bottle of Maryland rye. He didn't wait to look for a glass, but tilted the bottle to his lips. Luz had followed him to the bar, and the other women were watching them without trying to hide their curiosity. Longarm lighted a cheroot and took another swallow of the rye.

"You'd better be out there with the others, fighting the Yaquis, than swilling that devil's brew!" one of the women said.

191

Luz whirled to face her and retorted angrily, "This man is the federal marshal who's responsible for anybody at all being out there fighting the Yaquis! You should thank him instead of finding fault with him!"

"Now that's all right, Luz. The lady didn't know."

"What's going to become of us, Marshal?" the other woman asked. "Are the Yaquis going to kill all of us and cut off our scalps and burn our houses?"

"Oh, I don't reckon that's going to happen, ma'am," Longarm said cheerfully, much more cheerfully than he felt. "We'll hold off the Yaquis all right, but there's going to be a lot more shooting before this is finished."

As though his words had called for them, a ragged volley of shots sounded outside. The two women jumped from their chairs and ran to the batwings, peering out into the darkness. Longarm hurried to the door, pushed his way between the women, and swung into the saddle. A sliver of moon was showing above the horizon's rim. The volume of firing increased as the town's defenders began responding to the new Yaqui attack.

"Longarm!" Luz called. He turned to look back, and as he heeled the Morgan down the street she raised her voice so that her parting words reached him.

"Be careful, Longarm!" she called. "I want you to come back to me!"

Chapter 17

Before Longarm reached the sentry post, the rifle fire from the Yaquis had dwindled to an occasional stray shot. Sloan was lying prone, carefully spacing his shots. The men from town were strung out in a line on both sides of the trooper, shooting more enthusiastically, all but the combat veteran getting off two or three shots to each one Sloan fired.

Sliding his rifle out of its saddle scabbard, Longarm found there was barely light enough to aim by, but let off a pair of shots at two of the blurred, shadowy forms he saw moving among the Indians. Over his sights, he saw that the vague forms of the renegades were growing smaller and even more blurred, and realized they were retreating.

"Hold up, men!" he called. "No use wasting good ammunition. They're pulling back now!"

"How come them worthless bastards jumped the gun, anyhow?" the man named Frank asked complainingly. "They wasn't supposed to do nothing till the moon was full up!"

"They figured that's what we'd all be thinking, mister," Sloan said. The barely disguised tolerance of the professional soldier for the civilian novice showed in his tone. "All they was doing was trying to keep one jump ahead of us. Lucky we was ready, or they'd be all over us about now."

"He's right, Frank," Perk said. "You got to think a leetle bit ahead of the other fellow when you're in a ruckus like this."

"Well, this is the first one I been in like this," Frank retorted. "And far's I'm concerned, it can be the last one!"

"Better not talk like that till we wind this one up," Longarm cautioned. He moved up to join the others. "But they've tested us out now, and found out they couldn't catch us napping. I got a hunch they'll let us alone till daylight."

Longarm's hunch was correct. The Yaquis had pulled back far beyond rifle range, following their aborted surprise attack. When the moon waned at the approach of day, and the gray pre-sunrise light revealed the flat desert area around the town, Longarm could see that during the night the Indians had apparently scouted the defense areas selected by him and O'Rourke, and had formed their forces in groups around Mina Cobre, the Mexican adobes, and the Papago village.

Looking along the bank of the draw, Longarm saw a cluster of the attackers roughly opposite the two defensive positions that were visible from where he stood. There were about an equal number of Yaquis in each of the groups. The Indian encirclement was far from being an unbroken line, but in spite of that, it very effectively surrounded the town and its subsidiary settlements and enclosed the defenders.

He could also see what the darkness had hidden: that the Yaquis had surrounded the Copper Queen as well. The distance was too great for details to be visible, but there were Indians on ponies sca red along the low bluff on which the mine buildings stood, and the figures of men milling around could be made out. So could the puffs of powder smoke that blossomed now and then like miniature white clouds from the buildings and the area surrounding them.

Sloan had also observed the evidence that the Copper Queen was being beseiged. He remarked to Longarm as they stood looking at the activity around the mine, "That might be what saved our bacon last night. Bastards had to split their force to handle the town and the mine."

"How many of 'em you figure's in that bunch up at the mine, Sloan?" Longarm asked.

Sloan studied the distant figures for a moment. "Fifty, at least. Maybe sixty or more."

"About what I guessed," Longarm nodded. "I been tallying how many we got out in front of us here, and I make it to be right around twenty. It looks to me like there's about that many in the other bunches along the draw north of us."

"That'd make a hundred or so," Sloan said.

"Give or take a few," Longarm agreed. "Take in that bunch up at the mine, and that's a hundred and fifty, which is close enough to make no never-mind to how many I figured when they jumped me yesterday."

"Pretty big odds, with only five or six of us at each post," Sloan observed. "They'd've had us last night if they'd knowed how bad we're outnumbered."

"They know now. I look for 'em to try again, soon as they can put their heads together and get something planned out."

"They're sure to," the trooper agreed. He looked around and pointed to the peak of the low slope that ran up to the edge of Sonoita Draw. "If it was up to me, I'd pull back from where we are now, and get on the other side of the hump, down in the draw. It ain't a trench, but it's a hell of a sight better than where we are right now."

Longarm looked where Sloan was pointing. "Hell," he said, "let's do it. And while you're getting set there, I'll ride on up the line and see that the others do the same thing, if they ain't already figured it out for themselves."

While Sloan and the others moved back to the better-protected position, Longarm rode up to the next defense post. Trooper Martin and his seven civilians were still where they'd been during the night, on the downslope facing the Yaquis.

"You and your bunch better get behind the edge of the draw," he told the young cavalry trooper. "Scrooch down behind it, and you'll be less apt to take a bullet."

"We got along all right last night," Martin said. "Held the redskins off our post."

"Day and night ain't quite the same thing, son," Longarm told the youth. "Last night they were shooting blind. When they come at you next, they'll be aiming."

"He's right, by God!" one of the civilians put in. "Come on, boys! Let's move!"

Longarm watched them for a moment as the found places on the safe side of the draw, then rode on.

As he approached the post north of the Papago village, Longarm saw Carvajal pacing angrily around Boyd, waving his arms at the young trooper. When the sheriff noticed Longarm riding up, he left Boyd and came to meet Longarm. Today, Carvajal's shirt was black silk.

"You are here just in time, Marshal Long!" Carvajal exclaimed. "What kind of men do you have as soldiers in your army?"

"Pretty much the same kind you'll find in any army, I'd imagine, Carvajal. Why? What's the trouble?"

"This young man is most obstinate!" Carvajal sputtered. "He refuses to obey my commands! You will please tell him who I am, and that by virtue of my position, I am in command here!"

Longarm lighted a cheroot before replying, Then he said, "Well now, Sheriff, I'd better find out both sides of this business before I start butting in. Mind telling me what you ordered him to do?"

"He insists that we crouch down behind the crest of that rise and sit there like stones. He says he will do nothing else until the sergeant of your federal cavalry arrives to give him orders!"

"That ain't what I asked you," Longarm reminded the sheriff.

"We are brave men, Marshal, my *gente* and me!" Carvajal said. "We wish to fight like men, not act like lizards who seek safety by hiding!"

For the first time, Longarm looked closely at the half-dozen men standing beside Boyd; all of them were Mexicans.

Carvajal continued, "We have our guns! The Yaquis are there in front of us! I have told him that we must attack them before they overwhelm us!"

"Maybe I better take a look at what kind of guns your men have got, Carvajal," Longarm suggested.

He dismounted and went to where Boyd and the Mexicans were standing. Two of them held rifles so old and battered that Longarm did not recognize their origin. Another carried a Gras rifle that had been made for the army of the third Napoleon. The other three guns were also French, Chassepot rifles at least thirty years old, relics of the French occupation of Mexico under Louis Napoleon. All the weapons were as limited in range as most of the rifles the Yaquis were using.

Longarm did not want to damage the morale of the defenders or anger the sheriff; the volatile Carvajal might storm away, taking his men with him. He looked at Boyd. The young recruit lifted his eyebrows and shook his head.

"Let's you and me step over here and have a little talk," Longarm suggested to Carvajal. He led the sheriff aside, out of earshot of the others. Pitching his voice to a low, confidential tone, he said, "Don't blame young Boyd for not doing what you wanted him to, Carvajal. He can't take orders from nobody except a U.S. cavalry officer. Now, I know you and your *gente* want to wipe up on the Yaquis, but storming out at 'em ain't the best way to do it right this minute. We'll hurt 'em more if we hold on and let them try to get to us."

"But that is not the way brave men fight!" Carvajal protested. "We must charge them! Yes, charge them with our guns blazing!"

"Sure. And we'll most likely be doing that, later on. But for right now, you and your *gente* just do what the rest of us are doing. Wait for the Yaquis to attack, then fight 'em off."

"You are sure this is what everyone else is doing?" the sheriff asked.

"I'm sure."

"Then no one can say we are cowards if we do the same."

"Not a bit of it! Now, I got to be getting along. You just do what the trooper says, and stick tight here, and we'll get around to going out after the Yaquis later on."

"Very well, Marshal. As long as I know it is the proper thing to do."

"It is, Carvajal," Longarm assured him. "And don't worry about what anybody says. You'll know you're doing what you'd ought to."

Longarm mounted and rode on. He was about halfway between Boyd's post and the one manned by Wimberly, opposite the Papago village, when the Yaquis attacked.

No warning preparations, no war-whoops, preceded the attack. Since first daylight, when Longarm had started watching them, the Yaquis had never dismounted. There had been a few who'd gotten off, but most of the Indians had stayed aboard their ponies. In response to some signal only they understood, the entire Yaqui band began galloping toward the defense positions.

Sunup had made it possible for Longarm to watch Wimberly's outpost, a quarter-mile ahead of him on the east bank of the draw. He saw the six or seven men grab their rifles and begin firing even before the thudding of the onrushing Yaquis registered on his ears. At the same time a crackle of gunfire from Boyd's position sounded behind him. He glanced at the renegade force and saw it sweeping toward Wimberly's post, a solid line of riders.

Wimberly's men were putting up a good defense. While he

was whipping his rifle from the scabbard he saw a horse go down, and a moment later one of the Yaquis dropped off his mount. Longarm took careful aim with his Winchester at the nearest Yaqui, and squeezed off a shot. The Indian fell forward over the neck of his mount and, a few seconds later, slid off while the horse kept galloping ahead.

Looking for his second target, Longarm saw over his sights that his first shot had drawn the attention of the Yaquis riding behind the man he'd just dropped. Two of them left the main band and started galloping toward him. Gunfire was sounding on all sides now—faint shots from across the draw, louder reports from the posts closer to him.

These details registered on Longarm's mind unconsciously while he was picking his next target. He fixed the vee of his rifle sight on the closest of the two Yaquis galloping toward him, and brought the man down.

Without taking the rifle from his shoulder, he swiveled to pick off the second rider. The quick shot was low. The Yaqui's horse pitched forward, but the rider rolled to his feet and ran to get on the horse that had been ridden by the Indian felled by Longarm's first bullet. The main Yaqui band was closing in on the outpost now, and the Indians began bunching up, preparing to sweep over the rise. Longarm kicked the Morgan into a gallop as the Yaqui riders got within pistol shot of the crest that sheltered the defenders.

He was still a long rifle shot distant when he saw O'Rourke stand up. The sergeant had discarded his slow-loading carbine and drawn his heavy Colt Dragoon revolver. Longarm saw the trooper jerk under the impact of a bullet just as O'Rourke's first shot toppled the Yaqui in the lead of the band. Taking deliverate aim each time he fired, his body shaking repeatedly as Yaqui lead struck it, O'Rourke dropped a Yaqui rider with each of his four remaining shots. Then the gun sagged in his hand and the veteran trooper crumpled to the ground.

Longarm was within range now. He levered the Winchester with the speed gained from experience, shooting low, bringing confusion to the attacking renegades by killing their horses and throwing their charge into confusion. The Yaquis milled for a moment; then, with a frantic twisting of bridles, they turned their ponies and galloped away in full retreat.

Longarm reined in and let the Morgan breathe while he took cartridges from his pocket and reloaded the Winchester. Seeing that the Yaquis had retreated out of rifle range, he toed the horse ahead and rode on to the outpost.

The remaining defenders were just beginning to stand up. O'Rourke's bullet-riddled body was lying on the slope he'd defended with his life. At his feet lay the bodies of the five Yaquis he'd brought down. Lower on the slope, two dead ponies were lying and a wounded one was trying to struggle to its feet.

Slowly recovering from their shock, the survivors of the Yaqui attack stood gazing at the dead trooper with somber eyes. There were seven of them, including Wimberly, the cavalry recruit. Longarm saw that Trent and Purdy were among them. The constable's revolver was still in its holster. Longarm pulled up and dismounted.

"We better get O'Rourke's body here, where the Yaquis can't get to him to chop his scalp off when they come back again," he told the still-dazed men. "It's the least you can do for him after what he did for you."

"He didn't even have to be here," Wimberly said, his voice still dull with shock. "We lost a man here last night, and the sergeant took his place. Said we needed another man. If the Yaquis broke through us, they'd take the town."

"They would've, too," Longarm said. "Well, some of you take O'Rourke and put him with the other body."

Four of the men picked up O'Rourke's corpse and carried it down the inside slope of the draw, where a blanket-covered form lay. As they started back up the slope, Longarm recognized one of the party; he was Purdy, one of the trio who'd objected to Naylor's effort to profiteer on the sale of rifles. Trent was still staring into space, his eyes glazed with shock.

"That sergeant was a right good man," Purdy remarked as he picked up his rifle—a new one—and began reloading it. "He seen what it was going to take to stop them Yaquis, and he done it. We could use a few more like him." As he spoke, he looked directly at the constable.

"Yes, he was," Longarm agreed. "But you men better get ready in case they hit this post again."

Purdy looked across the flat at the Yaquis. They were still

moving around aimlessly, not yet organizing another rush on the post. He said, "We got time enough for me to get something off of my mind." He turned to face Trent again. "How come you didn't pull out that pistol of yours and help the sergeant, Trent? He sure as hell called you to."

"I'm damned if he did!" Trent retorted. "Hell, it all was happening so fast, there was so much shooting, I didn't hear him say anything!"

"You was closer to him than me," Purdy said quietly. "And I heard him yell, 'They're close enough for pistols now! Come on, give me a hand.' And you're the only one of us wearing a pistol."

"If he said that, I sure didn't hear him," Trent protested.

"Would you've helped him if you'd heard him, Trent?" one of the other men asked mockingly.

"Well, damn you!" Trent snapped. He took a half-step in the direction of the man who'd asked the question.

Longarm stopped the constable's movement with a hand on his arm. He said, "Never mind him, Trent. Turn around a minute, will you? I want to see something."

"See what?" Trent asked, turning to face Longarm.

"This." Longarm ripped the constable's shirt open, sending its buttons flying. He did the same for the top of Trent's balbriggan underwear, and bent his head to look closely at his hairy chest and stomach.

"Long, what in hell you think you're doing?" Trent exploded.

Longarm straightened up and stared coldly into Trent's eyes before saying, "I just wanted to see how much yellow's showing on your belly, that's all."

Trent opened his mouth to reply, but what he saw in Longarm's grim face stopped his words. He stepped away and began rearranging his clothing.

"It was O'Rourke's job to check the posts," Longarm said. He went to the Morgan and mounted. "I guess I'll be taking his place doing that till this thing's all settled." Then, looking down at the seven remaining defenders from saddle height, he added, "Now, you fellows better check your guns and stay ready, because they might try the same thing again." He added pointedly, "And this time you'll only have six *men* to stand 'em off."

There was still one more post for Longarm to check, the one between Mina Cobre and the Mexican settlement. When he'd passed the bright frame houses of the town, the sides of the draw grew steeper, and he pussyfooted the Morgan down the slope to the road. Curtin, the remaining recruit, had only five men with him. One of them was Corky; the barkeep looked at Longarm and grimaced wryly. Longarm grinned back before turning his attention to the post's situation. Here, the road ran through a gully, with a steep rise leading down to the flat where the Yaquis sat on their ponies, apparently waiting before launching another attack.

"Your bunch all right, Curtin?" Longarm asked as he swung to the ground and dropped the Morgan's reins so the horse would stand.

"We've stood 'em off so far, Marshal," the young trooper replied. "If the ammunition holds out, I guess we can too."

"Are you real bad off for cartridges?"

"We've got enough to last for one more fight, if it's not a very long one. Sergeant O'Rourke was going to try to get some more for us, but he hasn't brought it yet."

"And won't. O'Rourke's dead," Longarm said bluntly.

Curtin gulped. His face twisted and his jaw dropped; it was obvious that he was having trouble controlling his emotion.

Longarm said quickly, "I'll go see what I can find. What do you men need?"

"I'm all right," Corky said. "Remember, Marshal, I got a spare box from the store yesterday. Good thing I did, too."

"I can use some .44-40s," another said.

"Spencer .52s, Marshal," said a third. "There's two of us needs them."

"I'll see what I can do," Longarm said.

Clattering down the road back to Mina Cobre, Longarm swung out of his saddle in front of Naylor's store. The door was shut, and when he tried it, he found it locked. He pounded on the panels for a moment, then drew his Colt to shoot out the lock. He had the revolver's muzzle pressed to the keyhole when the key grated in the lock and Naylor's face appeared in the crack of the opening door.

"Long? What kind of trouble are you bringing with you this time?" Naylor asked. He swung the door open. "Well, as long as you're here, come on in."

Longarm went inside, glancing around the empty store. A barricade made by stacking up wooden boxes stood opposite the door. From slits left when the boxes were stacked, the muzzles of three double-barreled shotguns protruded.

He told Naylor, "The men holding off the Yaquis need ammunition. I want .44-40s and .52 Spencers. And don't tell me you ain't got any. Half the men in town use one or the other."

"Who's buying it?" Naylor asked. "Them, or the government?"

"You are, unless you want to be using those shotguns when the Yaquis bust through and take the town. Now make up your mind, because if I go out of here without the shells they need, that's just what's likely to happen."

"I don't hand out—" Naylor began, then stopped short. "Oh, hell! You'll get what you want out of me one way or the other, Long. Come on. I'll give you the ammunition."

His saddlebags heavy, Longarm galloped back to the defense post. He handed out the ammunition and then scrambled up the side of the draw to look around. The Yaquis directly in front of him were mounted, their horses turned in the direction of the Copper Queen, their eyes fixed on the mine.

There had been no sounds of gunfire coming from that direction since he'd gotten within earshot, Longarm realized with a start. He looked to see what the Yaquis were watching. There were no Indians milling around the buildings, no puffs of powder smoke coming from outside the mine area or from the guards in the Copper Queen's buildings. There were, however, at least forty Yaqui riders coming at a quick trot toward the town.

It took him only a couple of seconds to figure out what was happening. Where before, the Yaquis had been divided into two bunches, those besieging the mine and those whose objective was the town, now they were joining forces to concentrate their firepower on one group of defenders—those who were protecting the town.

Chapter 18

Longarm dropped down to the road. He looked toward the mine, but found that the high side of the draw hid the section of road where he'd seen the Yaqui reinforcements. He told the others, "You might as well know it now as find out later. The Yaquis that've been trying to take over the Copper Queen are coming to join the ones we been fighting down here."

"Godamighty, Marshal!" Curtin exclaimed. "How many more is that going to make for us to fight?"

"Between forty and fifty."

"We've had our hands full, holding off the ones we've been fighting all night," one of the men said. "I don't see how we can take on a bunch more."

"Looks like we've got to," Longarm said soberly. Then he grinned and added, "Seeing as they didn't ask us if they could come join the fracas."

"Fracas, hell!" the man snorted. "Battle's more like it!"

"Call it what you want to, it's going to be a fight," Longarm said. "And don't be surprised if the Yaquis change the way they been fighting. If they do, we'll have to change too."

"Why should we change?" Curtin asked. "We've done all right so far."

"But they ain't," Longarm replied. "I'd sort of look for 'em to pick out one place and hit it with every man they got, except what few they'd need to keep the other posts tied down."

"What do we do if they do that?" one of the men asked.

"Two or three of you stay here and the rest go to wherever the fighting's heaviest." Over his shoulder, as he remounted, Longarm added, "I need to get to the other posts in a hurry and tell everybody what's happening. You men do the best you can."

Galloping back to Wimberly's post, Longarm looked over his shoulder as soon as he'd reached a section of the road where he could see the Yaqui force that was coming from the Copper Queen. The Indian riders had covered half the distance to the town, and were still moving fast.

Longarm saw that he'd have no time to warn all the posts before they got in position. Cudgeling his brain for a solution, he remembered the walking wounded he'd seen going to the saloon, and made a quick change in his plans. Instead of leaving the road, he followed it into town and went into the saloon.

Inside, he found four freshly wounded men. One was still awaiting attention; the others were sitting at tables, where the women were dressing their wounds. Luz was working at the table closest to the door. A tall, gray-haired Mexican man with a sweeping mustache and an old-style goatee was doing his best to help her with the bandage she was applying, in spite of the handicap of his own bandaged arm.

She asked Longarm, "What's wrong? Don't say anything, because I can see from your face that something bad has happened."

"I wasn't figuring on lying to you," he told her. "The Yaquis that've been fighting up at the Copper Queen are on their way to join up with the ones that's been trying to take the town. There's maybe forty of 'em, and I got no time to tell the men over on the west side what's happening. There's only two of the posts to cover. Is one of the men here able to ride?"

"I don't know," Luz replied. "I can—"

"I can ride, Marshal Long," the man who'd been helping Luz volunteered. "This scratch on my arm will not bother me."

"No, Don Diego!" Luz protested. "It is too much for you to try to do!"

"Don't talk nonsense, Luz. If Eusebio were alive, he would volunteer, no?"

"Of course. But you're not as young—" she began.

"I am not too old, either," he retorted sharply. "Leave this to me, Luz!" He turned to Longarm. "You may have noticed, Marshal. Young people think their elders are weak and infirm. My daughter-in-law is like all the others. Now. We have not met, but Luz has told me of you. I am Diego Parrejo, Marshal. *A sus ordenes.*"

"You got a horse, Don Diego?" Longarm asked.

Luz said quickly, "If you insist on going, take my pony. It's in the shed at the side of the building, already saddled."

Don Diego nodded gravely. "Thank you, Luz. Now, Marshal. Tell me the message that you wish me to carry."

Quickly, Longarm explained to Don Diego the possibility that when the Yaqui reinforcements arrived, the Indians might change their tactics and select one point for a massed attack.

"If they do," he went on, "We'll need every man we can muster wherever we're getting hit." He paused long enough to touch a match to the cheroot he'd been holding in his hand. "I'd give a pretty if there was some way to let everybody know where they ought to come. Shots won't work for a signal, there's apt to be shooting going on most of the time. But I can't—"

"A smoke signal, perhaps?" Don Diego suggested, indicating the plume rising from Longarm's cheroot.

"That'd do, but I ain't got a thing to burn except cigars."

"Rags," Luz said. She indicated the bottles on the shelves behind the bar. "Pour liquor on them. Here." She picked up a bundle of cloth from which the women had been tearing bandages and thrust it into Longarm's hands. "Now Don Diego will need only tell the men to watch for the smoke signal you will send up and to hurry to it."

Longarm took the cloths, grabbed a bottle of tequila from the saloon's stock, and hurried to get back in the saddle. As soon as he'd passed Mina Cobre's last buildings, he looked for the Yaqui reinforcements. The riders had reached the flats east of town by now, and were moving steadily toward the gap between the buildings of Mina Cobre and the Papago village.

"Looks like they're going right for the middle," Longarm muttered as he watched the Yaqui band. "Wimberly's post, most likely. Or between that one and Curtin's." He made a mental estimate of distances and times. "We got twenty minutes, half an hour at best. And we ain't halfway set for 'em."

Bypassing Wimberly and his men, Longarm galloped beyond the Papago huts and pulled up at Boyd's post. He told them of the changed situation with as few wasted words as possible, then wheeled the Morgan and galloped back to the center position.

Even before he reached the group, Longarm could see it was larger than it should have been. The men were gathered in a knot up the slope from the spot where the shrouded bodies of O'Rourke and the other casualty lay. When he got closer, he saw that the original seven had been joined by twice that many more. Then he was near enough to identify the new arrivals as Papagos; they wore the baggy white cotton trousers and jackets of the tribe.

"What in hell are they doing here?" he asked Wimberly as he swung off the Morgan.

"They say they want to fight the Yaquis with us," the young trooper replied. "Came marching over here from their houses just a few minutes ago."

"Now, everybody knows Papagos don't fight," Longarm said. "I never heard of a Papago fighting man in my whole life."

"Well, I guess these do," Wimberly told him. "Of course, all they've got to fight with is bows and arrows and spears. I don't see they'd be much use to us."

"I guess I better talk to 'em," Longarm said. "Help's help, when you're between a rock and a hard place."

As Longarm walked toward the Papagos, one of them stepped out of the group and came to meet him. In one hand the man was carrying a long spear, a six-foot length of some wood Longarm did not recognize; its tip had been sharpened and thrust into coals to harden it. In his other hand the Papago held a bow almost as long as the spear, and a cluster of slender arrows made from some sort of reed and tipped with needle-sharp ocotillo thorns.

"You are chief?" the Papago asked.

"I guess. As much of a chief as we got here."

"Good. I am Ah-koh-tah. Chief of Papagos." He extended his weapons for Longarm to inspect. "We fight Yaqui too."

"How come, Ah-koh-tah?" Longarm asked. "I never heard of your people fighting anybody."

"Papago not like fight. When got to, fight. Yaqui kill us. We kill Yaqui."

"Well, we'll be proud to have you join up with us. I won't try to tell your men what to do. You tell 'em. Understand?"

Ah-koh-tah nodded. "We fight, then." He returned to where

206

his men waited, and spoke to them in their own language. When he'd finished, the Papagos drew off to one side, where they stood silently watching while Longarm went to talk with the other defenders.

Wimberly's first words were, "We been watching the Yaquis coming down from the mine. Looks like they're getting ready to try and finish us off, Marshal."

"Not much mistake about that," Longarm agreed. "But we'll get some help from the other posts, and the Papagos over there are going to be fighting on our side."

"Papagos! Shit!" Trent snorted disgustedly. "Everybody knows Papagos don't fight!"

"Don't downgrade the Papagos," Purdy put in. "Up on the Gila, in the old days, they was damn good fighters when they took the notion. Many a time I seen them long arrows of theirs go right through a man."

"Ak-koh-tah says they'll fight," Longarm said. "They want to work off their grudge against the Yaquis for raiding their village the other night."

"That's what got this whole damn thing started!" Trent complained. "And it's your fault we're in the mess we are, Long! If you hadn't took El Griego prisoner, none of this fighting would've happened!"

"Maybe not. But if they'd got off scot-free from that raid on the Papagos, how long you think it would've been till they raided Mina Cobre, Trent?"

"Not as fast as they've come at us this time!" Trent shot back triumphantly. "This fight here's what comes from messing with something that wasn't our business!"

"Is that why you turned yellow-belly when O'Rourke needed you to help him?" Purdy asked. He turned his back on Trent and asked Longarm, "How long you think it's going to be until they move?"

"Not very much longer. They're most likely picking out the place they'll hit right now. And I've fixed it up for some of the men from the other posts to hustle over here if the Yaquis hit where I think they're going to, here or between us and Curtin's post, south a little ways."

"How in hell can anybody from the other posts get here in time to do us any good?" Trent asked. "They won't be no more help to us than them damn Papagos will!"

"Looks like we'll have a chance to find out," Longarm said quietly. "The Yaquis are finally forming up. And judging from the place they're bunching, it's us they're aiming to hit."

All eyes turned to the flat. The Yaqui band was pulling into a formation of sorts, a mass shaped like a vee, its point just a bit below the defense post. Longarm went to his horse and took out the rags Luz had given him, and the bottle of tequila.

He piled the rags in a loose heap and emptied the liquor over them, then flicked a match across his thumbnail and dropped it on the alcohol-soaked cloth. The oily liquor burned at first with a transparent smokeless flame, then the rags caught and a thick column of smoke began rising into the bright late-morning air. Longarm stepped back and watched the smoke winding upward. The eyes of the others followed his, and they missed the first movement of the Yaqui band.

Hooves pounding the hard-baked desert soil quickly drew their attention from the signal fire. There was a moment of confusion as the men grabbed for rifles that had been laid aside during the lull, and dropped to the ground, training their weapons on the onrushing Yaquis. This time the attackers did not advance in a thin line. The center of the Indian horde was a solid mass of horsemen, five or six deep, with a front line that was a dozen riders wide and widened at the rear to two or three times that many. Two smaller groups, fifteen or twenty men in each, were galloping forward with the main body.

"Hit the horses first!" Longarm shouted over the increasing thunder of the advancing hoofbeats. "Never mind the little bunches! Aim right for the middle of the big one!"

Within minutes that seemed as short as seconds to the post's defenders, the Yaqui band came within rifle range. Guns spoke, and a Yaqui horse, then another and still another, dropped. The center of the Indian line faltered, then split to ride around the downed animals and came sweeping forward.

As the range closed, the men holding the post raised their sights. Men as well as horses began falling, but the range had closed for the Yaquis too, and their guns began barking. Slugs thudded into the banks of the draw. Then the Yaquis were sweeping up the slope, and on their ponies they were above the low, earthen line that had protected the defenders before.

One of the men slumped, his rifle rolling from lifeless hands. A slug hit the gunstock of the man next to him and splintered it; he reached for the weapon dropped by his dead neighbor and kept on firing.

When the first Yaqui riders were only thirty yards from the crest of the draw, the Papagos leaped to their feet. Ignoring the bullets that sang past them, they loosed their slender arrows, and over his sights Longarm saw a Yaqui, transfixed by one of the shafts, drop his rifle and fall from his horse.

One of the Papagos pitched forward on his face beside Longarm, blood streaming from the hole made by the bullet that had passed through his body. Behind him, Longarm heard a sharp, high-pitched cry of pain as another Yaqui slug found a Papago target, but the slim arrows continued to fly.

Just when it seemed to all those behind the low bank that the horde of ponies and yelling, shooting Yaquis was going to sweep over them, the Indian charge broke.

Almost as one man, the Yaquis wheeled and galloped away. The Mina Cobre men kept up a withering fire to encourage the retreat. El Griego's men kept going until they were safely out of range of the defenders' guns. On the flat between the combatants, a half-dozen horses and twice as many Yaquis lay sprawled.

Surprise in his voice, Wimberly exclaimed, "By God! We turned 'em back!"

"About time, too," Longarm told him.

He was sitting up, reaching for a cheroot, looking around at the defense post. Three of the Papagos and one of the Mina Cobre men were dead. A Papago was sitting on the ground, his hands clamped around a bullet hole in his thigh, trying to stop the blood that welled up between his fingers. Purdy had his shirttail out and was sawing a strip from it with his knife to bandage a bullet-torn ear from which a trickle of blood dripped and ran in a rivulet off his chin. Most of the defenders' faces wore the dull, stunned look that follows sanguinary combat.

"We got off light," Longarm remarked to nobody in particular after he'd finished his survey. "But we better be getting ready instead of setting around like gut-stuck hogs, because those Yaquis ain't wasting time out there."

"We won't be fighting 'em by ourselves, though!" Wimberly said.

They turned to look. Men from Boyd's command were coming toward them from the north, and from the south a group from Curtin's post was hurrying to join them.

"There'll be more in a minute, too!" Longarm told the others. "All we got to do is hold on till they get here!"

Across the flat, the Yaquis had re-formed. They did not put out flanking groups this time, but spread in a staggered line, four or five riders deep, that stretched from the Papago village to the center of Mina Cobre.

"Spread out!" Longarm commanded. "We're wide open on both sides! Fill up the gaps so they can't break through!"

Taking off his hat, he waved it to attract the attention of the men coming from Curtin's post, and indicated by gestures that they were to take up their positions along the top of the draw to the south of the men already in position. Then he turned his attention to the group arriving from Boyd's post, and gave them signals to fill in the spaces along the north side of the draw.

When all the newcomers had moved into place, a widely spaced line of defenders, which stretched from beyond the center of the Papago village to the edge of Mina Cobre, stood waiting for the new attack. Only the Papagos stayed together. Their white clothing made a bright cluster opposite the huts of their own village.

As yet, the Yaquis had not moved. They were still spreading laterally, opening gaps between riders, staggering themselves so that when horses were shot, the ponies behind them would not collide with them and spill their riders.

"They learn fast," Longarm commented as he watched the Yaquis taking up their new formation. "This time it ain't going to be so easy to bust 'em up." He told the man on his left, "Pass the word down the line. Don't try for the ponies like we did last time. Take plenty of time to aim and knock the Yaquis down!"

Time stretched taut while the sparse line of defenders waited for the attack to begin. Just as the Yaquis started their advance, the men from the western posts appeared, coming across the draw between the huts of the Papago village and pushing their way through the livestock that was still in the corral at the edge of Mina Cobre.

Purdy was next to Longarm in the line. He called across the gap that separated them, "You think them extra men's going to get here in time, Marshal?"

"Hell, Purdy, don't worry about them! They're hurrying as fast as they can! Put your mind on stopping the damned Yaquis!"

Longarm took for himself the advice he'd given Purdy. He watched the uneven Yaqui line as it gained speed until it was coming at them at a full gallop, cutting the distance quickly, the ponies straining under the kicks of their riders.

He picked his target as El Griego's renegades advanced, and his was the first shot to ring out. The Yaqui he'd picked slid off the rump of his pony and lay huddled on the ground.

Choosing another target, Longarm had time to squeeze off a second carefully aimed round before the galloping Yaquis were so close that sheer firepower replaced aiming and he was firing as fast as he could lever fresh shells into the Winchester's chamber.

Unimpeded this time by getting entangled with falling ponies, the Yaqui band swept up the slope. When they were almost at the rim of the draw, and Longarm felt the hammer of the rifle click on an empty chamber, he dropped the rifle and drew his Colt. The Yaquis were well within pistol range now, and Longarm concentrated on those who'd gotten closest to the defenders' positions.

Along the line, he could hear other pistols barking, their duller reports sounding baritone notes in contrast to the sharp, harsh cracking of rifles. Without really being aware of it, he noted the slap-slap sounds of the .44s carried by Trent and Carvajal, the heavy boom of the Dragoon Colts fired by the troopers, the quick sharp barks of the pocket pistols a few of the Mina Cobre men carried.

It was the quick fire of the revolvers that finally turned the second Yaqui assault, aided by the spear-thrusts of the Papagos, who left their positions to rush at the hated Yaquis and impale the riders with upward thrusts of their six-foot spears. When the Yaqui riders turned to retreat, only half of the Papagos who'd joined the defending force were still alive.

211

Not just the Papagos, but the defenders from Mina Cobre and the troopers suffered too. Longarm looked along the rim of the draw while the Yaquis were still retreating across the flat. He counted four bodies, including two clad in the red-striped pants and gray flannel shirts of the U.S. Cavalry. There were still more wounded. Here and there an arm dangled, blood dripping from fingertips, or a man sat on the ground, trying to stanch the flow from a leg wound.

Now the calls came from along the draw: "Who's got some extra .44-40 shells?" . . . "Anybody got a few .54s?" . . . "I need .48s, if anybody can spare 'em!"

"Share out what shells you can, men!" Longarm shouted. He'd turned his eyes to the Yaquis after his quick count of the toll taken by their attack. Across the flat, they were re-forming quickly. It was apparent to Longarm that they intended to make still another charge without giving the defenders time to recover from the last.

Longarm reloaded his Colt and slid it back into its well-worn holster, but before he could pick up the Winchester, El Griego's renegades had turned and were galloping back to renew the fight. As he pressed cartridges into the rifle's magazine, he saw the Yaquis kick their horses into motion.

"Get ready, men!" he called. "They're coming back!"

He looked along the defense line. Half of the men were still reloading. Some were out of position, seeking sheels for empty guns. There was no time left to rally the men; all Longarm could do was set them an example and hope they would respond. He did not drop to the ground this time, but took a stance with widespread feet on the rim of the swale, and brought his rifle to his shoulder. He found a Yaqui in the sights and waited for the onrushing horde to come into range.

Chapter 19

Longarm held his eyes fixed on the Yaquis in spite of the tempation to look along the defense line and see how the men were responding to his call to get ready.

In the vee of the Winchester's sights, the Yaqui he'd picked for a target grew larger and larger as the renegades galloped across the flat toward the draw. Longarm was holding the rifle rock-steady, his finger tightening around the trigger to squeeze off his first shot, when a blare of liquid sound cut through the broken drumming of the Yaqui ponies' hooves. It sounded like a trumpet blast, but he knew that nothing of that sort could be possible.

Again the sonorous sound reached his ears, this time broken into an almost melodic, half-familiar series of staccato bursts. The Yaqui on whom he had fixed his rifle sights suddenly veered and began moving away from the draw. Longarm raised his head from the gunstock and looked around.

Galloping toward the Yaquis' flank from the direction of the lake he saw a band of riders, a disciplined troop of cavalry in a uniform he'd never seen before. The raiders wore white pants and blue coats, with white crossbelts across the chests and brass buttons in lines down the front, that caught the sun and broke its rays into sparkling darts of golden light. In front of the troop rode the trumpeter, his instrument a glare of polished brass that once again sounded the strange staccato air.

Longarm tore his eyes away from the cavalry troop and looked at the Yaquis. They had abandoned their charge on the draw and were galloping north, running in front of the cavalry, which was slowly overtaking the tiring Indian ponies. He looked at his men, scattered along the draw. They were standing in the same frozen stance that he was, watching the developing chase.

As the cavalry troop thundered past the defense line, the riders were drawing carbines from saddle scabbards without slacking the speed of their pursuit. A short distance beyond the Papago village the troopers began firing. The Yaquis wheeled and returned the fire, but the cavalrymen still did not lessen the speed of their headlong dash.

Yaquis began dropping from their ponies as the troop overtook the Indians. The Yaquis gave up the thought of fighting back, and turned again to run. The final moments of the battle were almost out of sight of the men from Mina Cobre, but the distance was still not too great for them to see sabers drawn as the troop overtook the Yaquis and rode into them, blades flashing in the bright, high sunlight.

It was a fierce fight, but a short one. The Yaquis had made three charges, many were wounded, their horses were tired. The cavalrymen slashed and hacked, the Yaquis fought back with gun butts and knives, but the unequal struggle could have only one outcome. While the final moments of the encounter were still taking place, Longarm saw three riders leave the battle and start back toward the draw.

"Any of you men know what the hell that cavalry outfit is, or where it came from?" Longarm demanded. "It sure don't belong to the U.S. Army. I guess that means it's from Mexico, but what I'd like to know is, what's it doing on our side of the border!"

"There ain't but one thing it could be," Purdy said. "I never did see it before, but I sure heard about it. That's got to be the bunch they call the *cordada azul.*"

"Damned if I ever even heard of it," Longarm said. "Never heard the word *cordada* either, that I can recall. *Azul*, sure, that's blue. But what the hell do they signify together?"

"Well, I never was that curious about Mex lingo," Purdy replied. "I'd guess them fellows riding at us can tell you, if they talk American, that is."

Longarm stepped forward to wait for the three riders in their bule-and-white uniforms. Two of them wore short-billed military caps, the other had on an odd cylindrical cap that Longarm could see as they drew closer was made of lambswool. The

214

riders stopped in front of him and the one wearing the lambs-wool cap saluted.

"You are the leader from the men who are fighting the Yaqui, I am think?" he said. Longarm frowned, something about the man's voice struck a familiar chord in his memory. The rider went on, "Gregor Basilovich, is me. Colonel, *Gendermería Fiscal de la Republica de Mexico* and commander-in-chief of *la cordada azul.*"

"Like hell you are!" Longarm replied. His memory had meshed when he saw the man's face at close range. "Your name's Gregor Basilovich, all right, but you're a spy for the Tsar of Russia!"

For a moment Basilovich stared at Longarm, then his square face broke into a smile. "Longarm!" he exclaimed. "Federal Marshal Long! My friend, is my heart that seeing you does good! And it is more the better because I have just to you paid a beeg debt vhich too long I have owed!"

"Basilovich, just what in hell are you talking about?" Longarm demanded. He was conscious that Barney Trent was standing a few feet away, staring in wide-eyed amazement. He went on, "The last time I seen you was in the south part of Kansas, and you were working with a woman spy."

"Good is your memory, Longarm! Ilioana Karsovana!" Basilovich shook his head. "Beautiful, Ilioana vas! I vonder vhat to her is happen."

"I wouldn't know," Longarm replied. "I never seen her after I finished my case in Junction."

"Junction!" the Russi_n repeated. "Sooch a terrible place Junction vas! Like Siberia!"

"Maybe you'd like to tell me what you're doing in Arizona Territory, dressed up like a Mexican Army officer," Longarm said. "And what's more to the point, what in hell you're doing leading Mexican troops into the United States."

"*Nyet!*" Basilovich protested. "Not is just dress up! I am wear uniform to which I am entitle! But army it is not, is uniform from Gendermería Fiscal, my friend, what is by your people call *rurales*. Of which I, Gregor Basilovich, am colonel, made so by President Díaz. Is true this, Longarm. To you I do not lie."

"You sure don't look like any *rurales* I ever run into. And

215

I've seen enough *rurales* to know what I'm talking about."

"You have the Policía Federal met with, of this I now remember I am to hear. My *cordada* is to the Gendermería belong. Is not the same, Longarm. On the Policía Federal, bah! I speet! They dogs are, not like my *cordada*."

"I will say your outfit looked mighty good when you galloped by here after those Yaquis." A suspicion was growing in Longarm's mind that in spite of its totally improbable sound, the story Basilovich was telling was true. "Look here, Basilovich, I'll listen to your tale later on. Right now, there's wounded men here I got to look after. You stick around, and we'll talk after I finish."

"It is for help you from them that we have come back," Basilovich said. "I have my surgeon and my orderly bring. They will for your wounded men care. Bandages, medicines, all what they will need, they have."

Turning to the riders who'd been sitting their horses just behind him, the Russian snapped a string of orders in Spanish. The two men dismounted, one of them produced a surgical kit from his saddlebag, and they moved at once to care for the wounded. Longarm became aware that Barney Trent was still standing, listening.

"Maybe you better give Colonel Basilovich's men a hand," he told the constable. "You know enough of their language to help 'em find out how bad our boys is hurt."

"I don't—" Trent began, then, seeing the look in Longarm's eyes, followed the two Mexicans.

"Longarm," Basilovich said, "The men of my *cordada* will the job of collecting the rest of the Yaquis finish. Is a place we can go, where we can talk? Is much from tell you, I have."

"I don't know how legal what you're doing is," Longarm told the Russian. "But I'm damned glad to let you go ahead and finish up this mess. We been fighting those renegades since yesterday evening, and all of us is about give out. Come on, we'll go into town and have a drink at the saloon while we talk."

Sitting at a corner table in the saloon, a bottle of *tequila anejo* in front of the Russian and his Maryland rye before him, Longarm looked at Gregor Basilovich. The saloon had been cleared of wounded by the *cordada*'s surgeon and a few troopers he'd brought to help him, and the women had gone home. The bar was lined with men, rehashing the fighting. From time to time they looked curiously at Longarm and Gregor, but none of them interrupted their conversation.

"So when you are so near to kill me in Kansas," Basilovich was saying, "I am decide to give for the Tsar my life, I do not wish. I am go, then."

"I'll say you went! Dropped clean out of sight. And I didn't have time to try to find you, I had my hands full with Ilioana and the Brethren and the rest of it," Longarm said.

"It is from make me run, make me see I do not want more to be spy for Tsar, it is for this I owe you beeg debt, Longarm," the Russian went on. "Debt I today am pay, *da*? Is best thing to ever happen from me. I run to Mexico. So to keep Tsar's spies from find me, I am join Gendermería Fiscal. I am Cossack-born, you weel understand, so I am know to ride good. President Díaz, he is see me, promote me queek—sergeant, lieutenant, captain, and so now colonel. I am make my *cordada* best in Mexico, because I use Cossack ways I know from Russian army, before I am start spy. Some day, general I weel be."

"By God, I'll bet you will, at that," Longarm grinned. He lighted a fresh cheroot and asked, "But how'd you happen to ride into Mina Cobre just in time to save our bacon today?"

"These Yaquis, they are from band of one El Griego, you are know this, Longarm?" When Longarm nodded, Basilovich said, "Him I am long time to chase. I am tell you of my *cordada*, is from all Mexico most best. On border here, is not man, is not beast, is not even snake or scorpion, that is move and I not find out fast. Remember, I am spy for Tsar, I know trick to find out. So, I am hear El Griego is lead Yaquis to raid, I am track him to here. You are know rest, you see it. You believe, Longarm?"

"Yeah, I believe you, Basilovich. Your damn yarn's just crazy enough to be the truth. And I guess you just crossed the U.S. border by mistake. Anyhow, that's what I'm going to put in my report."

Basilovich drained his glass of tequila, refilled it, sighed, and shrugged. "Is only one thing bad. My men are finish

Yaquis, but is not with them himself El Griego."

"Maybe that's because I got him locked up in a shed at the copper mine. And I'll be glad to hand him over to you, let you take him back to Mexico. I guess you got enough on him down on your side of the border to put him away a good long time."

"You have El Griego!" the Russian exclaimed. "Now I am owe you new debt, Longarm! But I will pay someday." He drained his glass and grinned at Longarm. "Do not worry about El Griego be put away. We have in Mexico good law. Is call *ley del fuego*. You know this law, *da*?"

"I've heard about it." Longarm sipped his rye. El Griego would never stand trial, he knew. Somewhere in the desolate land Basilovich and his men would cross as they returned, the Yaqui renegade would be shot "while trying to escape."

Basilovich stood up. "Is best we go now. Is not wise too long on this side of border to stay. You give me El Griego, and so fast we ride back."

"I'll ride up to the mine with you on your way out, and you can have him," Longarm said. "And don't worry about you owing me anything for him. As far as I'm concerned, you done enough today to make us even-steven."

"Is good," Basilovich agreed. "But we are from now friends, is true, Longarm? And friends have not owing and paying between them. Is so in U.S. of America? Is so in my new country."

"Let's say it's so as far as you and me are concerned. Now, if you'll give me a minute to get somebody to help those cavalry troopers get ready to start back to Fort Huachuca, we'll ride up to the mine and I'll hand El Griego over to you."

Apparently the Yaquis had been too busy to pay any attention to the cottage. When Longarm stopped at the little house on his way back from the Copper Queen, he found it undisturbed. The idea of a bed after the strenuous twenty-four hours he'd just put in was too appealing for him to pass by. He did not take time to undress. Kicking out of his boots after hanging his gunbelt on the bedpost, he dropped off at once into a deep sleep.

How long he'd been sleeping he did not know, when noises from the kitchen wakened him. It was dark, and might have been any hour from just after twilight until midnight. He only knew that he felt refreshed and ravenously hungry. Rolling off the bed, he padded barefoot into the kitchen. Clarita was standing in front of the stove, an empty skillet in her hand. She saw Longarm and rushed into his arms.

"*Ay*, Longarm *mío*! I am so worry over you!" she exclaimed, punctuating her words with kisses. "I am hear guns, boom-boom, and wonder eef you are shot!"

"Didn't your owl tell you I was all right?" he asked.

"Ees not come to me, the owl. And I remember I tell you, first when you get here, ees terrible theengs to happen! But ees all finish now, no? And you are all right?"

"There ain't a thing wrong with me that a steak and some potatoes and coffee won't cure."

"And *baño*? You like bath? Ees water hot. And ees clean clothes, I wash for you before Yaquis come."

"That'd be good. And getting rid of this damn bandage will make me feel better too. You fix up the tub, Clarita. I'll go in and have a drink, and then after I get bathed I'll eat some supper."

While he savored the Tom Moore and a cheroot, Longarm took his Ingersoll watch out and looked at it. Surprisingly, it was only eight o'clock. He slid out of his clothes and went into the kitchen. Clarita had the washtub filled with steaming water, and insisted on helping him bathe. When her hands strayed in loving, exploratory caresses, Longarm gently lifted them away.

"Not right now, Clarita. It ain't that I don't feel like it, or don't want to, but I got business to take care of in town. But it'll only take me a little while. There'll be lots of time after I get back."

"You are go to see Luz?" Clarita asked, her eyes snapping in anger. "She ees stay weeth Don Diego, *esta dañado, su suegro*."

"I know he got a bullet in the arm. But I ain't going to see Luz. I've got to get on with what I came here for, Clarita. I've got an election to watch, and there's things to do first."

"*Tengo celos de Luz!*" Clarita said. "I am one you peek first, Longarm! *No engañarme ahora!*"

"Is that why you and her was arguing, the night the Yaquis

219

come?" When Clarita nodded, Longarm went on, "Now, there ain't any reason for you and Luz to fight. I ain't going to pick one of you over the other. You're both fine girls, and I'd be a fool to try to pick between you. I like both of you the same, Clarita. You understand what I'm saying?"

Clarita sighed. *"Sí."*

He nodded. "A man in my job can't be tied to one woman, nor one place. It don't work out."

"Ya lo creo." Clarita said. "I onderstan'." Then she smiled and reached out to tweak him gently. *"Y tienes verga enorme, bastanta para los dos.* Ees all right, Longarm. I don't got jealous for Luz no more."

"Good. Now, you fix supper while I get dressed, and I'll wind up my business in town and be back before too long."

Longarm left the Morgan at the hitch rail in front of the saloon, but before going in, he crossed the street to stand beside the door of Naylor's store and take a covert look inside. The fat storekeeper was sitting in his usual corner, Barney Trent with him. Except for the two of them and the straw-haired clerk, the store was empty.

Smiling with satisfaction, Longarm went back to the saloon. Like the store, it was without customers, but Corky stood in his usual place behind the bar. Longarm looked at the empty tables and the barren bar.

"Where in hell's all your customers?" he asked. "Place was jammed when I was in here earlier."

"Hell, you know how it is," Corky said, setting the bottle of rye and a glass in front of Longarm. "For a while after a man's been fighting, he feels like celebrating. Then the tireds catch up with him and he goes home to bed. I tell you, if I didn't have to stay, I'd be in bed too."

"So'd I, Corky, if that election wasn't coming up day after tomorrow. But I came here to see it was run fair and square, and all this business with the Yaquis just sort of happened to get in the way of my real job."

"You figure Naylor and Cross and Trent got a joker up their sleeves?" Corky asked.

"Oh, sure they have. Cross has been gone a few days. Or at least, if he got back he sure didn't show up to help do any fighting. But I got an idea where he went, and what he did."

220

"I don't guess it'd be any use me asking questions, so I won't," Corky grinned. "But from the way you figured out how to stand off the Yaquis, I guess you can handle them three. If there's any way I can help..."

"It just happens there is. Think you could spare me one of those lemons you keep on hand?"

"Sure. Spare you a half-dozen, if you want."

"One's plenty. But slice it real thin for me, will you?"

Corky brought out the lemon and cutting board, and sliced the lemon, his brow furrowed in thought. When he'd finished, he pushed the cutting board across the bar to Longarm.

"Well, there you are," he said. "You want to take it with you, or do you plan to chew it here?"

"It's just fine the way it is."

Longarm took his freshly washed bandanna from his pocket and spread it on the bar, being careful not to smooth out the folds Clarita had ironed into the big red handkerchief. He placed a row of lemon slices along the center fold, brought the edge over to cover them, and repeated the process at each of the fold lines. When he was through, the bandanna was again in a neat square, and very little thicker than it had been before the lemon slices had been folded into it.

Corky shook his head. "First time I ever saw a man make a bandanna-and-lemon sandwich. I don't think I'd care to try it, myself."

"Nobody's asked you to. And I'll be obliged if you just forget you saw me make up this sandwich," Longarm told him, as he eased the lemon-laden bandanna back into his hip pocket.

"I didn't see a thing, Marshal," Corky said soberly. "Even if I told somebody about it, they wouldn't believe me."

"I'll be moving on," Longarm said. "Thanks for your help."

Crossing the street, Longarm went into the store. He saw that Cross had returned from wherever he'd been, and was sitting with Naylor and Trent in the storekeeper's pet corner. The three men looked up and exchanged a few words in a whisper before he reached the corner where they sat.

"Well, Marshal," Naylor said, "I like to see a man come in to pay his bill promptly. I guess that's why you're here, isn't it? To square up for those cartridges you bought while the fight was going on?"

"Now don't pull any of your tricks, Naylor," Longarm replied. "You *gave* me that ammunition, and you know it."

"Did I, now?" Naylor frowned. "It must've slipped my mind. But if you say I did, your word's good. If it's not the ammunition, you must have something else on your mind, then."

"I'd imagine you know what it is. Day after tomorrow's election day. I've got a little job to do before the ballots get passed out. You said the other night they didn't have numbers on 'em, so I figured I'd just count 'em and make sure there's not any spare ones that might get counted by mistake."

"I don't see what good that's going to do," Trent said, frowning.

"It's like this, Trent," Longarm said in the manner of a schoolteacher trying to instruct a backward student. "If the printer that made up the ballots wasn't careful, he might've printed up a lot too many. It'd be right easy for the fellows that hired the printing to mark the extra ballots for the ones they wanted to see elected and stuff 'em in the ballot box."

"Oh, hell!" Naylor snorted. "You told us you're going to be watching the ballot box, Long. We'd be fools to try to pull a stunt like that. You'd catch us too easily!"

"Well, I'll count 'em just the same, Naylor. They're still all wrapped up like they come from the printer, you said, and locked up in your safe."

"They sure are. If you're so set on counting them, that's all right with me. I'll get them for you."

Waddling to the safe, Naylor twirled the combination, opened it, and took out an oblong package wrapped in brown paper. He came back and handed the package to Longarm.

"Here they are. Not opened, you can see that. Go on and start counting."

Longarm looked around, saw one of the boxes that Naylor had used as a barricade during the Yaqui attack, and dragged it over to the corner. Putting the ballots on the box, he dragged up an empty chair from the corner, sat down, and tore the wrapping paper off the package. Naylor and Trent watched him impassively.

For the first few minutes after he began counting, Longarm's fingers were unusually clumsy. He lost count twice and had to start again, he had trouble separating the rough paper on which the ballots were printed, and after a few minutes he shook his head and pushed the stacked ballots aside.

"My fingers are awful dry and stiff," he said. "And right now my mouth's too dry for me to lick 'em." He took his bandanna from his pocket and went on, "Lucky I got a fresh bandanna. I'd better go dip it in your water barrel, Naylor, if you'll tell me where it's at."

"Standing right by the back door," Naylor told him.

Carrying the bandanna, Longarm went to the barrel. Shielding his movements with his body, he squeezed the bandanna, crushing the lemon slices. Their juice quickly moistened the bandanna. He went back and put the wet bandanna on the box beside the ballots.

"Now, then," he said. "Maybe I can do better."

Longarm had surprisingly little trouble counting the ballots after he'd re-started. He rubbed his fingers over the moist surface of the bandanna from time to time, and soon had the job finished. He wrapped the ballots loosely and handed them to Naylor.

"Now, both of you watched me count," Longarm said. "Maybe counted along with me, for all I know."

"We said your word was good," Trent told him. "How many did you come up with?"

"An even two hundred."

"That's what we ordered," Naylor said. "There are seventy white men in the town and sixty Mexican men live in the 'dobes. They're the only ones that vote in the town election. Up at the Copper Queen, there's about fifty Mexican men that've signed up to vote, but they only get to vote for sheriff."

"Which leaves about ten extra ballots," Longarm said. "All right. Now I know there won't be more'n two hundred, I can keep my own tally when the votes get counted."

Trent asked, "Are you satisfied, then, Long?"

"I sure am. No reflection on you men, of course. It's just that I'm responsible for seeing there's a square vote, and I sure wouldn't want anything to go wrong." He stood up and nodded at Naylor and Trent. "Well, I guess that does me for tonight. I'll see you men at the vote-counting on election day."

Chapter 20

Luz did not return to the cottage until the morning of election day. When Longarm went in before breakfast, he found her chatting with Clarita as though there had never been angry words exchanged between them.

She smiled at Longarm and explained, "I did not come back to work sooner because I went with Don Diego while he asked the men to vote for him. I did not want him to go alone because of his wound. Today it will be decided, so he is staying at home."

"He's likely to get a lot of votes, Luz," Longarm said. "Folks see him with a bandage on, they're going to remember he was one of the ones fighting for the town."

"But Raoul Carvajal fought too!" she exclaimed.

"Sure he did. But he didn't get a scratch."

"And that makes a difference?"

"Always seems to."

"Men and elections!" Luz sighed. "I am afraid I will never understand them! I am glad women do not have to bother with such stupid things!"

"Oh, elections ain't all that bad. Only if you got a bunch like Naylor and his cronies trying to steal 'em."

"You will not let them do that, will you?" she asked.

"Not if I can keep 'em from it." He turned to Clarita. "If I was to set down at the table, you think you could find me some breakfast?"

"Ees cook now. Go seet down, I breeng."

"No, Clarita," Luz said firmly. "I am back now. We will do as we have always done. You will cook, I will serve."

For a moment Clarita looked as though she were going to argue, but she shrugged and said, *"Como te gustes."*

When Luz came in carrying his breakfast, she asked Longarm, "Will you be very busy today?"

"I'll be at the voting place till it's all finished and the votes are counted. Why?"

"I thought we might ride out on the desert, where we could be alone." She caught his eye and repeated, "Alone, Longarm."

"Tomorrow, maybe. It's likely to be late before I get back. I don't want either you or Clarita to wait up for me. You got to remember, I'm used to looking out for myself."

"Very well," she replied stiffly. "I will tell Clarita."

Finishing his breakfast, Longarm donned vest and coat and rode into town. He took time for an after-breakfast drink at the saloon before crossing the street; Naylor's store had been selected—by Naylor, in his capacity as selectman—as the polling place. The storekeeper had made no elaborate preparations. A wooden box with a slot cut in the top, its lid nailed closed, had been prepared to receive the ballots; it stood on an empty flour barrel upended in the center of the store. The counter nearest the barrel gave the voters a flat surface on which to mark their ballots with a pencil.

Naylor watched silently while Longarm inspected the arrangement, then asked, "Well, Marshal? That suit you?"

"Looks all right to me. I'll just pull up a chair and sit down and watch."

Naylor pointed silently to a chair, and went to his usual corner to settle down. Longarm made himself as comfortable as possible, shifting position or standing and stretching as the day wore on and the hard chair Naylor had provided grew even harder.

Most of the men who came in knew him by now, and he'd have been drunk before noon if he'd accepted all the proffered bottles or the invitations to step across the street for a drink at Corky's. Since he had no way of escaping, he listened to at least twenty different versions of the battle with the Yaquis, and gave twice that many noncommittal replies to questions about his opinion of who the election winners would be.

Slowly the hours ticked off. The men of Mina Cobre, the Mexicans from the adobes, the workers from the Copper Queen, came in, marked their ballots, and deposited them in the box. Then, according to the color of their skins, they

226

crossed the street to Corky's or went down to the cantina to wait for evening.

Late in the afternoon, the store began to fill up. Purdy arrived, and a short time later Cross came in and joined Naylor in his corner. Carvajal swaggered in, wearing a brilliant purple shirt decorated in the *china poblano* style, with its seams outlined by sequins. Neither Trent nor Don Diego Parrejo put in an appearance. The candidates avoided one another after a somewhat embarrassed exchange of greetings, but groups of their supporters congregated around them, and discussions in hushed voices became the common pattern.

It was a dragging day for Longarm. He breathed a silent sigh of relief when the interior of the store grew dim and the straw-haired clerk began making the rounds of the kerosene lamps that were fixed in brackets on the walls.

Longarm watched while the clerk took down each lamp, removed its glass chimney, touched a match to the wick, replaced the chimney and adjusted the wick until it stopped smoking, then put the lamp back in place. When the last lamp had been lighted, Longarm stood up, ready to announce that the polling was ended and the votes would be counted. Before he could make his short speech, a half-dozen shots rang out from the street. Keyed up by memories of the Yaqui raid, the men in the store joined in a concerted rush for the door.

Longarm pushed his way through the press and got to the street. Braney Trent stood in the center of the roadway, his still-smoking pistol in his hand, a broad grin on his face.

"Just what the devil are you celebrating, Trent?" Longarm asked the constable.

"Why, the end of election day, Long." Trent flipped open the Colt's cylinder and began to reload. "We got damn few clocks in town, so I thought it'd be a good idea to shoot off a sorta sunset gun, let everybody know the votes is about to be counted."

"It was a damfool stunt, with everybody still jumpy from that set-to with the Yaquis," Longarm said. "But now that you've got the tomfoolery out of your system, come on inside. You're right about one thing. It's time to begin counting."

Amid a buzz of conversation, the men crowded back into the store. Longarm went to the improvised ballot box and

227

looked at the nails securing its lid. He said to Cross, who was standing near by, "You know where things are better'n I do. Get me a hammer so I can take the lid off the box."

Cross rummaged around behind a counter and came back with a hammer. Longarm pried the cover off the ballot box and tossed it on the floor. He upended the box on the barrel lid and dumped the folded ballots out. The men jostled one another, trying to get closer to watch what was going to take place.

Longarm raised his voice and said, "Now, all of you know what I'm doing here. I was sent to make sure this election was run fair and square, and I aim to do the job right. I want three of you men to get a piece of paper and a pencil and write down the names of the ones that're running for election, and keep track of the votes they get when I call 'em off the ballots. That way, there won't be any chance of making mistakes."

There was a confused flurry of motion as men unwilling to volunteer themselves urged friends to step up and do the tallying. Three were finally persuaded and took their places at the counter.

Longarm looked at the heap of ballots for a moment, then called to the clerk, "Sonny, you mind getting one of those lamps off the wall and putting down here so I don't make any mistake about the marks?"

Quickly, the clerk took down one of the kerosene lamps from the wall and placed it on the barrel lid. Longarm lifted the first ballot and held it close to the lamp chimney. He said, "I guess I better just call out the names for constable and sheriff, they're the ones you're all interested in. We can do the other ones later on. Anybody object?" He waited, and when no one protested, he announced, "I guess we're ready, then. Here we go."

Ballot by ballot, Longarm called off the vote and the volunteers at the counter marked down their tallies. The process took a little more than two hours, and finally Longarm picked up the last ballot from the barrel lid, held it up to the lamp, and called off the names marked with Xs. He laid the ballot down on the stack of those already counted, and turned to the talliers.

"All right, men. Call out what you got on your lists, one at a time," he told them.

"Well, in the town election, I make it out to be forty votes for Barney Trent, twenty-six for Caleb Purdy. In the county, where everybody votes, it's a hundred and fifty for Jim Cross and fifteen for Carvajal, and thirty-five for Parrejo," the first tallyman said loudly.

"That's what I got too," the second agreed.

"My figures come out the same," the third announced.

A buzz of voices had begun when the first tally was read. It grew louder as the other two called out their figures. Barney Trent's voice sounded from the rear of the crowd.

"I guess that settles things, then. Looks like I'm elected for another term," he said.

"Just a minute, Trent!" Longarm called over the buzzing of the crowd. "We better count the *real* ballots and see how *they* add up."

"What d'you mean, the real ballots?" Trent demanded. "Hell, Long, I hear you been watching that box all day. You seen every ballot that was put into it! What're you trying to pull off?"

"Why, Trent, that stunt you and your friends Cross and Naylor tried to pull so you could steal this election wouldn't fool a two-year-old baby!" Longarm replied. When the clamor from the crowd increased, he raised his voice to override it. "Now, everybody be quiet! I don't want any of you to miss what I'm going to show you!"

Lifting the lamp, the empty ballot box, and the stack of ballots from the top of the flour barrel, he put them on the floor. Then he lifted the barrel. On the floor underneath it stood a second box, identical to the other.

Longarm lowered the barrel to the floor and picked up the second box. "Here's the real ballot box I've been watching all day. When Trent let off those shots out in the street and everybody ran outside, Cross switched the real box for this other phony one that him and Naylor and Trent had fixed up."

"You'll play hell proving that, Long!" Cross called from the corner where he stood with Trent and Naylor. "But go ahead and try, if you think you can make it stick!"

"Oh, I'll make it stick, all right, Cross," Longarm said.

He put the unopened box on the barrel top and placed the lamp beside it, then took the hammer and pried open the lid. A murmur began rippling through the crowded store when the men saw that the freshly opened box was filled with ballots identical to those that had already been counted.

"How you going to tell 'em apart, if one set's real and the other's not?" Caleb Purdy demanded loudly.

"Why, that's easy, Purdy," Longarm said. "I marked the real ballots the other night. Had me a hunch Naylor and Trent and Cross had this kind of trick up their sleeves. You know," he said, addressing the crowd now, rather than Purdy, "if somebody's trying to steal an election, printing up two sets of ballots and switching boxes is the oldest stunt in the game. And you men keep in mind, it was Naylor and Cross had those ballots printed in Tucson. All they had to do was order two sets."

"Now wait a minute, Long!" Naylor called. "Cross and Barney and me, all three, watched you count those ballots. And all three of us will swear in court that you didn't put a mark on a single one of them!"

"That's where you're wrong, Naylor," Longarm replied calmly. "I marked all them ballots, you just didn't see me. Look here."

He held a corner of one of the ballots from the new box up to the lamp chimney. Slowly, a dark brown spot became visible in the corner. Longarm held up the ballot so that the men in the rear who were craning their necks to see could get a clear look at it. While he held up the first ballot, he put another close to the lamp chimney and a second brown spot slowly appeared.

Until the second mark appeared, the crowd had been listening quietly. Now the voices started to him again. Before the confusion became too great, Longarm raised his voice once more.

"I guess you men are wondering how I did my marking, so I'll show you." Reaching into his pocket, Longarm brought out the lemon he'd gotten earlier in the day from Corky. He tossed it to one of the men at the tally counter, and told the man, "Just cut that open and rub your thumb over the cut side. Then press your thumb on a corner of your tally sheet and hold it up. Let everybody see it don't show where the lemon juice touched it."

When the tallyman had followed the instructions, Longarm

said, "Now hold the corner of that paper up close to the lamp over the counter and watch what happens."

In total silence, the men in the store watched a brown spot appear and grow dark in the corner of the sheet of paper.

"You men satisfied?" Longarm asked. When the roar of assent had subsided, he went on, "All right. Let's start over and count the real ballots this time."

A buzzing fly would have sounded louder in the store than a locomotive's whistle while the genuine ballots were being counted. When the counting ended and Longarm called for the tallymen to report, the silence continued until the last total was announced and then the crowd exploded into a pandemonium of cheers and shouting.

In the second count, the real ballots gave Trent only fourteen votes, while Purdy received fifty-two. For sheriff, Cross had sixty votes, Carvajal got only twenty-five, and Don Diego Parrejo stood high with one hundred and five.

Longarm watched the faces of Trent, Cross, and Naylor change from smug satisfaction to anger while he waited for the tumult to die down somewhat. Then, speaking loudly enough to be heard above the din, he called to the room in general, "All right. I'll be putting that last set of figures down in my official report. We'll count the votes for the other races tomorrow. Seems like to me everybody's had enough vote-counting for today."

Pushing his way through the crowd, Longarm left the store. He stopped outside before the road crossing to the saloon, to light a cheroot. He had just touched a match to the tip of the long, thin cigar when, over the noise spilling from the store, he heard a bootsole grating on the hard earth behind him. Before he could turn, Longarm felt the unmistakable prod of a gun muzzle in his back.

"All right, Long," Barney Trent's angry voice grated in his ear. "Take out your pistol and hand it to me. We're going to take a little ride together out on the desert."

As he slid his revolver out of its holster, Longarm said quietly, "This ain't going to change a thing, Trent. Everybody in town knows you lost the election."

"Don't you think I know that?" the constable asked hotly. "Tonight's the second time you've made me look a fool in front of everybody, Long! And it might not change the vote, but I'll know I made you pay for it!"

"I guess you got in mind taking me out to the desert to get rid of me?" Longarm asked, handing his Colt to Trent.

"You're a good guesser." Trent stuck the pistol in his belt and went on, "But if you give me any trouble while we're mounting up, I'd just as soon shoot you down here and run for it. I'm finished in this town anyway. Now we'll get on our horses and ride away before the men start coming out of the store."

Longarm's hand was already on his watch chain. He waited until Trent stopped beside the Morgan to slide the derringer attached to one end of the chain into his hand.

"You mount first so I can keep an eye on you," Trent commanded. He started to return his own pistol to its holster.

Longarm brought the derringer up and triggered it. The ugly little snub-nosed gun spat. Its slug plowed into the constable's heart. Trent dropped, his Colt falling from his lifeless hand.

Longarm waited until the first men came rushing out of the store so that they could see him retrieving his own Colt from the dead man's belt. He saw Cross pushing his way to the front of the crowd. He waited, still holding his revolver in his hand, until Cross reached the road.

"I guess you and Naylor knew what Trent had on his mind when he left in such a rush," he told Cross. "It would've been better if you'd stopped him." Cross was looking down at the constable's body and did not answer. Longarm added, "You and Naylor have had more experience handling carrion than I have. I'll leave him for you to take care of."

Mounting the Morgan, Longarm rode out of town toward the cottage.

A lamp glowed in the parlor. Longarm unsaddled his horse and went in. Luz was asleep in one of the easy chairs. She woke when he closed the door and sat up, blinking drowsily.

"I know you didn't want us to wait up, but I had to find out about the election," she said. "Clarita wasn't interested in it, she went to bed a long time ago. Did Don Diego—"

"He won it," Longarm told her, reaching for the rye bottle.

"Beat out Carvajal and Cross. Looks like your daddy-in-law's the new sheriff, Luz."

"I don't know whether to be glad or sorry. Glad, I suppose, now that El Griego's renegades won't be giving the town any more trouble. Don Diego can take care of anything but them."

"You sleep on whether you're glad or sorry." Longarm put the bottle down and recorked it. "Now I'm going to bed. You better too. I'm aiming to ride out tomorrow by noon."

"So soon? But, Longarm—"

"My case is closed, Luz. I got to report back to Denver."

"Well . . ." Luz stood undecided for a moment, then started for the door. "I'll see you in the morning, then."

Longarm carried the lamp into the bedroom. He smoked a final cheroot while he undressed, tossed the butt into the spittoon beside the bed, and blew out the lamp. The glow from the newly risen moon through the windowshades eased the room's darkness without dissipating it. Longarm had just closed his eyes when a whisper of fabric drew his eyes to the door. Luz stood there, her nightgown shimmering in the soft glow.

Through the darkness, she said softly, "You knew I'd come to you tonight, didn't you?"

"I halfway thought you might."

Luz moved to the bed with a soft shushing of bare feet, and Longarm watched the white shadow of her nightgown fall with a brushing of silk on skin. Her figure shimmered in the transparent moonglow, a slim white column with dark dots of nipples and a darker shadow between her thighs, then settled onto the bed beside him.

She lifted herself on an elbow to lean over him and Longarm saw her face above his, dark eyes and a gleam of white teeth between lips parted in a smile. The tips of her breasts brushed his chest, then their firmness was crushed warmly soft against him. Longarm raised his lips to hers, and Luz's darting tongue entered his mouth. Her hand moved down his body to his groin and found him, her fingers moving along him in a light caress.

Longarm lifted her to kiss her breasts. Luz was squeezing and stroking him at the same time now, bringing him erect. He rolled over and she shifted to lie under him, opening her thighs to receive him.

233

He went into her slowly, Luz gasping and squirming as she moved her hips from side to side to help him penetrate her fully and deeply.

"I had to feel you inside me again," she whispered. Her hips began to move as though to draw him deeper. "Now give me what I came to you for!"

Longarm stroked, gently at first, then his stroking became hard lunges as Luz's breathing quickened and she started writhing and squirming, bringing up her hips to meet him, until he felt her beginning to stiffen and tremble. He tried to slow his tempo, to prolong her beginning orgasm, but she would not let him.

"No! Keep on, Longarm! I must let go now!"

Longarm plunged on, each thrust bringing Luz closer, then her spasm began and her body arched beneath him while he drove on until her deep sighing and moaning died away and she lay still. He rolled away to lie on his back. Luz turned to look at him, saw his erection jutting up in the moonlight.

"Can you wait until I've caught my breath?" she asked, her breasts rising and falling as she gasped to fill her lungs.

"Ees no need he waits," Clarita said from the doorway.

Both Luz and Longarm rose up in surprise and watched as Clarita came to the bed. She was nude, her full breasts billowing in the soft light, their nipples outthrust like fingertips.

"*Dame su tronchudo magnifico*, Longarm," Clarita went on. "*Vuelve a Luz cuando me ha chingado completamente.*"

Before either Longarm or Luz could speak, Clarita straddled Longarm's hips, impaling herself on his erection with a quivering sigh of contentment. She began to twist her hips as they rose and fell rhythmically, and then leaned forward, her breasts quivering in time with the motions of her body.

"Clarita!" Luz said indignantly. "*Quita de ahí!*"

"*No querellarse, Luz!*" Clarita gasped as she crouched over Longarm to raise her hips higher. "*Longarm tiene duraza hora detras hora, es bastante de su verga para dos mujeres!*"

For a moment Luz lay silent. Then, with a happy lilt of acceptance in her voice, she said, "Enjoy Clarita, Longarm. I will be ready again when you are. She is right. You are enough man for both of us."

234

Longarm said nothing. He kept his lips pressed to Clarita's breasts. There would be time enough for him to answer Luz, and more than answer her, during the long hours that stretched ahead.

SPECIAL PREVIEW

Attention LONGARM readers!

Here are the opening scenes
from

EASY COMPANY AND THE SUICIDE BOYS

the first novel in Jove's exciting
new High Plains adventure series

EASY COMPANY

Next month, Jove will launch a new and completely unique Western adventure series—the adventures of EASY COMPANY, a company of mounted infantry stationed on the High Plains during the peak years of the Indian wars. The men of EASY COMPANY are a tough, gritty, colorful crew. From First Lieutenant Matt Kincaid to Sergeant Ben Cohen to the soft spoken, Indian-wise scout, Windy Mandalian, they are Indian fighters, hot-blooded lovers, High Plains heroes. Each new EASY COMPANY adventure will feature plenty of Indian fighting, personal drama, sultry ladies, and fascinating historical detail. Look for books 1, 2, and 3 in the EASY COMPANY series next month!

Book 1   *EASY COMPANY AND THE SUICIDE BOYS*
Book 2   *EASY COMPANY AND THE MEDICINE GUN*
Book 3   *EASY COMPANY AND THE GREEN ARROWS*

And don't miss *Longarm in Northfield,*
also coming next month from Jove.

One

THE SUMMER SUN rose early on the High Plains of the Wyoming Territory, and a distant bugle was sounding reveille as the Cheyenne slithered up the slope on their bellies in the summer-brown but dew-wet grass. There were nine of them, stripped for action to breechclouts and paint, despite the morning chill. The strawflowers braided in their hair matched the indigo stripes on their faces as they topped the rise to peer over the ridge, their features desperately calm, hearts pounding against the prairie sod. They were far less frightened by the U.S. Army outpost over on the next rise than they were by their own audacity. The flowers in their hair were lawful camouflage, but they were "suicide boys," as their own people called them—young, untested, would-be warriors, out to prove their bravery—and they had painted themselves without consulting the older men of the Dog Soldier Society. Medicine Wolf had said he didn't think anyone should count coup on the Americans until The People Who Cut Fingers found out where the other bands had scattered after the Custer Fight at the Greasy Grass. The young men scouting the outpost from this rise knew it was possible that they were doing a bad thing.

Twisted Rifle rose on his elbows behind a clump of soapweed and stared disdainfully across the shallow draw at the limp flag above the sod ramparts of Outpost Number Nine. Unlike his comrades, Twisted Rifle had painted half of his face black. The older men had not yet invited him to join the Contrary Society, but Twisted Rifle was an independent thinker, even for a Cheyenne.

A moon-faced youth at Twisted Rifle's side said, "The American fort is bigger than you told us it would be. Those sod walls are thick. The Americans built cleverly. It is one big, hollow square. They made their houses and ramparts as one. The Americans can run freely along the level rooftops, save for that lookout tower by the far gate. They have a singing wire, too. Do you see those poles running over the horizon to the east?"

The Indian on the other side of Twisted Rifle said, "Hear me. I don't think this would be a good place to fight. Lame Calf is right about the strong walls. They have been clever about clearing away all cover within rifle range, too. Long before we could wear them down, they would get help over the Singing Wire and—"

"Red Lance speaks like an ignorant person," cut in Twisted Rifle, adding, "Long before I led an attack, I would make certain the singing wire was cut. But I am not a fool. I said nothing about attacking the Americans behind those walls. They have horses, many horses, grazing on the far side, to the south. Look over there, those black dots against the sunrise, two rifle shots from the fort's northeast corner."

Red Lance squinted into the brightening horizon. "I see maybe fifteen tipis circled over that way. What of it? None of our band would be camped so close to an American outpost."

Twisted Rifle's voice dripped venom as he said, "They are evil people. Indians and half-bloods who trade and shelter near the blue sleeves of the American chief in Wah-shah-tung."

The normally amiable young Lame Calf frowned and Red Lance bared his teeth as he hissed, "Does my brother mean they are Pawnee or Crow?"

"Worse," said Twisted Rifle. "They used to be People Who Cut Fingers. That is the band of Gray Elk. They have made peace with Wah-shah-tung. They live near the Americans because they know all Real People hate them now."

Lame Calf sucked in his breath and said, "Ai! I have heard the old men speak of Gray Elk in the Shining Times! He was once a Crooked Lancer. They say he counted coup on the Utes. They say he once stole a woman from the Pawnee. In his youth he stole many ponies from the Crow, and he lifted Crow hair more than once, too!"

Twisted Rifle sighed deeply. "Once was a long time ago. . . ."We don't have enough young men, yet, to really hurt those people over there. First we will have to show everyone how easy it is to make them look foolish. We will count a few coups in fun. I intend to make a man of each of you. Then we will be able to get others to follow you. Hear me. Each of you will be war chiefs if you do as I say."

Lame Calf said, "I would like to be a war chief. What will you be in the new Shining Times to come, Twisted Rifle?"

"I will be a *big* chief, of course," Twisted Rifle said.

None of the others laughed.

They knew he meant it.

Twisted Rifle was said to have good medicine, and nobody had ever caught him in a lie.

First Lieutenant Matt Kincaid had pulled OD that morning. He walked the perimeter of Outpost Nine atop the sod roofs of the quarters built into the outpost's sod walls. The parade stood empty in the slanting sunlight, although Easy Company was up and getting ready for another boring day of frontier routine. He was walking over the married enlisted men's quarters at the moment, and he noticed that someone was cooking corned beef for breakfast as he passed one of the stovepipes, rising waist-high above the sod. Corned beef was a cheap as well as an unusual breakfast, but the fortunate noncom who could afford to keep a wife out here on his base pay and fogies was probably enjoying breakfast more than were the privates in the mess hall catty-corner across the parade.

Matt came to the southwest corner of the post, and the guard on duty there snapped to attention and presented arms. Matt thought hard and said, "as you were, Harper. What's your first general order?"

The private licked his lips and stammered, "Sir! My first general order is to walk my post in a military manner, keeping always on the alert and . . ."

"That's enough. Carry on, soldier."

Matt knew the recruit was feeling greatly relieved as he continued his rounds. He felt relieved, too. It was a bitch to remember every man's name, and it was a good thing Harper was a recruit. An older hand would have caught Matt's mistake in not returning the rifle salute while desperately trying to remember a new man's effing name. Matt shook his head to clear it as he told himself to wake up, for God's sake. They'd be holding morning report in a few minutes, and he shuddered to think of making a mistake in front of the first sergeant.

Matt moved up the west wall, noting how the slanting light exposed thin spots in the sod. He'd have to order a sod-cutting detail once he finished his tour as officer of the day. Housekeeping in sod quarters was a bitch even when the roof didn't leak.

Walking with his eyes down, Matt didn't spot the next man atop the ramparts right away, but the man spotted him and stiffened awkwardly to a parody of attention. Lieutenant Kincaid was said to be a nice gent, for an officer, but the second in command at Outpost Nine was West Point and looked it. Matt Kincaid was a tall, clean-cut New Englander with wide-set gray eyes that smiled a lot, but could knock a fuck-up clean off his horse. The nervous private waited as Matt took a few more steps, looked up, and stopped with a quizzical frown.

He said, "Private Malone, I hope you have some reason for standing there with a rifle on each shoulder and your pack on backwards. I don't remember you at guard mount, either."

Malone said nervously, "Please, sor, it's the first sergeant's orders and I know it's a fool I look. I've been trying to figure out how to present arms with two Springfields in me hands, but for the life of me . . ."

"You do have a problem, don't you, soldier? Forget the salute. I don't see how it could be done, either. How did you get on Sergeant Cohen's bad side this time, Malone?"

Malone said, "Och, it was only the honor of the outfit I was after defending, Lieutenant, sor."

"I see. You were brawling with the feather merchants in town again, eh? Goddamnit, Malone, the last time I saved you from a court-martial, you promised to behave yourself off post. How in the hell can a man your size get fighting drunk on three-point-two beer?"

"Jesus, Mary and Joseph, I was cold sober this time, sor," Malone protested righteously. "I swear I was minding me own business in the Drover's Rest when this damned auld buffalo skinner looked me right in the eye and called me a cavalry trooper."

"What happened then?"

"Well, sor, I was patiently explaining the difference between mounted infantry and them sissy yellow legs, when a couple of other feather merchants took exception to the way I was gintly tapping him with me fist for emphasis, and then the damned auld regimental MPs came in, and, though I know you'll think I made it up, the MPs was after *helping* as the whole crowd lit into me!"

Matt rolled his eyes heavenward and sighed, "Right. So after the MPs brought you in and turned you over to Sergeant Cohen—"

"Och, what do you take me for, sor, a quartermaster corpsman? Sure and no two MPs born of mortal woman could take a Malone, drunk or sober. I just left peaceful, when I saw I wasn't among friends in that dreadful place. Unfortunately, me blue neckerchief became misplaced in the free-for-all, and Regiment wired the first sergeant about some glass that seems to have gotten broken as I was making me departure."

"Oh, damn, that means we'll probably have to pay for the damages from the company slush fund. I'd take it out of your pay, if you weren't still paying off that last fine I managed to get you off with."

Malone shook his head and said, "If you please, sor, it won't be necessary. It's me understanding that Sergeant Cohen was after informing Regiment he had no idea *who* sort of shoved that cowboy through that window. I heard him tell Four Eyes to put that on the wire just before he called me a worthless son of a bitch and put me up here on company punishment."

It wasn't easy, but Matt managed not to laugh as he said, "All right. As long as the first sergeant has a handle on it, carry on. While you're up here walking double dutch, you may as well keep your eyes open. We have some kids scouting us from that rise to the west."

"Och, I have them spotted, sor. I make it eight or nine of 'em, crawlin' on their bellies like reptiles over there. They'll have another holding their ponies for them on the far slope, and—"

"I said carry on, Malone. This is my second tour out here. If you see 'em, you see 'em. I don't need a lecture on Mr. Lo."

Matt walked on, secretly pleased. Malone was a truly terrible garrison soldier, but a born fighter with a good pair of eyes. The first sergeant had picked the perfect company punishment for him. Malone couldn't see very far, digging the usual pit latrine, and as awkward as he must feel with a rifle on each shoulder, everyone knew that in a pinch Malone could fire right-or left-handed, sharp.

Matt was walking over officer's country, now. The voice of Miss Flora, the CO's wife, lilted up a stovepipe as Matt passed it. He didn't stop to eavesdrop. Flora Conway might not have really been the most beautiful white woman west of the Big Muddy, but there wasn't a man in Easy Company who wouldn't punch you in the nose if you suggested there was a worthy rival to the captain's lady. As a bachelor officer, Matt was a little uncomfortable as he walked above their bedroom, trying not to picture Miss Flora in a nightgown with her long raven's-wing hair unpinned.

Actually, Flora Conway sat stark naked on her bed as she watched her husband, Warner Conway, Captain, Mounted Infantry, overage in grade, finish dressing in front of the pier glass on the sod wall. Conway was a handsome man in his mid-forties, and his ramrod figure was still slim in the slightly faded blues he was buttoning methodically. His wife smiled fondly and said, "Heavens, you look stern this morning, darling. Please don't scold that poor young soldier in the mirror. I'm rather fond of him."

Conway met his wife's eyes in the mirror, and his stern visage mellowed. He said, "I'm rather fond of that shameless hussy I see peeking at me, too. But that fellow in the mirror has a good chewing-out coming to him.

He keeps breaking promises to a lady. But honestly, Flora, if they pass me up on the next promotion list, I swear I'll tell them what they can do with these railroad tracks."

Flora rose and came over to him. Despite the fact that they'd just made love, his breath still caught at the sight of her ivory curves in the dim light. She leaned against his back and put her arms around his waist, resting a cheek against his blue-wool-clad shoulder blade as she soothed, "Stop it, you adorable bear. We both know the army is your life. It's not the War Department's fault that that silly old President Hayes won't give them any money."

Conway turned around and took her in his arms, suddenly wanting her again as her nude flesh pressed against his forage dress. But the men were scraping their mess kits just across the way, and the bugle was about to sound assembly. He said, "Jesus, Flora, this is no life for a man and wife who met at a Baltimore ball one night when floors were waxed and walls were papered with satin and—"

"Hush, dear heart," she cut in, adding, "I won't have you carry on so about unimportant trimmings. We have each other, and that's all that matters. Do you really think I'd trade you for a cut-glass chandelier? I knew you were a soldier when I met you, and a very handsome soldier, too, I might add."

He said, "Yeah. Everybody was a soldier that year. When we married, I was a lieutenant colonel and the War was almost over and . . . Jesus, I fed you a line, didn't I?"

Flora stood on her bare tiptoes to kiss him before she shook her head, tossing her black curls, and said, "Poo, you old silly. I never married you because you were a short colonel. Stop feeling so sorry for yourself. I'm not complaining about this new post. I think it's rather fun. The carpets from home cover most of the rammed-earth floors, and once I hem those new drapes for the windows . . ."

"Flora, for God's sake, you were raised in a gracious Tidewater mansion, and look what I've brought you to, this time. It's worse than Fort Leavenworth. The whole damned place is made out of mud and grass. I've seen Indian pueblos more fit for a white woman to set up housekeeping."

"You just run along and let me worry about housekeeping. It's my house and I love it. Wasn't that the assembly call, just now?"

He said, "It was. I've got to get over to my office. We're expecting visitors."

"Visitors?" she cut in, brightly.

He said, "Yes, the IG's sending some big mugwump to inspect us. I can't get those new repeating rifles and half my men need new boots, but somehow they can always manage an infernal inspection."

The hope in Flora's eyes faded, but she turned her head so her husband couldn't see it as she said cheerily, "You'd better run along and do something inspectish, then. I have to get dressed. This depraved young man I'm living with keeps me in a state of shocking nudity, and I wouldn't want the neighbors to find out."

245

Conway laughed, kissed his wife, and left.

Flora walked over to the pier glass and stared soberly at her naked reflection in the cruel light that filtered through the bottle-glass windows. She saw a woman, still attractive but no longer young, and even if her breasts were still firmer than those of most others her age, and her torso was still unflawed by stretched marks, time had tempered its kindness by refusing to give her husband the son she knew he wanted.

Dear Warner never complained, and he certainly treated her as lovingly as ever, but—

"That's enough of that," she told herself as she turned away to see just where she should begin another attempt at putting her new home in order. Like many a frontier wife before her, Flora had the shocking but pragmatic habit of sweeping and dusting in the nude. The dust raised in a soddy was awesome, and it was far easier to wash one's hide than one's sparse wardrobe.

Flora took a broom and went to work as, outside, she heard that nice young Lieutenant Kincaid shouting, "First Sergeant, take the report!"

Flora swept as the men outside went through their own seemingly pointless routine. One by one, each platoon leader bellowed something that sounded to Flora like the chant of a tobacco auctioneer. She'd been Army long enough to know that what sounded like "Bowowowfer" really meant, "First platoon all present and accounted for."

In the years she'd followed her man from post to post, she'd never grasped just what the point of it all was. What did those men get out of all that stamping about in boots and yelling at one another as if they were about to have a fight?

She swept a stripe of rammed-earth floor, and while a cloud rose to film her shins with mustard-colored dust, the floor looked just as dirty as ever. Which was reasonable enough, when you thought about it. The dust got all over everything. Her mock-Persian nine-by-twelve rug looked as though it had been buried and dug up again by ghouls. She thought about letting the floor go and just dusting. As she stared hopelessly around for a place to begin, a dry straw fell from the wall and fluttered down to tickle her bare instep. She bit her lips to keep them from trembling, and after a couple of deep breaths, she knew she wasn't going to scream, after all.

Outside, boots were tramping up and down, as if there weren't already enough dust in this goddamned little mud-pie outpost. Flora put the broom back in the corner and said, "Oh, hell, I may as well get dressed."

American Tears wore no paint today. He was dressed in the hand-me-down army shirt and pants of the BIA, with a folded red blanket kilted around his hips and a Remington repeater cradled in his left arm. But his feet were clad in beaded moccasions of white deerskin, and his pomaded hair was roached with indigo quills and a fox tail. He was traveling incognito, but that was no reason to look like a poor person.

The young men scouting atop the ridge saw American Tears as he strode grandly up the slope toward them. Twisted Rifle moved back to cover and rose to meet him, saying, "Heya! Be careful, Uncle. The Americans are just over the rise."

American Tears stared down at the youth as if he'd just noticed a fly in his food and said, "I know this, puppy. It is called Outpost Number Nine. The men there are from Easy Company, U.S. Mounted Rifles. Their chief is named Conway, and he fought well against the Southern bands in the Buffalo War three summers ago. His subchief is Kincaid, who fought well and counted coup on the Staked Plains when they sent him there. There are at least two hundred guns in that stronghold. What do you children think you are doing? Medicine Wolf sent me to get you. Your mothers are worried about you."

Twisted Rifle tried to look older as the other young men moved down to join them. He struck himself on the chest and said, "Hear me, Uncle. I am too old to be called a child. I know I have never hung from the Sun Dance pole. I know I have never lifted hair. But that is not my fault. You older men obey the agent from Wah-shah-tung and refuse to lead us, so—"

American Tears slapped Twisted Rifle's face, stared down at the black paint on his palm as if he'd just noticed it, and said, "The name of the place is *Washington*. If you're going to talk about the Americans, learn the words they use. What is this shit on my hand? If I didn't know better, I'd think my sister's baby had painted himself as a Contrary. When did the Contrary Society start inducting little boys with the smooth chests of girls too young to fuck?"

247

Twisted Rifle's face turned red where it wasn't covered by smeared paint. He knew he'd die on the spot if he raised a hand to a Crooked Lancer, so he threw his gun down and stamped on it, shouting, "You struck me! That was cruel! Everyone knows the Americans beat their children, but even if my uncle is angry, we are Those Who Cut Fingers. We do not even beat our women, unless they have done something truly dreadful!"

American Tears shrugged and said, "Some people say I am bad-tempered for a Cut Finger. But if I had been a member of the Contrary Society, my naughty nephew would be dead right now. I want you boys to wipe that silly paint off. Real People would laugh at you. Those Americans on the other side of the rise might shoot you if they noticed it and took you for men."

Twisted Rifle grunted disgustedly. "The fools don't know we are scouting then. We thought maybe after dark we might slip in and cut out a few ponies or—"

American Tears grabbed Twisted Rifle's arm in a viselike grip and dragged him along as he strode boldly up the slope, growling, "By Manitou, my sister must have stepped on your head when you were a suckling. Come with me. It is time someone took a hand in your education."

As they topped the rise together, Twisted Rifle gasped, "They can *see* us, Uncle! Why are we standing here against the skyline like this?"

American Tears raised his Remington and waved across the draw to a soldier walking the walls of Outpost Nine. The soldier hesitated and then waved back. American Tears said, "They already know we are here, painted puppy. Look over there to the south. Tell me what you see, mighty horse thief."

Twisted Rifle squinted at a rise to the south for a time before he shrugged and said, "I see an old dog coyote, watching the army horses in the paddock over on that side of the fort, my uncle."

"You do, eh? When did God's Dog start stalking full-grown horses? What is a coyote doing in broad daylight, near a place where men with Springfields even shoot rabbits? Use your head, child! That's no coyote. It's one of those damned Delaware scouts the army has working for them. I know the chief scout working for Conway. He is called Windy Mandalian by the Blue Sleeves. He is good. One day one of us is going to lift the other one's hair."

Twisted Rifle looked sullen as he asked, "If they are so good, why have they not attacked us?"

"Oh, Great Manitou, give me strength!" sighed American Tears. Then he said, "They haven't attacked because nobody has started a war this summer. Can't you see they have other Indians camped nearby for water and protection? They probably think you are children from that friendly band, playing at war games. They are not far worng. Would *you* be worried if you commanded that company over there?"

"I still think we could steal some horses, after dark."

"The horses are only pastured outside the walls, under guard, during the daylight hours. Before the sun goes down, they will herd them inside, painted puppy. Come. Let us be on our way before some nosy Delaware moves in to ask questions."

American Tears waved to the "coyote" on the far rise and led the abashed Twisted Rifle down to his subdued young comrades. Red Lance asked, "What do you think, American Tears? Are you going to lead us into battle against this Easy Company?"

American Tears said, "Don't be silly. Medicine Wolf and the other old men say they are not ready for another fight, just yet."

"Medicine Wolf is getting *too* old, if you ask me," Twisted Rifle said. "I think we should hit the Americans now, before they've fully recovered from the Custer Fight."

American Tears said, "Listen, boys, it's not that simple. It is true we bloodied them at the Greasy Grass last summer. But Washington sent others to replace the five troops we wiped out. The Seventh Cavalry is back to full strength and burning for revenge. Three-quarters of our allies are hiding out in Canada, and even if they were not, there are more Blue Sleeves out here now than there were when we beat Custer. You can see they just sent out that infantry company and—"

"Infantry fight on foot, like Paiute," cut in Lame Calf, "I am not afraid of any man on foot. My pony, Dancing Fox, can catch or outrun any man on foot."

249

American Tears sighed patiently. "A little knowledge is a dangerous toy for a growing pup. Nobody *walks* on the High Plains. Easy Company is what they call *mounted* infantry. They fight like dragoons. Weren't you just talking about stealing their damned horses?"

"Yes," Red Lance replied. "We were wondering about that. Why do those soldiers call themselves infantry if they ride horses like everyone else?"

"I don't know," American Tears admitted. "The army talks funny. I guess they needed more cavalry out here, so they took an infantry company and put them on horseback. They carry infantry rifles with them. That might be it."

Twisted Rifle said, "If I were Wah-shah-tung—I mean, Washing-tong—I would be worried about having inexperienced fighters out here. My uncle says we are young and inexperienced. But how could those soldiers be any better? If I were Medicine Wolf, I would lead the people against them *now*, before they have time to learn about the way we fight out here."

American Tears shrugged. "Medicine Wolf is the one everyone listens to."

"He is old and has no heart for fighting," Twisted Rifle insisted. "The people would listen if *you* told them it would be a good fight against green troops, my uncle."

American Tears started to shake his head. Then he frowned and said, "I don't think so. I am very beautiful and have counted many coups, but I have never been a leader."

"Hear me. *We* would follow you, American Tears."

The Crooked Lancer stared around at the eager young faces as he thought about that. Lame Calf said, "We know we have a lot to learn. But you are wise. I think you are wiser than Medicine Wolf, and we know you are braver."

"Listen, boys," said American Tears. "I know how you feel and I like you, even though I think you're silly. I was young like you, one time, and my heart still soars every time I remember my first good fight."

Twisted Rifle said earnestly, "We could still have a good fight, my uncle. You say you know these new men. You say you know how they think and fight."

250

"I do. I have told Medicine Wolf I think I could make them look foolish if he'd let me put on my paint, but—"

"Put on your paint, American Tears! Lead us against the Blue Sleeves, so that the maidens will smile at us when we dance our scalps as real men."

"I don't know, boys. You're all just children and there aren't enough of you to hit anything really big."

"Then lead us against something small," pleaded Twisted Rifle.

Red Lance said, "Hear me. There are other young men like us. Many. They would not follow Twisted Rifle because he has no reputation yet. They would gladly follow *you*. I alone could gather six or eight cousins."

"Me too!" said Lame Calf, and a quiet boy named Broken Pipe spoke for the first time. "My two older brothers laughed at me when I said I was going on a raid. If I told them *you* were leading, they would follow."

American Tears was stone-faced as they pleaded with him but his heart pounded as he studied the golden opportunity Manitou seemed to be offering.

It was a dangerous idea to consider, but Medicine Wolf *was* getting soft and he, American Tears, was a bold as well as a beautiful person.

The Dog Soldier Society would punish him if the elders told them to. But what could the elders say if he did great deeds and counted many coups for the band?

The Americans would hang him as a renegade if they caught him breaking the treaty he'd made his mark on when the band had surrendered to draw rations and have hunting grounds assigned to them by the Great White Father. But how could any Blue Sleeve tell one Real Person from another, and how could they hope to catch anyone as cunning and clever as he?

As he strode grandly away to get his pony, Twisted Rifle fell in at his side to ask, "What are we going to do, my uncle?"

American Tears took off his shirt, exposing his muscular torso and Sun Dance scars to the sky and spirits. Then he handed the shirt to the boy and said. "Carry this and walk behind me. I am seeking a vision."